A DYSFUNCTIONAL FAMILY SEEKS IN A QUAINT TOWN, BUT IN ADDITION TO PACKING UP THEIR OWN PERSONAL DEMONS, THEY DISCOVER THE LOCALS AREN'T SO WELCOMING.

The quaint town of Lawrenceton, Missouri isn't sending out the welcoming committee for its newest neighbors from Los Angeles—the Samples' family. Shannon Lamb's "Like a Virgin" fashion choices, along with her fortune-telling mother, Wendy Samples, and her no-good, cheating, jobless, stepfather, Dale Samples, result in Shannon finding few fans in L-Town where proud family lines run deep. Only townie, Eddy Bauman, is smitten with Shannon and her Valley Girl ways. *The Bystanders* is a dark coming-of-age story set in the 1980s when big hair was big, and MTV ruled. In a quiet town of annual picnics and landscapes, the Samples' rundown trailer and odd behaviors aren't charming the locals. Shannon and Wendy could really use some friends but must learn to rely upon themselves to claw their way out of poverty and abuse if they want to escape Dale. *The Bystanders* pays homage to Americana, its small-town eccentricities, and the rural people of the Northern Mississippi Delta region of Southeast Missouri, a unique area of the country where people still speak Paw Paw French and honor Old World traditions.

Early Praise

"Without a doubt, Dawn Major is thoroughly schooled in the full-blown existence of jealousy, lust, love, confusion, pettiness, mystery, violence, hope, et al, exhibited by small-town denizens. *The Bystanders* stands tall in the world of coming-of-age novels"—**George Singleton, author of You Want More: Selected Stories**

"Dawn Major has written a gritty and hard-hitting novel *about* a couple of teenagers trapped in poverty, violence, and addiction. This colorful novel is set in the small real town of Lawrenceton, Missouri, whose dark side Major exposes in prose that is vivid and sensate. In the end, thankfully, Major shows that even a tragic world offers a way out. Major is a writer to watch."—*Janisse Ray, author of The Woods of Fannin County and Ecology of a Cracker Childhood*

"Intelligent, humorous, and sublimely original, Dawn Major's debut novel, *The Bystanders,* entwines short story narrative into a master tapestry of rural Missouri life in the 1980s, offering an insightful study into how people distribute responsibility and excuse their own inaction."—*Robert Gwaltney, award winning author of The Cicada Tree*

"Full of passion and punch, the characters in Dawn Major's gritty debut novel, *The Bystanders,* grab hold and don't let go. Living with her family in a trailer on the outskirts of Lawrenceton, Missouri, teenager Shannon feels outcast from her peers, as her mother Wendy continually combats an abusive husband. Mother and daughter struggle to fill empty places in their hearts in this commanding story sure to touch the reader."—**Susan Beckham Zurenda, author of *Bells for Eli***

"*The Bystanders* is a deliciously dark novel. Major created a cast of characters that are at home in a Flannery O'Connor story. Readers will not put this book down until they finish the last page."—***Ann Hite, award-winning author of Haints On Black Mountain***

"Flannery O'Connor and Eudora Welty move over, there is a new voice on the stage, Dawn Major's first novel, *The Bystanders*, is about to enter the ranks of Southern Literature."—***J.M. White, Author of Pulling Down The Sun and The Beyond Within***

Excerpt

"This is wrong, Eddy thought. This is all wrong. He felt the blow inflicted by the man as if he had taken it himself; he could not bear its injustice. Yet, deeper down, he knew his part to play here would only be that of an enraged bystander. He wanted to stop it, protect the girl, but he was just a kid. He couldn't stand up to a man. They all knew it—Fritz, the girl, her mother, the man, his sisters. He felt cheated, an unknown soldier glued to some shit store's floor."

THE BYSTANDERS

Dawn Major

Moonshine Cove Publishing, LLC
Abbeville, South Carolina U.S.A.

First Moonshine Cove Edition March
2023

About the Author

Dawn Major has a graduate degree in creative writing from Reinhardt University's Etowah Valley Creative Writing program. She was a recipient of the James Dickey Literary Review Editorial Fellowship, the Dr. Robert Driscoll Excellence in Writing Award on Regional Themes, and Reinhardt University's Faculty Choice Excellence in Writing Award. She is a member of Atlanta Writers Club, Broadleaf Writers Association, Horror Writers Association, and Georgia Writers Association. She is a member of the William Gay Archive and has written about his artwork and prose, as well as edited the late author's posthumous books.

She lives in the Old Fourth Ward in Atlanta, GA with her family.

While she considers herself a literary fiction writer, she has gravitated into speculative fiction more recently.

Publications and more at:

www.dawnmajor.com

Foreword

In *The Bystanders*, debut writer Dawn Major, writes with subtlety, compassion, and understanding about a time and place in the world that many authors have tackled but few have mastered. Set in the heartland and partially in the Deep South, *The Bystanders* is one of those rare works that is able to capture remembrances, and to remind us all why those moments are worth remembering. Major is an insightful and funny storyteller whose characters become amusingly alive with their dialogue and quirks as they walk straight off the pages and into our hearts, all while teaching us to accept life and live it as best we can. There is nothing better than a simple story told well, and this book certainly falls into that category. *The Bystanders* will stay with you long after the final page has been turned. It seems that when Dawn Major puts pen to paper—to quote Arthur Miller—attention must be paid.

—Raymond L. Atkins—*Set List, Sweetwater Blues*

Preface

First, I'd like to say that I've always been interested in the psychological phenomenon known as the bystander effect ever since I learned about the tragic story of Kitty Genovese from whence the term originated. As it turns out not everyone in that situation "failed to act," and the news sensationalized much of it. Still, it was a tragic and senseless act. With this book, I wanted to explore how it felt to be a bystander. As a child, I found myself in situations where I could not act when I wanted to act, which is vastly different from not acting because you believed someone else would or it wasn't your business. I'm sure I took liberties with this term and its true meaning. Please don't fault me. Sometimes, writers like the sound of a word or phrase and experiment with it.

I also wanted to mention that I never wavered from using real places to craft this story because I found the small-town settings of Lawrenceton, Bloomsdale, Sainte Genevieve to be so inspirational. Certainly, these towns were vital to my upbringing and made me who I am today. Keep in mind the scenes, events, and characters are fictional.

I also want to note that when I moved from Los Angeles to French Village, Missouri in the early 1980s, I felt overwhelmed by my differences and oftentimes felt like an outsider. Though I struggled living in a small town initially, I also believe small towns make up the fabric of America and are fodder for great stories. I worry over their loss. Having lived seven years in such an extraordinary part of the country, I was deeply saddened to leave this place and the people who I counted as my friends. They say authors are always seeking a hometown. I suppose that is why the towns stayed with me all this time. While I call Atlanta my home and have lived in the South longer than anywhere else, Southeast Missouri will always hold a special place in my heart.

The Bystanders

The day the Californians invaded Lawrenceton, Missouri, didn't seem much different from any other days ending in "y," except it was the same day Eddy Bauman and his family made their annual trip to St. Louis. There was an air of anticipation amongst the Baumans. They were going to shop in an actual mall, as opposed to the rinky-dink shops in the nearest "town-town" of Sainte Geneviève. The kids had saved their allowance all year for this occasion and carefully chose an outfit that their mom ironed as soon as they returned from St. Louis. It would hang neatly in the back of the closet, away from school uniforms and everyday clothes, until picture day. At the next dance it would appear again and, later, at Christmas Eve Mass until it faded into the regular wardrobe, another year passed by, and it was time to head down Highway Y, to I-55, back to St. Louis. Even though Eddy looked forward to going to the city, he also knew he would never live there, that he'd always return to Lawrenceton. He felt sorry for those types who couldn't settle or know the comfort of a hometown.

Eddy's sisters would embarrass him today. They'd insist on picking out his outfit. He'd push carpet around with the toe of his sneakers outside the fitting room and do anything to not look up when the saleswomen told him how cute he was and asked about his girlfriend. He didn't have one. He was twelve.

"Eddy, you should let your *favorite* sister pick out your outfit," Abby said.

"Shut up! You're not his favorite. Tell her, Eddy." Theresa poked him in the shoulder, "You know? What you told me the other day?" And then coyly turned towards Abby, "Sorry, Abby, this is going to hurt."

"*Girls*, leave him alone," his dad said, "It's too early to start this."

Eddy's family were French/German and lived in Lawrenceton in the outskirts of Sainte Geneviève—Missouri's oldest European settlement on the west bank of the Mississippi River. The area was originally colonized by French Canadians in the early 1700s with virtually no outsiders living there until the Germans and Anglos arrived, and then later, when the territory was sold through the Louisiana Purchase. Even today, some of the old ones still spoke Paw-Paw French. In time, the French and Germans married, blending families so that now the Leroys and Lalumandiers were cousins with the Hoffmeyers and Hermanns. The Germans drank the Beauvais and celebrated Jour De Fête, and the French ate the leberknödel prepared by the stout German ladies at St. Lawrence's annual picnic.

Because spring floods always threatened to swallow up the town, the original settlement of French Colonials was moved to higher ground, but even then, the great river crept up. Year after year, the town gathered to sandbag the banks and around the settlement. Kids were let out of school to fill bags. High school boys and men piled one sandbag on top of the other, building a protective wall around what their ancestors once called home, and what was now theirs to keep. Last year Eddy was old enough to fill sandbags.

Eddy nudged his sisters from the back seat and whispered that if one of them would take out the trash for him for a week he'd give her full decision power.

Theresa answered both of them, "We're not doing your chores."

"No one is doing anything different," his mom said, "And I have final say." This was true, but she, like his dad, was soft on her children. They were raised right.

Before getting onto I-55, his dad pulled off to fill up at Fritz's, the local market and gas station on the edge of town. He parked in front of the gas pump, turned off the engine, and then slightly leaned upward reaching into his back pocket for his wallet. He had carried the same wallet since Abby made it for him in 4-H. The letters DAD

11

was burnt into the leather, and it was held together by leather twine crisscrossing around its edges.

He pulled out fifteen dollars and waved the cash over the back of his seat, waiting for his children to pluck. They were allowed a piece of candy and a soda for the trip. He gave them way more than they needed, but this was his small treat, and Eddy's mom would pretend she didn't notice.

Everyone clambered out from the back of the car; only his mom remained inside.

"Can I pump the gas, dad?"

"Not this time, son." He was already opening the latch and inserting the nozzle into the gas tank. "Keep your hands clean for your snack."

His dad was fit enough for forty with only a slight pudge around the middle. But all dads were allowed a belly. He worked hard, sometimes doubles at the lime kiln in Sainte Geneviève. On Fridays he often fell asleep on the couch with the television still on. Over his snoring, Eddy giggled until his mom got up and slowly slid the half-finished can of Busch beer out of his hand, placed it on the coffee table, and tucked the Afghan that had fallen on the floor back around his shoulders.

Eddy stopped to watch as his dad flipped the windshield wipers up and dragged the wet foam part of the squeegee across the glass. It didn't matter. Lime dust covered every inch of the town within a twenty-mile radius of the plant. You knew who lived in town and who was visiting by the accumulation of lime dust on the vehicles.

Eddy walked towards the market, combing his fingers through his sister-gelled hair with the two of them yelling behind him to leave it alone. Inside, he headed to the candy aisle, picked up a Snickers, and was considering the sodas when he heard a door slam shut. He turned his head in the direction of the women's bathroom and peered over the shelves. His sisters heard it, too. They glanced up from their *Tiger Beat* magazines, then quickly resumed their debate on whether Ricky Schroeder or Kirk Cameron was cuter.

The slamming door made Eddy curious. He walked closer and stood near the restroom, listening. Through the door he heard the muted sounds of a woman crying. She was telling herself to breathe, to keep it together, just breathe.

Just as he was wondering what she was trying to keep together, the door suddenly flew open, banged against the wall, and the woman darted out. She would have knocked him over if she hadn't used both her hands to brace herself against his shoulders. He could smell her shampoo — an intimacy unfamiliar to him — and his cheeks and ears started to burn. The woman steadied them both and then pushed him aside without an apology, leaving him with only the clanging bell from the exit door.

His sisters caught onto the drama and came over to ask what was going on. Eddy shrugged. "She was crying about something." All three gathered in front of the glass exit door to watch. Outside, there was a man, another woman, and an argument.

The woman from the bathroom ran towards the phone booth from the curb next to the entrance to Fritz's, and for a moment Eddy wasn't sure if she belonged to this scene. It was as if the gas station had two stages on both sides with two plays going on at the same time. On one side his family car and on the opposite side, an aqua-blue and white, convertible Chevy Blazer where a different woman stood in the backseat with one foot above the fender to balance her other foot on the upholstery. She was tossing luggage and trash bags helter-skelter around the gas pumps. As soon as the woman heaved a bag out onto the pavement, the man picked up the same bag and hurled it back inside. She tossed a bag. He flung it back. Back and forth. Back and forth. A demented factory line where progress wasn't the goal.

The woman in the Chevy had long auburn hair that kept getting in the way of the fight. She yelled, "I never should have agreed to this!"

She yanked her hair away from her shoulders, tossing it back like a comic-strip heroine. "Why am I so stupid?" She tore at her mane with her hands. "You never change." She pulled something off her wrist — a rubber band — knotted her hair into the band, managing to secure it into a messy ponytail.

Eddy was close enough to tell she wasn't wearing a bra. His eyes gravitated over her chest; the fitted face of Garfield spread tightly over her nipples and if it weren't for the violence, he may have gotten lost there.

The man yelled back, "Your daughter's out of line. You know it. She ain't going to talk to me like that. Needs some fucking discipline."

Daughter entered Eddy's brain. The woman from the bathroom, who Eddy realized was *not* a woman at all, but a girl dressed like a woman, she was the daughter of the woman in the back of the Blazer. He studied her now. This girl/daughter combo who resembled the female DJs on MTV — tight, black leggings paint-spattered in neon colors, a cropped, white lace top, and an exposed neon yellow bra. Eddy did the strange math in his head. The daughter was much smaller in size compared to the mother, not as curvy. But what added to his confusion was the mother didn't look like any mother he'd seen before, and her clothes completed his mistake. His eyes logged her toned, suntanned legs, her coffee-colored, fringed moccasins, cutoff jean shorts, and then there was that Garfield tee. Eddy's eyes gravitated to it again. He thought, it must belong to her daughter, but his thoughts were interrupted by the girl who bolted from her position at the phone booth and rushed the man.

She screamed in his face, "What? What do *I need*? What di'ya say, asshole?"

"Oh my God," Abby said. "What's he going to do to her?"

And as if echoing his sister's words, the girl screamed, "What? Whatcha gonna do? Hit me? *Hit me again?* Go ahead. See what happens. Go ahead!"

14

When the girl ran towards the man, the mother had leapt from the back of the Chevy. She pulled at her daughter's arms, trying to draw her away from the man, but the girl wrenched free. Inches from his face, she repeated her mantra, "Go ahead."

The man's face flushed. The tendons in his neck bulged. He rolled his arm back like a baseball pitcher or a viper poised to strike, and his arm shook as though restrained by an invisible rope he was using all his strength to free himself from but could not. And then his face became empty of feeling, he lowered his arm, grabbed hold of the girl's shoulders, and headbutted her. Hard. Hard enough to hear his skull collide into hers, enough to make her stumble backwards. She lost her balance and fell onto the concrete, holding her hand to her head. Her courage crumbled. She began to sob and repeat over and over, "I hate you. I hate you."

The mother began shoving the man, but with each push he arched forward. He was tall, prison strong, and he made sure she knew he was not going down. His stance said, "not for her, not for anyone," and he bobbed back and forth with his feet firmly planted to the oil-stained cement like an arrogant rooster.

"Don't you ever, don't you *ever* touch her again," and she then began to sing the same song as her daughter. "What? You going to hit me? Go ahead."

The man's voice took on an edge of perverse calmness. "Wendy," he said, "Nope, I'm not. As much as you want me to."

Eddy's sisters tugged at him. "Let's go. Come on, Eddy. Let's get daddy."

He couldn't leave. How could he? He needed to do something. He sensed it was his role to step in and stop it, but he was also intensely aware of his own insignificant boy frame and his inexperience with this type of situation; so, he stayed. Stayed stuck to the yellowed, peeling, linoleum floor and did nothing while his sisters ran outside to get his dad.

Eddy noticed before the girl did. She was bleeding. With the back of her hand, she wiped away blood from above her lip. That he had made her bleed seemed to enrage her again. She jumped between the man and her mother, pushed her mother backwards, tilted her neck back, and spat at his face. She missed her mark, though, mostly hitting his neck.

The girl staggered back now, stunned by her own actions and then like a fearful dog cowered behind her mother.

The man wore a sinful smirk. Using the corner of his tee he wiped off his neck. He silently shook his head. Finally, he spoke, "Little girl, you better back it up if you're going to spit in a man's face." An uncomfortable ceasefire set in where no one said a word waiting for the man to act and when he did, he laughed, pounding on the Chevy's hood like he was patting the back of friend who just told him a joke, and then laughed some more. "Shanana, I'm going to let you have that one. I got to." He slapped his thigh. "That takes some balls to spit in a man's face or try to...*Goddamn.*" He seemed strangely proud of her. He walked towards them and said, "Get in," and his voice lost all sense of humor.

When the man approached them, the mother encircled one arm around the girl, behind her back, and then reached her other arm out to press her hand against the man's chest — making sure he literally stayed at arm's length. "Dale, we have an audience."

The man took stock of where he was. He peered into the market, where Eddy watched from behind the glass door, and gave him an innocent little girl wave. The mother and daughter followed his stare. They were all looking at Eddy now. He'd gone from being a spectator to a contestant in a game he'd never played before.

Eddy jolted backwards from the door running into a postcard stand that held faded cards of colonial Sainte Geneviève no one ever bought. Fritz, who was behind the counter flipping through an *Auto Trader*, said, "Careful there," without looking up.

"Mr. Herzog?" When Fritz didn't acknowledge him, he repeated louder, "Mr. Herzog? Those people out there are fighting."

Fritz continued flipping through the pages, unconcerned, but responded this time. "Yep."

"That man hurt that girl."

"Yeah. What's that got to do with us?"

"But they're your customers, sir."

"Son, ain't any of it our business."

Fritz turned away from the counter surveying the wall of cigarettes. A cardboard box of tobacco products sat on a shelf under the wall. He began restocking them.

This is wrong, Eddy thought. This is all wrong. He felt the blow inflicted by the man as if he had taken it himself; he could not bear its injustice. Yet, deeper down, he knew his part to play here would only be that of an enraged bystander. He wanted to stop it, protect the girl, but he was just a kid. He couldn't stand up to a man. They all knew it — Fritz, the girl, her mother, the man, his sisters. He felt cheated, an unknown soldier glued to some shit store's floor.

"Pussy," he mumbled.

Fritz moved onto the loose tobacco. Eddy said it even louder. Fritz heard this time. His shoulders dropped in resignation, yet still, he ignored Eddy. He didn't turn around, just carried on with his task.

"Pussy!" Eddy yelled. He'd only ever heard it, never said it before. His hands shook.

Fritz flung the Red Man chew back in a cardboard box. "Who you calling that?"

"You," and as if feeding off the girl's suicidal energy he accused him again, "You are."

"'Cause I don't get in the middle of some white trash episode out there?" Spittle flew out of Fritz's craggy mouth. He glared through purple-veined, hooded eyes and shook his palsied finger at Eddy.

"Yes."

17

"Why don't you get your daddy, tell him what you just called me? Go on. Get him. Tell him. 'Sides we don't know those people. They want help, they're welcome to the payphone. Far as I can tell they got fingers."

The bell on the door jangled and panic surged through Eddy's body fearful that a crazed man would share the same small space with him, but it was his dad who tossed cash for the gas on the counter just as Fritz started to say, "Your son..."

He grabbed Eddy's arm and led him out to their car.

"Dad—"

"Not now, Eddy."

"But—"

"Not now." He opened the car door and urged Eddy inside.

His sisters were already buckled up. His mom adjusted the radio. She looked back at him, shook her head and said, "You didn't get anything either. I don't know these children of mine."

His dad turned the key in the ignition and slowly drove around the other side of the market. He stopped in front of the Chevy. Two bulls pawing dirt.

"Why're you stopping, Gary?"

"Hold on."

When they pulled up to the Chevy, Eddy felt a momentary sense of satisfaction wash over him. He would get his fight. His dad, a surrogate hero.

When his dad didn't explain, his mom asked, "Gary, what's going on here?"

His sisters kept their eyes on the floorboard. Eddy stared out the window at the scene that had evolved into capturing clothes that had busted out of garbage bags.

"Oh, we should help those folks," his mom said, "Their luggage must have fallen out, and look," she pointed out their newly cleaned windshield, "their clothes. They're blowing up the road. Those poor women. Eddy, girls, come on." His mom opened the car door, but his dad pulled her arm and said, "No, Margaret. Wait." She shut the door.

"Wait? Why? Their clothes will get ruined."

"Just give it a second, Marg."

His mom must have trusted his father's tone, because she gazed at the scene as if she might decode their waiting.

At some point, the girl had put on sunglasses. They didn't fit, and she kept pushing them back up the bridge of her nose. He thought it must hurt wearing them. There was a sense of an iconic Hollywood movie star about her, hiding behind sunglasses.

She was like no one he'd ever seen before. Nothing like the girls at school. He might as well have been on a safari, observing exotic wildlife. Watching her lace top blow in the wind, he imagined how it must feel to her, tickling her smooth pink abdomen. She wore her long, coppery-blonde hair in a ponytail on one side of her head. Some strands had escaped her scrunchy, and were stuck in the top of her waistband, pulling, asking for help. His body simply reacted. At first, he wanted to protect her, save her, but the violence had ended, and the sensation changed with it. She was as pink as a strawberry popsicle. He wanted to lick her lips.

"Look," his mom pointed towards the girl, "Look, Gary. That woman's practically is in the middle of the road, and not paying attention." A car whirred past the girl, honking wildly. But she seemed not to notice, or care. "Oh, my God. *Where* are her *shoes?* She, she, she must..." His mom stopped talking, finally tuning in to what the rest of the family had seen: The woman wasn't a girl at all.

The girl was very tall for her age, and Eddy imagined she was twelve years old, like himself.

"That's a girl." His mom went from sympathy to judgement in thirty seconds. "What's her mother thinking letting her dress like that? She can't be much older than Eddy."

When she said his name, his mom turned her head to look at him in the backseat and found him staring at the girl — a look of hunger on his face.

"Eddy?"

Eddy didn't answer, spellbound by the girl.

"Eddy," she said louder still. "*Eddy,* stop. You stop it right now."

He was back. "What Mom? What? What I do?"

"I'm not going to embarrass you in front of your sisters." Her voice trailed off, "...but you know."

The chorus of girls started singing, "What? What is it, Mom? Tell us."

"Hush. All of you," his mother said to the backseat, and then to his dad, "Gary, Gary. No. What're you doing? Just go. Let's go. We don't know these peo—"

Eddy watched his dad roll down the driver's window, tilt his head cautiously out, and ask, "Everything all right here?"

Their car was still running. Eddy was annoyed with his dad who wasn't getting out. Then, he recalled his own dilemma moments ago in the market. His dad could only face the man from the safety of their car. He was no better than himself, or Fritz. They shared a secret cowardice in their DNA.

The man sat against of the hood of the Chevy with one heel of his cowboy boots wedged into the metal bumper, the other leg stretched out comfortably in front of him waiting for his family to finish gathering their clothes. He smiled at Eddy's dad as if he were expecting them. His hair was brownish, wavy, and just hit his shoulders. His T-shirt was too short, so when he leaned back on the hood of the Chevy, part of his brown flesh was visible, his abdomen was muscled. He was smoking. Ashes fell on top of his boot.

The man queried the air, never addressing his family who had returned from the road. "I don't know. Is everything all right, Wendy...Shanana?"

"It's Shannon. Stop calling me that."

The mother didn't respond.

"Okay, Shanana. Sorry, *Shannon.* Have it your way." The man stared into Eddy's glaring eyes, mocking him. "No complaints here. How about you, buddy?"

"I'm fine, but that girl —."

"Eddy, *no,*" Theresa cried. She squeezed his calf in her hand to silence him.

Eddy slapped Theresa's hand away. He felt like the tiny Looney Toon cartoon dog who circled the big dog, egging him on to chase cars, to beat up a cat, starting a fight the big dog would inevitably need to finish, but his dad wasn't going to finish anything today.

"How about you? You doing all right?"

"All right." Eddy watched the back of his dad's head nod. "You needing some help with your stuff?"

The man unhooked his heel from the bumper. With his thumb and index finger, he flicked his cigarette in the direction of his dad's driver's side. The mother and girl sat laconically on the ground, stuffing clothes back into the trash bags. The sunglasses kept falling. The girl kept pushing them up. They could have easily been gathered around a campfire instead of the gas station concrete, so natural was this behavior as if every day they ran around gas stations chasing their wardrobe or worse.

"Girls, you hear this. This nice family asked if we needed any help."

The mother looked up from her task, her expression a mixture of acceptance and humiliation. "Thank you, but no. I think we'll be okay." And though her words spoke of being fine, her eyes asked, why did you make me speak? Eddy wanted to leave now.

The man sighed. "Said they're okay but we *do* appreciate the offer...Very neighborly to stop and check."

He didn't have a southern accent, but his speech was slow and unhurried. Not the type who would do anything in a hurry, for anyone. And again, he took his time before speaking.

21

"Now, wait. There is something, buddy." Eddy's dad had been demoted to a buddy like him. "Where's the nearest liquor store? This market ain't got shit. Excuse me, ladies. You know how long road trips can bring out the worst in folks. We thought we'd have little welcome home party."

"Sorry." Eddy winced at his dad's apology. "It's dry after the line."

"*Dry?* No shit, buddy? Doll baby, we got trouble. This place is dry."

"There's a liquor store maybe three or four exits up...heading west," his dad said.

Eddy kicked the back of his dad's seat, but he ignored him. Abby reached across Theresa before he got another chance to kick again and pinched him. She shook her head no, glaring at him like this was all his fault.

"West? Christ, we just came from there. You already kicking us out of town?" The man huffed in mock offence.

"I don't understand your meaning," his dad said.

The man didn't elaborate. He had walked closer to their car, eyeing the inside as though he was summing them up. Eddy mean-mugged him from the back. The man snickered slightly at him and made a funny face back at him like you might a baby.

His jeans fit tight down the length of his lean body. He adjusted himself and stretched his arms above his head, completely unconcerned he was baring his abdomen. The action evoked a memory of a water moccasin Eddy once saw slip off a tree branch into the creek behind his house. One mean piece of muscle. He wasn't unattractive, but in a roughneck way.

Finally, he spoke, "Meaning we're home. You live in town?"

His dad cleared his throat. "Yes, well a little way out in Lawrenceton, but Sainte Geneviève's the biggest town, anyways."

"Well, neighbor. Maybe we'll see you around."

They lived here. How could they live here? Eddy was shocked. He couldn't place these people in his town.

"All right. Have a good day," his dad said rolling the window back up.

"Shurnuf."

The man got into the driver's seat. With his family, his possessions packed up now, he started the engine, and pulled the Chevy around their car. His brown arm hung out the window and he casually palmed the metal door as though rubbing a dog's belly. Then he studied on his fingers, for the first time feeling the lime dust that had collected there.

Eddy and his family watched the man pull the Chevy out on the access road towards Highway Y, heading towards their town. They craned their heads to read the blue and gold license plate. It all made sense now. Eddy said out loud what everyone was thinking. "California."

Nativity

Lena and Holda were twins; however, most parishioners didn't see them as two eccentric hens, but as one big lady who cracked in half. They lived in a ninety-eight-year-old house that once served as the rectory for St. Lawrence Church. After the last full-time priest passed away, the diocese decided the new priest, Father LeClair, should split time between the two town parishes — Lawrenceton and Bloomsdale. Hoping to preserve one of few original structures left in town, the ladies bought the rectory, and moved in. In turn, the parish supplied them a tiny income to keep up the church. They attended every Sunday Mass, every wedding and every Baptism. They never missed a feast day or a St. day but the holiday or event that was most to the ladies was, Midnight Mass — they'd overseen Christmas almost as long as Christ.

The sisters kept a strict routine, waking up without alarms, never asking what should be done today. On Monday, they polished pews. Tuesdays, they rolled out buckets of water, applying liberal amounts of Murphy's Oil to the hardwoods — the scent of oranges lingering in the air for Sunday Mass. Wednesday, windows. On Thursday, while Lena wiped down the altar and baptismal font, Holda replaced the votive candles and cleaned any dust found in the crevices of St. Lawrence himself. On Friday mornings, they put out the Sunday programs and wrote the hymn list. Saturday needed a quick once-over and a broom to the steps under the bell tower.

The rectory sat on a hill overlooking the church, cemetery, and the homes of the few families who lived in Lawrenceton. The two sisters watched Eddy Bauman raking leaves with Anna Schmidt standing over him with a piece of paper in her hand, gesticulating passionately with her hands as if giving him orders.

"Boy, Lena, that Anna Schmidt sure trimmed up. *Poor thing.* Kids can be cruel. Her mom put her in some camp, called, camp what's its name? Go, go...mmm...go something."

They walked into the church, dipped their hands in holy water, and genuflected. The church had a lonely feeling when it was empty, like it was waiting for everyone to return, but the ladies shook off the feeling and got busy.

Holda opened a new box of votive candles. She was rambling about the Samples family, the newest members of the parish. But Lena wasn't really listening to her sister; she needed to confess something. Church was the perfect place for it. Her sister couldn't get upset on sacred ground.

Lena put the cap on the polish and said, "Holda, I know we've discussed this for quite some time, but we really must do something for our nativity this year, and so..."

Holda started into her "I know, but the cost" speech, but Lena wouldn't hear it this time and interrupted her. "I've found the perfect nativity, and I ordered it already so there's nothing left to it."

It was true. The old nativity had plagued them since last year's Midnight Mass when the re-glued head of Joseph fell off his body into Baby Jesus' manger. The figures were in too bad of a state for another coat of touch-up paint. They had considered replacing the main characters, and reusing the old animals to reduce the expense, but the thought of attaching another hoof onto an already limp lamb seemed unsuitable. They *must* invest in a new scene.

"Lena, you devil sister." She didn't mean it. "And yes, how much?"

"Oh, it's worth it, Holda. The Vatican commissioned it, so you know the Pope, himself, approved it and besides, I chucked the old one. You pay as you go, and we get a new piece each month."

That did change things for Holda. Though pricey, it seemed more precious, almost holy, being a Vatican edition. Who could put a price tag on perfection?

On the first day of seventh grade, Anna took one look at Shannon Lamb, and it was instant hate. She had spent her entire summer at Go-Go Girls, a fat camp disguised as a girl building experience, daydreaming non-stop about Eddy, had lost thirty pounds, but when Shannon climbed the bus steps, he went goo-goo eyed.

Tonight, she had to look her best.

Anna had snuck her mother's makeup bag upstairs to her bedroom and was concentrating on applying eyeliner to her lower lids. The lighted magnifying mirror showed every single blemish on her oily cheeks. She smeared too-dark foundation over her face. With her pale neck, the makeup gave her face the effect of wearing a mask, but she decided it was better to cover up her blemishes.

She was wearing her brand new, pink, puffy-shouldered sweater with horizontal white and purple hearts and blue unicorns from JCPenney's. It had taken two months' worth of allowance.

Tonight, her seventh-grade class was having its first dance at RollerRama Rolling Rink. She wanted Eddy to see what he was missing.

Anna stood up inspecting herself in a full-length mirror and did her best impersonation of a Valley Girl. "Like, duh, Eddy." She flipped her hair the way Shannon did. "Totally...For sure." Something as off. Her vowels didn't sound as bratty as Shannon's.

"What's that, honey? I can't hear you."

"*Omigod.* Nothing, mom." And under her breath, "Dipshit."

Anna's bedroom was in the attic above the dining room where the family weren't allowed access but twice a year. Her mom kept it for company. The staircase leading to her room was walled off with a door at the bottom. Tonight, the door was open, and Anna could easily overhear her mother and Doll Mueller's conversation. She walked downstairs to close the door — it was nothing for her mother to tell Doll the most embarrassing things about her, which is how Go-

Go Girls got around, but today, nope, they were bitching about the increased prices in baked goods. Really, banana bread? Get a life!

Halfway down the stairs, she caught Shannon's name; she stopped to eavesdrop. If her mother and Doll were fans, she would puke. On top of everything else, she read a note from Eddy to Shannon asking if she'd go with him tonight. When Anna asked Eddy who he was going with he rolled his eyes and said, "I mean....no one is really *going* with anyone."

This was almost close to true except April was going with Dan and Becca was going with Brian, but mostly everyone else was just showing up so she dropped it until Eddy incriminated himself. On the bus ride home Shannon tossed a folded piece of paper at Eddy and said, "Sure, I'll go," while doing her hair flip, the one for the boys.

Eddy, dumbfounded by Shannon's verbal acceptance, stood up quickly causing the letter to fly off his lap. It slid under Anna's seat, and she snatched it up. She held it high above her head while Eddy jumped around her like a bouncing Pomeranian. Eddy almost had it once, if the bus bully, Danny Wegman, always tuned into tyranny, hadn't yanked it from Anna's hand.

Danny doubled over with glee when he saw its contents. Above the barking bus driver telling the kids to sit down, he shared the letter with the entire bus:

Shannon,
Do you like me? Check the following:
YES __*
NO __
MAYBE __**
*Do you want to RollerRama with me?
** We can still go as friends.

Danny crumbled the letter in his fist into a tight wad and pegged Anna in the back of the head with. She kept it in her nightstand, torturing herself with nightly readings.

Those words (and out loud on top of it) nearly killed her. Of course, in front of everyone else she acted like she didn't care and equally tormented Eddy and Shannon with Danny's new chants—"Yes, no, maybe" or "Want to go to RollerRama?" when they boarded the bus.

And then she did something so, so, so stupid. She asked him about it. Why, why, why?

"Why'd you say you weren't going with anyone and then ask Shannon?"

"I don't know. Me and you. We're just friends."

Just friends. Just friends!

She needed to punish him, but more than anything she wanted a note like that for herself. Why not me?

Doll interrupted her thoughts. "You weren't as close as I was last Sunday. Did you see what that child was wearing? Where do you even buy clothes like that?"

At Sunday Mass, Shannon, who looked like she just walked off the stage of Dance Party USA, pranced in wearing an oversized Frankie Goes to Hollywood "Relax" t-shirt. If it weren't for her mother, she would have listened to her Walkman the entire service. Who does that?

"A lingerie store (gulp wine), her mother's underwear drawer (cackle)."

Fridays was her mom's Blue Nun night. They'd get louder as the evening progressed, but Anna didn't mind because it felt good to have Doll and her mom on Team Hate, even though she wished she had Shannon's clothes.

"I guess some mothers allow makeup at thirteen, but not me. Top up?" Doll didn't have any kids, just opinions on other parent's kids.

"I *know*. Well, Anna is always asking, but I say not until you're sixteen, and even then, there's limits."

It was silent for a bit and Anna was about to head upstairs and find a coat with a hood to cover her face when she heard Doll whisper, "Trashy." It was what Anna thought every time she watched Shannon board the bus. She smiled.

They weren't exactly neighbor, neighbors. Anna lived in a two-story brick Colonial near the town limits, and Shannon lived in a trailer on the edge of town. The distance between passing the "NOW ENTERING LAWRENCETON" sign and the "NOW LEAVING LAWRENCETON" was but a mile, but the townsfolk early on decided the homes closest to the church were where the respectable people resided. If there was a bad side of town, Shannon lived there. The trailer demanded this designation.

The trailer itself was a rusted, run-down contraption that when new, once housed a nice elderly couple who died in a tragic car accident trying to cross a flooded road. They never got to build their dream cabin on the lot. Their son listed the property for over a year before giving up and started slum-lording first to potheads whose feral children played barefooted in nothing but their underwear and grimy, men's white t-shirts until they were kicked out when a teenager was busted for selling weed, he'd bought from them. The next tenants were construction workers, in town for the Goose Creek development. They built bunkbeds from floor to ceiling and raised huge bonfires mere feet from Highway Y. There were failed pleadings to the landlord and then petitions that resulted in temporary cleanup jobs.

The two Samples and the one Lamb should have been an upgrade. A family is what the Lawrencetonians needed, but they did not see it that way. The town was nestled between an old wood forest on the Fourche a Du Clos Creek with a sprinkling of neat brick ranches and tidy, white farmhouses with tidy red barns much like a scene out of Currier and Ives. They wanted the trailer and its inhabitants erased from their once perfect landscape.

The Samples could have been better neighbors, too. It wasn't one-sided. Their front door was smeared with muddied paw prints and gouged with deep scratches as though a werewolf had tried to slash its way through. This work was caused by their half-rabid dog, Rebel, but they could have wiped the mud away. They left trash bags piled up outside, waiting to be delivered to the dump that Rebel inevitably tore into and spread down the road. Cats had gone missing. When Rebel wasn't chained to an ancient, grey-weathered, picnic table, he crouched in a ditch and terrorized cars traveling down Highway Y. He loved to bite at tires, and he ran many cars off the road. Dale, not one for keeping with working hours, was usually sprawled in a lawn chair chain smoking and immune to burning rubber and squealing brakes. But God help that one man who knew Rebel was waiting and tried to hit him. He was the lesson for any others who may have considered messing with Dale's dog again.

There wasn't a driveway, just hardpan mud Dale would park his Chevy all squirrelly on and as close to the front door as possible. No porch, neither. Stacked, cement, cinder blocks made up their steps and rocks gathered from the creek created a pathway from the front door to the road.

When it rained the rocks on the pathway became wobbly in the mud and Anna would hold her breath, hoping just once Shannon's feet would lose their balance and she'd fall in the muck. She prayed, lips silently moving, "Just one time, Lord, and I'll never ask for anything wicked again. I'll stop cursing. I won't even think bad words." The image of Shannon's too short plaid jumper muddied and wet and with clumps of sludge in her mane of copper hair made her laugh out loud, but Shannon knew those rocks well. She never once fell. There was a grace in her dance, zigzagging from rock to rock, towards the open bus door.

The unfortunate thing for Shannon was she was one of the last to be picked up, which meant all her trashiness was on display for a full bus. There was no hiding it with a long drive or shrubbery. Rebel, who despised the screeching bus brakes, sprang out from under the picnic table in full snarl while Danny Wegman taunted him from an open window in the back of the bus.

Anna heard her mother say, "That stepfather, *now*, he's a looker...if you're into America's Most Wanted type (cackle, cackle)."

"With an eye on him, too. The few times he's been at church I've caught him staring," and then in a voice she must have believed was low said, "practically undressed me with that stare."

Gross, gross, gross, gross. Doll was delusional if she thought Dale Samples was undressing her with his eyes. The only mistress she'd ever hope to be was Lawrenceton's postmistress.

"*Anna*! You almost ready up there? Daddy just went out to the car...he's waiting."

He's not waiting. He's just sick of listening to you two. She climbed to the top of the stairs so as not to sound too close, stood on the top step, called back in a faraway voice, "coming," and then waited for more dirt on the Samples.

"Oh, she's a sweetie, though, and Go-Go was so good for her," her mother said.

They were back on her again. So annoying. Her mother whispered-yelled, "Well, she started her period at camp."

With this comment, Anna ran back down the stairs and slammed the door. Her dad could wait all night. She didn't want to walk out in front of Doll now.

Why can't they stick to the church hags price gouging their stupid pies?

* * *

After Sunday Mass, Father LeClair asked the sisters if he could speak with them briefly. When his congregation finally left, the sisters stayed behind to lock up and Father LeClair waited in the shade of the bell tower. The weather was cooling down and with it the fall bake sale was fast approaching, set for the first week of September, and before anyone knew it there would be icy mornings and soft layers of snow blanketing the parish, and then of course, Christmas would be here.

Lena and Holda bustled down the steps with Father LeClair behind them. They were pleased to have company, and content to discuss the bake sale — recipes for Dutch apple muffins, quick breads, and maple-nut-chocolate chip, cookie bars swirled through their heads. They never sensed something else would be on Father LeClair's mind.

Lena said, "Now, why don't you come up to the rectory (they still called it the rectory) and we'll put on the kettle for some tea, or coffee if you prefer —"

"Lena, Father is a coffee drinker. Oh, I hope you remembered the flavored creamer he likes."

"Ms. Lena, Ms. Holda —"

"Was it on the list? Holda, I don't think it was on the list."

"No, don't you remember. You were already in the car. You said not to worry. You —"

"Ms. Lena, Ms. Holda —"

"Well, if it wasn't on the list, Holda, you can't —"

"Ms. Lena, Ms. Holda —"

The ladies were halfway up the hill before either of them noticed Father LeClair had stopped following them.

"Please. Just please." Father LeClair put his hands out. "Listen. I'm awfully sorry, but I can't stay. Next time. Just a quick chat this time."

"Well, it's a good thing since Lena forgot your flavored creamer."

Lena huffed and then huffed again but before the argument resumed, Father LeClair spoke, "There's been some grumbles around the rise in prices for the fall bake sale. I understand everything costs more nowadays, but we should remember not all of us in the parish have the means." Father LeClair swallowed hard. "And I'm afraid it may send a message...not the one I'd like, or, or, or that is... what... I'm sure you ladies intended. Is there a reason for the increase?"

This was the speech he said to himself on the way to morning Mass — words put into his mouth from another source, Doll Mueller, but now it came out rushed and more than a little guilty-sounding. He did not like quarrels, even if they were minor spats. Differences of opinions led to clashes and clashes led to him acting as a mediator. All Father LeClair wanted was for the two parishes to be happy and to get along. There was always a Doll, though.

The sisters glanced sideways at each other, their eyes like those of startled children. There was no getting out of an explanation, and so they told him about their *new* nativity. This Midnight Mass would surpass all others. A Vatican edition nativity scene naturally justified higher priced mini-berry pies.

The news traveled throughout the parish and the church board approved the increased pricing. The church saw a record high turnout for the fall bake sale. Of course, Father LeClair told someone about their new nativity scene coming all the way from Rome, and that person told someone, and that person told someone, and on and on until the first delivery arrived. It was no surprise when Doll called from the post office. It wasn't just the parish ablaze over the new nativity; the entire town was. Even some of the Christmas-Easter Christians made an appearance and bought more than their share of zucchini bread.

* * *

"Ms. Lena, this is Doll. You've a delivery here, three actually. See, two arrived yesterday, and then this one. I hadn't noticed the first two packages, because Franc sorted them, but when he showed me the third and I said, 'Gosh Franc, I think these are the first of our nativity pieces from the Vatican.' Funny thing, they didn't come from Italy. No, the address is New Jersey."

When there was a tiny break in the chatter, Lena cut her off. "Thank you, Doll. You needn't have called, but we do appreciate it. I'm coming that way today, so I can pick them up later."

Doll was such a nosey thing, always wanting to know what was in everyone's packages. Without taking a breath, she continued, "It's no trouble, Ms. Lena...for me to come by. I mean, I drive right by the church, and Franc can load them in the back of my car."

Doll's drop-by wouldn't end until all the packages were opened. She could barely stop herself from unwrapping them at the post office; everyone had heard the gripes — though no formal complaints — about packages with tears and two different types of tape.

As Doll was saying she got off in an hour, Lena broke in, "I'll be there in thirty minutes. Bye, Doll," and hung up.

When Lena arrived at the post office, she left her driver's door open and popped the trunk before going in, hoping to make a quick getaway. Even with these tactics, Doll followed her outside, clucking behind Franc as he loaded the boxes inside the trunk. Lena was glad she hadn't rolled her window down for surely Doll would have stuck her talking head inside and never let her leave.

Back at home, although it was only a weekday, Lena waddled down to the cellar to pull a jug of elderberry wine. The cranberry glass pitcher and glasses, reserved for holidays and special occasions, were kept on the highest shelf in the kitchen cabinets. Lena struggled some but managed to get them down using a step stool.

Holda was already outside, perched in her chair, watching the sun go down behind the church. She looked up when she heard the porch door creak open and noticed Lena carrying the wine jug. "What's this about?"

"You'll see," Lena tutted, spreading a yellow linen tablecloth over the table between two, well-worn wicker chairs. Next, she brought out the wine glasses and two pairs of scissors. Finally, she lugged out one of the packages.

"*Oh*, is it really? Already? Let me help."

Once all three packages were out, they cheered to a festive Christmas, and like children in front of a Christmas tree, they tore into the packages. They knew, of course, what the boxes held. Mary, Joseph, and the Baby Jesus. They *knew* this deep in their hearts.

Holda was the first to make it through the packaging, but remained quiet, so Lena surprised by her sister's silence, stopped her scissor work, and asked, "What do you have, Holda?"

"It's, a, a lamb."

"Oh, but what a pretty lamb! Just look at the detail on his face. Let's see what I have here." Lena giggled nervously at her discovery. "I've got a cow."

Something was not right. Together, they opened the last package, and unable to hide their disappointment, they shook their blue-haired heads and sighing simultaneously and said, "An angel."

They reassured themselves it was the right thing to get the nativity. The pieces themselves were exquisite — hand-painted in soft honey colors and gold leaf. Pure perfection.

But the payment plan did not go as expected, either. They started receiving two to three figures per month instead of one. With all this inventory, the monthly payments increased way beyond what Lena calculated. The figures, stored in the spare guest room, were turning into quite a gathering. They peeked in on them daily. In those moments, some small bit of apprehension would melt away as they gazed upon their new roommates, until another box appeared *without* Mary, Joseph, or Baby Jesus.

As the months inched closer to December, they received shepherds, sons of shepherds, goats, cows napping in straw, sheep, and even the manger. An *empty* manger!

So much hope depended on that vacant space that held the form of Baby Jesus' little body. The indentations where his tiny elbows and bottom should meet the simple cloth laid out to protect the Lord was nothing more than a teaser. They felt sort of suckered, though neither would admit it.

Holda went through the paperwork, which didn't specify when and what pieces they would get, only the purchaser's commitment to an expensive pay-as-you go plan. With new characters showing up for the birth in Bethlehem, those convenient monthly payments were adding up. Who would have known it was a full house the night of the Lord's birth? Holda even consulted the Bible.

"Did you find it, Holda?" Lena impatiently stood over her while Holda flipped through the family Bible.

"Aha!"

"Read out loud. I can't hear what you're thinking! Christ!"

"I'm getting to Him. Just, just don't hover, Lena."

Lena retreated and Holda began to read. "And Joseph also went up from Galilee, out of the city of Nazareth, blah, blah, blah, into Judaea, which is called Bethlehem. Mary being great with child...but we know all this already...she brought forth her firstborn son, and wrapped him in swaddling clothes, and laid him in a manger —"

"Holda, who was there?"

Holda continued, "There was no room in the inn...and...yes, yes, here it is the...And, lo, the angel of the Lord came upon them... and said unto them: Fear not: for, behold, I bring you good tidings of great joy, which shall be to all people. For unto you is born this day in the city of David a Savior, which is Christ the Lord." Holda's voice shook some; she was quite taken by the scripture.

Lena gently took the Good Book from her sister's wrinkled hands. It was their family Bible and held the names of all their ancestors along with births, baptisms, weddings, and deaths. Their own names were scrolled there, but they were the last of them. Someone else would have to enter their dates of death.

No one was dying today, Lena thought. Today, we're getting to the bottom of someone's birth.

Lena skimmed the book looking for characters until she landed on an angel and read, "Suddenly there was with the angel a multitude of the heavenly host praising God, and saying, Glory to God in the highest, and on earth peace and good will toward men...the shepherds said one to another, let us now go even unto Bethlehem...and found Mary, and Joseph, and the babe lying in a manger. *Ahhh.*"

Lena stopped reading, allowing the beauty of those words to settle around them. She too was taken by their meaning until Holda blurted out, "Did you say multitude of angels?"

She had.

The sisters silently considered all the plurals of animals, insects, and people: a group of hummingbirds made a charm; a group of butterflies was called a kaleidoscope; seven people together were called a septet, but how many angels made a multitude? More than two, three, four? Fifty?

By November, when the first of the wise men arrived, and still no Mary, Joseph, or Baby Jesus, the sisters admitted they were in trouble. Doll made quite a stink about the number of packages coming in, and no one being allowed to see the characters. Hadn't everyone invested?

"I just don't understand, Lena. A wise man before Mary and Joseph? I thought we'd at least get the Baby Jesus after the crib arrived."

Being well-versed in their scripture, they knew for a fact the wise men were not present for the actual birth.

"It does seem better he isn't glued to his crib, though. More realistic, you know?"

"Yes, but I'm concerned, and why so many animals?" There was nothing in Luke about the number of shepherds, *nor* the number of animals they cared for, and then there was that "multitude" thing.

Joseph arrived, to their great relief, the first week of December, but still *no Mary or Baby Jesus.* They were in a pickle. Holda finally admitted it out loud.

"Lena, I think we must call someone. I mean what if we wait and they never show?"

"If it comes down to it, I suppose we could find a filler Jesus and heavily swaddle him, but without Mary..."

Holda picked up the phone and said, "I'm calling. Read off the number for me."

"Gosh, won't it be expensive to call Italy?"

A little frustrated with always being the one to set things straight, Holda snorted and said, "Lena, put on your glasses. It's at the bottom. See, the 1-800-number."

A nasally, New Jersey woman informed Holda there was a total of twenty-two pieces, but the next scheduled delivery wouldn't arrive until January. She was at least able to tell her what the next piece was, though. Another angel! The woman reminded Holda that the set was a limited edition and if she discontinued now, they wouldn't have all the figures. She'd never find matching pieces.

Holda was taken aback by a third angel knowing what she did about the multitude issue. "I see, well, can you tell me what's included in the entire set?"

In rapid-fire, the woman said, "Sure, you got Mary, Joseph, Baby Jesus, three angels, two shepherds, a shepherd boy, three sheep, one dog, one goat, one camel, two cows, one donkey, that was the one Mary rode on you know, oh and his crib, it's the one with the hay, but you should already have it, and three wise men."

The girl started in about a new collection based on Noah's Ark, but Holda had stopped listening. She thanked the woman, hung up, and delivered the news to Lena. A con job. It couldn't be. They were Roman Catholics. This was the Vatican, their Pope, and not some Baptist TV evangelist promising salvation for donations.

A nativity divined from the heavens wouldn't matter if the starring actors never arrived. At night, they sat wordless in their chairs, close to the fire, until it was time to go to bed.

The next morning at breakfast, before Holda could take her first sip of coffee, Lena blurted out, "I know what to do."

"Oh, Lena. I do, too!"

"A live nativity."

"You know that's what I was thinking, and it's never been done. I can't imagine anything more perfect, other than having Baby Jesus miraculously appear. Let's do it."

* * *

When they told Father LeClair about the plan for the live nativity, he thought it was a great idea, but nonetheless inquired into the Vatican nativity.

Lena mumbled and started fidgeting. Holda took over.

"Father, the truth is, there was a problem with the order. It's on backorder. Oh, but you should see them. Breathtaking, aren't they, Lena? By next Christmas we should have the full set. We think it's because they're terribly busy in Rome with Christmas and all. So, we thought, what a wonderful thing for the children."

"Backorder? Well, that's a shame. I know there're a lot of people looking forward to seeing it. I suppose you could just use the old one, mix in the new with the old pieces."

The sisters didn't respond, shamed into silence, and then Father LeClair realized what they couldn't say and asked, "You don't have it, do you?"

Holda answered, "No. We don't... Father, you saw the state of it. Remember last Christmas Eve? The incident."

"Oh, yes, the head. Joseph's, wasn't it?"

"It was and anyway the live nativity will be fun for the kids, and we could use the new animals and all the angels around the manger." Holda looked to Lena, who was bobbing her head in affirmation and adding, "And angels, loads of angels, a multitude even."

"Ladies, I'm sure it'll be simply heavenly, and if anyone asks, tell them it was my idea. No harm done."

"Thank you so very much, Father."

As Lena and Holda got up to leave, Father LeClair suggested it would be a nice gesture to offer the role of Mary to Shannon Lamb, the new girl from California. The transition from public school to

Catholic school was not an easy one, he imagined. She had a difficult time adjusting. He liked the girl. She was different, but he believed old towns benefitted from a little variety. And then there was the school principal, Sister Bienenkönigin, who was not a pleasant person. He heard the kids had nicknamed her Sister Evil.

"But, let me give Shannon the news," he said. "I don't want her to be overwhelmed by anything else."

After the discussion with the ladies, Father LeClair wasted no time in telling Shannon. It was easy to catch her by herself; he happened upon her later that week at school in the library. She was seated at a corner table flipping through a book.

"Hi, Shannon, how are you?"

She stiffened, tried to look serious as if she was actually reading *The Robe,* and said, "Good," and then as if recalling she was supposed to ask about him. "How are you?"

"I'm well. Thanks for asking." He paused a moment and then said, "Well, we do have a slight problem. We're in need of an actress for a serious role, and I was hoping you could help me."

"For real? Omigod, I mean. Sorry. Yes! What part?"

Father LeClair's fears of overwhelming her were clearly fabricated in his own mind. He told her it was fine to tell her parents, but no one else until he made the announcement on Sunday.

* * *

When Father LeClair asked the parishioners to remain seated after church and explained the live nativity, Anna's mother squeezed her leg in excitement and Anna didn't even mind, because she knew she was a shoe-in. Her ancestors were some of the founders of Lawrenceton; the church was named in honor of Henry Lawrence, Anna's great, great something. The entire Schmidt family had been baptized at the church. It only made sense that she would play the part of Mary. Father LeClair unfolded a piece of paper and read the names.

"Eddy Bauman will play the part of Joseph. Shannon Lamb will play Mary. Anna Schmidt has the role of the shepherd. The wise men are..."

The shock made Anna bolt straight up from the pew and scream (but only in her head), Are you kidding me? She gets to be Mary and I'm a Goddamned shepherd. A boy's part! She shouted a silent tirade of curses to herself. Her lips twitched, but she managed to remain mute until her mother pulled at her blouse to sit back down. If she could have crawled under the pew, she would have.

Father LeClair responded by asking the rest of the crew to stand so the parish could see the faces of their new nativity members. Anna's mother elbowed her, and she grudgingly stood up again. Eddy and his family were sitting three pews in front of her. He wore a smile like the donkey in the "Pin the Tail on the Donkey" game. She moved from his dorky grin to his eyes, but she already knew before she arrived at their destination that he was smiling at Shannon. Asshole.

* * *

For the most part, the live nativity created a warm buzz throughout the church. Weeks of listening to Father LeClair speak of Joseph's faith in Mary and their perilous escape from Herod to Egypt increased the anticipation, not only of the children, but also the adults. The investment in the new nativity was almost forgotten by the parishioners as parents looked forward to their young ones playing such important roles. There were a few people, however, and one particularly bitter twelve-year-old girl, who were not happy about the live nativity at all.

"Doll, I'm surprised at you." Lena gasped. "She's part of this parish now, too."

"Ms. Lena, maybe, next year give the role to her, but Anna Schmidt has been going to this church since she was a baby. Father LeClair baptized her. And, I'm just saying, more than a few of us are still disappointed about not having the new nativity."

Holda cut in. "We know perfectly well, Doll. We keep all the records but let me say something. Shannon Lamb struggles to fit in, and how many times do we have to tell you? It's on backorder. No one is trying to keep anything from anyone. We just wanted it to be a surprise. *And* there will be the animals, angels, shepherds..."

"Okay, I didn't want to say it, but she is tawdry. There, it's done. Not just me, but some of the mothers —"

Lena, who was topping up Doll's coffee, set the pot down and interrupted her, "Doll Mueller, really? To pick on her when Father LeClair himself thought she'd be perfect."

"Lena, hush," Holda said.

"What? Father LeClair? I had no idea, but why her?"

Lena held her hand to her lips, afraid to reveal more, and let Holda talk.

"Doll, it came from above. That should be enough. Now, we really are quite busy today."

Of course, Doll protested all the way out the door that Father LeClair didn't know any better.

On those final Sundays before Christmas, when mothers raised their brows in the direction of Shannon, the sisters scowled back at them, or rather squinted; they were incapable of true meanness. They had their Madonna, and nothing Doll, or the rest of the parish said would discourage them.

* * *

When the hour at last arrived, mothers guided their children to the stairs at the bottom of the choir and then took their seats with the rest of the congregation who were gazing tenderly at the shining new sheep (and cows, camels, donkeys, dogs, etc.) resting in hay around the manger. Three celestial angels surrounded the scene with upturned eyes and hands spread out. The feathers on of their wings were so realistic that a toddler who'd managed to escape his parents ran up to try and touch them. He was captured just in time. Fresh greenery of cedar, pine, and juniper adorned the pews, altar, and even the roof of the barn where the empty manger waited. "Silent Night" hummed softly in the air. Every man, woman, and child breathed in the scent of the garland and the wax from the burning candles and believed. It smelled like Christmas.

Teeny wise men trailed up the stairs to the choir. Their boyish feet stepped on long robes made too long that their mothers had cut from old white sheets. Lena lined them up in procession and fitted plastic crowns atop their heads, while Holda tied silky cords around their tunics recycled from gaudy Goodwill drapes. Eddy/Joseph wore a beige bedsheet and burlap tunic with a rope strung loose around his waist.

Anna petulantly tapped her staff, her eyes laser-focused on Eddy. She recently started calling him Judas. He was wearing his characteristic horsey smile and was cheerfully scratching under his headdress, which was cut from the same piece of itchy burlap as his tunic.

She wanted to hate him, but his complete indifference to her made her long for him more. She hated everything else about the night, though. The stupid sheet, the stupid staff, and the stupid stuffed sheep she was made to carry. More than anything she hated Shannon, who not only got Eddy, but also had a proper outfit made for the occasion. Any minute, Shannon would appear, gliding up the choir stairs in her blue silky gown that complimented her perfect shape, and a white lace veil draping over her glossy strawberry-blonde hair.

The only problem was it was already ten minutes to midnight, and there was still no sign of Shannon. Holda kept looking at her watch and repeating, "Where is she? I know we said 11:30?"

At 11:55, Shannon was still missing. Anna saw her opportunity. She casually mentioned to the group, "You know she's not coming, right? You *are* going to need to replace her."

"She'll be here, dear. It's Christmas. Everyone's busy. She'll show." Holda's reassurance was as much for herself as Anna.

"She thinks the whole thing is dumb," Anna said. "She told me at last practice."

Eddy said, "You're a liar! She never said that."

At least she got Eddy to finally stop smiling, but his treachery hurt. She refused to relent.

"Am not! She did. She also said you are the biggest dork she ever saw."

"Shhhh," Lena said. The sisters moved into a corner to discuss the possibility of converting Anna from a shepherd to Mary with only minutes left.

At 11:59 exactly, the organist started playing "O Little Town of Bethlehem." It was Mary and Joseph's cue to walk down the choir stairs and continue to the manger, to be followed by the shepherd and wise men. When he was nearly through the song he said, "What now?"

In hushed voices the sisters said, "Play it again."

He shook his head no, tormented by the idea of repeating a song. He held the last chord for as long as he could and then in a panic went with a Christmas favorite. After the second round of "Jingle Bells," the wise men began fighting over Anna's staff and Lena prepped an incredibly pleased Anna on what to do when she reached the altar.

"I know, Ms. Lena. I studied her part because I just *knew* something like this would happen. She's not reliable. I mean at school, um, like she sometimes turns in papers late."

"You're a liar!" Eddy said.

"I am not! Remember our last book report?"

"She was sick."

"Please, enough children," Holda said, but the two continued to argue quietly amongst themselves anyway, Eddy defending, Anna condemning.

"Yes, well, I just hope nothing has happened," Lena said to Holda.

The sisters were legitimately worried about Shannon and her family. Both went one more time to peek over the choir to see if the girl's parents were seated, and to their dismay they were. By the time the ladies turned back around to deal with the nativity cast, Shannon was bolting up the choir stairs. All the anxiety Lena and Holda felt in those last very tense minutes melted away; both gave one unanimous and giant sigh. The relief was short-lived, however, because Shannon looked more "like a virgin" than the actual Madonna.

Her eyelids were caked in frosty blue eyeshadow and the lace veil meant to drape elegantly over her head was rolled and tied into her over-sprayed, over-teased hair. Sharp streaks of deep rose blush meant to highlight Shannon's cheekbones, announced she was coming from twenty feet away. Her eyeliner, the darkest kohl black, had the effect of making one eyelid look feline and the other somewhere in the realm of a gypsy.

"Well, look at you, *Maarryyyy,"* Holda said emphatically to Lena and then, "Lena, get your hanky."

Lena dug in her bra where she kept everything from her keys to gum, but no hanky this time. Shannon apologized for her lateness and then listed off everything she got for Christmas, most of which had made it onto her face.

"Ms. Lena, Ms. Holda. *Look* at my eyes." Shannon kept her eyes closed while telling the sisters and the rest of the live nativity that her eyeshadow was called "Sparkle til' morning," and "look," she opened her lids and pointed to her electric blue eyelashes.

In the Christmas chaos, Lena and Holda had forgotten about poor Anna. They made quick adjustments to Shannon's face. Holda licked a thumb and managed to go over her lids, hoping to downplay the effect of "Sparkle til' morning," but only reassuring herself that she had at least removed a portion of her eyeshadow. Lena untied the oversized lace bow and draped it over Shannon's hair, creating a pseudo-veil she hoped would conceal the effect two tons of makeup would have on the congregation below.

"I put a little extra on, you know for stage makeup," Shannon said. "You're supposed to do that so the audience can see your face. It's true. I read about it."

Eddy beamed at Shannon, nodding his head in agreement.

Anna stood in a state of shock while one of the wise men poked her back with his newly-acquired-now-forfeited shepherd staff and told her to take it. Her face took on a shade of crimson. Her lips were moving — though nothing came out. Her brain roared with rage. And then, Eddy told Shannon she looked beautiful and that was the straw that broke the camel's back, the sheep, the goats, and the cows.

Anna shrieked, "You look like a whore!" and yanked the swaddled baby doll they were using for the absentee Baby Jesus from Shannon's arms. This time, the words did come out of her mouth. The organist stumbled on "Jingle" which came out more like "Jangle." There was an audible "ooohhhh" from the congregation below, and the littlest wise man asked, "What's a whore?"

The look on Shannon's face was worth it. Anna didn't care if she was grounded forever. Besides, she figured, you can't get grounded on Christmas.

Somewhere beneath all Shannon's make-up, were real eyes and now real tears began to well up, and slide down Shannon's rouged cheeks, fashioning Freddy Krueger-like slashes across her entire face.

Holda said, "Oh, it's not waterproof."

By this time Lena found a hanky and started wiping down Shannon's face while telling her she looked splendid, just slightly less stage makeup next time. Anna watched in shock and utter unadulterated fury as Lena rearranged Shannon's face. It was now or never.

"Come on, Eddy. Let's go."

Anna struck Shannon with her crozier, grabbed hold of Eddy's hand, and yanked him down the stairs. Eddy, unaccustomed to the workings of teenaged girls, stopped resisting once they made it to the aisle and were in public view. The wise men, or rather boys, trailed behind them, followed by Shannon, who was followed by Lena, who was followed by Holda.

The congregation rose to their feet with the arrival of the kids. Seeing the procession finally doing what it was supposed to do fifteen minutes ago, the organist raced through the last stanza of "Jingle Bells," and without skipping a beat switched to "Away in the Manger."

By the time the live nativity made it to the front of the church, it was as lively as anyone could have had hoped with the addition of first one Mary — Anna — being pursued by a second Mary — Shannon.

Doll Mueller, who was sitting next to the Schmidt family in the front pew, took one look at Shannon's face and blurted out so the entire church heard, "Good Lord, there are drag queens with a lighter touch than that girl."

"*Excuse me*, Doll," Wendy yelled, "that's my kid you're talking about." This was followed by Dale Samples nudging the man next him to tell him "Yo Mama so ugly" jokes. Though he replaced "mama" with "Doll Mueller."

With barbs flying from the front pews to the back pews, heads swiveled back and forth, their attention redirected from the kids in the nativity — most of which had made it to their assigned spots — to the argument at hand. Lena and Holda broke up another squabble between Mary, Mary, and Joseph and finally resigned themselves to the fact that there would be two leads tonight. Anna refused to forfeit Baby Jesus or put him in the manger, fearful Shannon would pluck him up. Finally, Lena and Holda worked out a compromise: Anna would stand on one side of the manger while Shannon and Joseph stood on the other side. Most of this was ignored by the churchgoers who were still invested in the Mueller/Samples takedown. The ladies found their reserved spaces in the front pews, plopped down, and took in the show that they had desperately tried to direct. Consigned now to stand like bystanders at some street performance, they watched St. Lawrence Church unravel, culminating in the final blow made by Dale. "It *means* you're battle-axe, lady. You can't cover up ugly."

This was too much. All eyes were on Doll who had inhaled the air from the entire Church. Even the flames on the candles seemed to flicker.

Father LeClair, recognizing his moment shouted, "You've ruined Christmas! All of you. Now, Shut up. Just Shut up!" And silence ensued but for an accidental chord struck by the organist's foot.

The priest skipped the introductory rites and launched right into the liturgy. "In those days Caesar Augustus issued a decree," and so on and so forth until the Savior was born.

Their live nativity was flawed. Yet, when Lena intwined her pudgy fingers in Holda's equally pudgy fingers and squeezed, they recognized it was their thinking that was flawed; a Vatican edition nativity scene wouldn't make Christmas any more perfect than it already was. With all its imperfections — soured eggnog, rock hard fruit cakes, foul-mouthed and harlotted virgins, spats between church members, and even with Lena and Holda's failures, it couldn't be any better.

Father LeClair delivered the news of the Savior born and everyone rejoiced, especially two sisters who realized they had found their multitude of angels amongst their town, who were presently singing carols at the top of their lungs, slightly out of tune, and more than a little slurred.

Summer Love

Eddy had reached the point of summer vacation when boredom set in and returning to school seemed almost appealing. Rather than serving time indoors and fighting with his sisters, who did nothing other than camp next to the window air conditioner, watching reruns of *Beach Bikini Bingo* and *Beach Party* (he succumbed to watching a couple of times) and the networks broadcasting black and white literary type movies he never understood nor cared to, he started taking longer and longer treks up the Fourche a Du Clos Creek and beyond. He tried to recreate the pirate games from his summers before and even *last* summer the land resembled Treasure Island, but lately, he couldn't muster boyish games. And then one day he strayed from his normal route, and everything shifted abruptly; his mind no longer lingered in the limbo between boy and teenager.

Eddy always took the creek path north simply because it was the same direction his school bus traveled to his school. The path was embedded in him, and it took him to his favorite places, places in the forest he'd even given names. He'd never once ventured further on foot than the edge of Lawrenceton, but if he wanted to, he could have walked the winding Fourche a Du Clos Creek that followed Highway Y, left Lawrenceton past Bloomsdale, turned onto Old U.S. 61 towards Sainte Geneviève, and beyond to the Mississippi River, sailed down to Louisiana, to the Gulf of Mexico, out to the ocean, to France and Germany, where his ancestors once lived. There were towers in cities where light polluted the heavens, cities he recognized deep down he'd never see, nor cared to visit. What his ancestors discovered here was fine by him; small towns nurtured their own.

Yet today would not be another day that slipped into the declining summer with his sister Theresa a/k/a Mother Theresa, calling mom at work to tell on him. *"Edddeee's* hogging the *Atariiii,* mom. He's been on it for two hours."

Eddy tossed the game controller at his sister and slammed the back-screen door, and then stopped to listen to the effect the door would have on his sisters. "Grow up, Eddy!" He trudged towards his path and stopped short again. Something new was sounding in his ears — the faint tinkling of distant music. For a second, he thought it was one of the ridiculous songs from his sisters' bikini movies and he imagined hearing Annette-whatever-pasta-sounding-last-name, goody-goody singing, "Summer's here...school is out...it's time to play...we're going to go to bikini beach..." or something about a dream boy or a dream girl; they were all the same. Yet, the music faded the further he walked down his path. He kept stalling, turning this way then that, trying to tune his ears to the music until he understood he was walking away from it and turned around completely, heading south of his home. The sirens called. He answered.

The volume increased as he stomped over the reedy, flood-flattened, tall grasses bordering the creek bed. He was ankle-deep in grasses so thick; he risked stepping on copperheads. Without a machete to clear a safe path, he had to move his mission to the creek. Removing his shoes, he observed dragonflies dip into the water, rainbows reflected off their iridescent wings. He left his shoes on the creek bed, and told himself to remember where he put them. Barefoot, he stepped into the cold water and crawdads bolted away from his feet to hide beneath rocks. It was hot and humid, his T-shirt was sweat soaked, but the water was cool and felt good.

His mind turned to Billy the Kid and momentarily he became an outlaw being chased by hired guns. Horses' hooves pounded in his ears. They were gaining on him. He high kneed it against the current slogging his way up the creek until he slipped on algae, and fell waist high in water. "Shit." He had stubbed his toe on a rock and now felt stupid. The fall broke his reverie enough to make him lose his outlaw ways. Eddy was back to being Eddy again, He couldn't understand why his head see-sawed between emotions. One moment he enjoyed pretending and then the next, he chided himself for being immature. "Grow up, Eddy!"

Gnats swarmed his face, gaining ingress into his ears, eyes, mouth, and Eddy swallowed a good many. When he found deeper waters, he dunked his head, but the baptism from boy to man only thwarted the gnats temporarily and soon he was swatting at his neck and face again. A water moccasin glided inches from Eddy's submerged thighs. He froze, holding his breath, observing it skate the surface of the water downstream like a black mourning ribbon Eddy once saw tied to an American flag floating in the wind.

The music was so loud at one point he thought he had found the source and he did a full 360. It unnerved him being surrounded by something that refused to show itself. He soldiered on. The creek finally opened to a treeless hill, and Eddy found himself in Shannon Lamb's backyard, staring at the back of her trailer. He never considered the same creek, what he thought of as *his creek*, also ran behind her trailer. In the mornings, when he heard the pneumatic "tsss" of the bus door opening, he watched with Cocker Spaniel eyes as she climbed the stairs not once considering her geography. He wished he had known this at the beginning of summer. They were tied by land, by water, by the stones beneath his bare feet. He likened himself to a Ponce de Leon, finally discovering the Fountain of Youth, drawn to the music like a monk called to prayer.

A boombox sat atop the Samples' trailer roof connected to several neon orange extension cords that hung down the side of the trailer and entered the back door where he assumed it was plugged into a socket inside. Madonna's "Lucky Star" blasted across the glittering water. All the sounds of nature — the gurgling creek, occasional screech of a hawk, the shuffling of squirrels on dead leaves, all this

51

faded into a single sound: "Star light, star bright, first star I see tonight." It was no nursery rhyme, though.

Eddy studied Shannon as she climbed the last rung of an aged wooden ladder tilted against the roof of the trailer. The sight rendered him immobile, every cell in his body bewitched by this vison. His first time appreciating live bikinied bodies. On the TV there were the MTV Spring Breakers, dancing girls in Day-Glo bikinis wearing Ray-Bans, but those girls were out of reach. And there were his mom and sisters who were always pale, bitchy, and in navy one-pieces and the 1960's icons — thirty acting to sixteen — who his sisters were oddly fascinated with this summer. But this — this was the real thing.

It was as though there were two religions in town, and he had discovered the pagans openly worshiping their sun goddess. His body hummed. Not quite raw passion, but a strong yearning. This vision branded into his brain would stay with him. Later, he'd carry it back home, taking it behind a locked door to his room.

Shannon spread out several bath towels, surveyed the scene, and then called down to her mom, Mrs. Samples, "Crap, mom, I forgot the quilt, and I can like totally feel the roof burning through these towels."

She did a sort of tap-dance right there on the roof and Eddy thought, cat on a hot tin roof, but that was one of his sisters' movies, and what he was experiencing was new, and not in black and white.

Mrs. Samples, who had also been watching Shannon, walked towards the open back door.

Eddy panicked, quickly ducking. It wouldn't have done him any good, because if either of them glanced up in his direction, they'd see him gaping-mouthed and erect as a sentinel.

By the time Mrs. Samples returned with the quilt, Eddy had retreated to the protection of a large cedar. She stood halfway up the ladder and handed Shannon the quilt. Then, Mrs. Samples, who didn't quite seem like a Mrs., climbed the ladder.

Eddy knew he was being a Peeping Tom, but he couldn't resist the sight of the two smearing suntan oil over their bodies. And though it was impossible to smell their lotion from where he stood, the scent of coconut and pineapple lingered in the air. They fidgeted with their towels, magazines, and drinks like two cats curling up to sleep until, finally content, they covered their eyes with gas station sunglasses and lay back, stretching their beautiful limbs in the full sun.

Aside from her green plaid jumper, Eddy had only seen Shannon in "street" clothes at Sunday Mass. Not that a bikini was considered normal attire, but it was vastly different than a school uniform. She once wore shorts to Mass, but only once — the entire parish made comments about the Californians and their odd ways. Even her mom and stepdad dressed differently than the rest of town. It was as if none of them knew they belonged in the category of mothers, fathers, and daughters. It wasn't just the way they dressed, though. They didn't talk like them, or act like them. And no one in Lawrenceton would ever think of climbing on top of their roof, buttering themselves up to tan in full view of Highway Y and all who passed by.

As much as he wanted to announce his presence, he knew a male lurking in the woods would unsettle them. He'd return the next day; a reason for being in their creek was already forming in his mind.

* * *

Eddy and Shannon lived in the parish of St. Lawrence but were bussed to St. Agnes School in the next parish over in Bloomsdale. A simple, white, one-room schoolhouse still stood near St. Lawrence Church, but it was last attended by children in 1947. The two parishes that fed into St. Agnes consisted of the more well-to do-kids from Bloomsdale chauffeured to school by a parent and the St. Lawrence kids bussed in from Lawrenceton and the surrounding countryside. St. Lawrence families were typically farmers. The parents of the St. Agnes kids mostly worked at the lime kiln in St. Geneviève which boasted being the second largest producer of lime in the world. A thin layer of lime dust covered the homes, buildings, and cars just else within fifteen miles of the plant. Finally, with the longest ride of all, there was a sampling of public-school kids (PSKs) who rode the same bus with Eddy and Shannon. Once the Catholics were dropped off at St. Agnes, the PSKs remained seated, to be bussed into the town of Sainte Geneviève for their free education.

A class divide existed amongst the two parishes and the PSKs resulting from one simple fact — paid tuition. Like the PSKs, the parents of the St. Lawrence kids did not, however, pay out-of-pocket for tuition. They did not go for free, either. Tuition was paid for from the proceeds of a huge annual picnic, and everyone worked with pride at the picnic knowing they were giving their children a *religious* education. In the unspoken caste system, St. Agnes ranked at the top, St. Lawrence in the middle, and then at the very bottom, the PSKs, the untouchables.

There was someone, however, who was ranked lower than even the PSKs and that was Shannon. Her trailer on the edge of Lawrenceton, where the bus stopped to pick her up, gave them ample fuel each day.

After Eddy played Joseph and Shannon played Mary in the live nativity at Midnight Mass, she started sitting next to him on the bus, unaware of the secret law that didn't allow girls to sit with boys.

Eddy would toy with the straps on his backpack, only permitting himself what he imagined were disinterested peeks until she arrived in front of him and sat down.

"Hi, Shannon."

"Hi."

"Hi," he said again like an idiot, and then to cover up he quickly blurted out, "Five more days."

"Huh?"

"Five more days before summer vacation. Thank God."

"For *reaall.*"

He loved her Valley Girl.

"Are you going anywhere?"

Shannon shifted on the bench. "Whatcha mean?"

"Like on vacation?"

She scrunched up her nose. "I don't know. We didn't talk about it. I mean Dale may go somewhere...for a job." The stepfather who all the women fawned over, even though the town knew he was jailhouse mean. Even his sisters talked about his "movie-star jaw," and his hair straight out of a shampoo commercial. He acted as though gunpowder ran through his veins instead of everyday human blood like the rest of the world. "Hopefully, he goes," and then, "hey, can you scoot in?"

He was hogging the seat and had failed to notice her long legs sticking out sideways into the aisle.

"Sorry." He whipped his legs over to the metal wall of the bus.

"It's okay."

He said sorry again anyway and then felt foolish for repeating himself. The whole ride to school he tried to get up the nerve to expand on the little information she provided, but nothing seemed right, so he focused on the bland landscape. All pasture and cows.

At the last stop before school, one of the PSKs, Danny Wegman, started making sounds from a porno soundtrack. Eddy didn't think it had to do with the second grader who just boarded. He went back to staring out the bus window when he saw it. In a small pond a bull had mounted a heifer. Shannon saw it, too.

Heat climbed his neck, his cheeks, until his whole face burned like a chastised virgin. Of course, he had seen this before, living near dairy farmers all his life. He had never seen the act done in a pond. The bull's nostrils were wet, and they flared. In the cool morning air, his breath steamed out like hot smoke. Its hind leg muscles bulged under the sheer weight of keeping itself on two hooves and manipulating its thrusts. The water lapped around both heifer and bull who committed the sacred rite as if to honor an ancient religion or some older god.

Shannon, being from Los Angeles and not being accustomed to farm animals, made the mistake of speaking out loud before catching herself. "What are they do — oh, grody."

This made all the boys in the back laugh. "Eddy, you haven't explained the birds and bees to your girlfriend, yet?" Danny Wegman, of course. "Or is it going to be another Immaculate Conception?"

Eddy and Shannon had been ridiculed endlessly since the live nativity.

"Shut-up, loser," Shannon said into the air.

"What? What was that?"

Danny plunked himself in the seat in front of Eddy and Shannon, crowding a third grader sitting into the corner. He was fifteen and obsessed with *Dr. Who.* Danny's mom knitted him a scarf, just like the one Dr. Who wore, and in the winter his elongated dirty scarf dragged on the ground; he never cared how muddied the bus aisle was, he'd step on it anyway. He used to attend St. Agnes but was kicked out the year before for carving graffiti on the church pews: "Kathy B. Sucks Dicks" (with the image of a penis next to Kathy B.'s name). The Wegman family made appearances at St. Lawrence on major holidays and had made it to the live nativity. He ran his hands through his greasy hair and leering at the two. *"Me* a loser? Look who comes out of a tin can every day."

"Leave her alone, Danny."

"Leave her alone, Dannee. You gonna make me, Casanova?" Danny puckered his lips and made kissy noises. Even though he was older, Danny was scrawny, and Eddy thought he had a chance, but the bus pulled into the parking lot of St. Agnes, and the morning drama had ended.

Shannon whispered, "Thanks."

* * *

The following day Eddy dug through his dad's tackle box and found some small lures. He didn't want to lug it all the way up the creek, so he put the lures in one of his mom's Tupperware containers. She wouldn't be happy, but he didn't care. In last year's school backpack he packed a thermos, an old beach towel, a peanut butter and jelly, and a small batch of deception. He grabbed a fishing pole and headed in Shannon's direction.

He had a let-them-see-him plan much like putting your hand down low for a dog to sniff and he posted himself with his back turned towards them as though he had been fishing and walking backyards until he suddenly ended up behind their trailer.

A kitchen timer went off and Eddy guessed they were flipping to tan their other sides. He tensed, anticipating their reactions on finally seeing him.

"Mom, *mom*, there's some dude in our creek."

"Hey, what you're doing over there?" He heard Mrs. Samples call out to him.

He feigned being startled, even making a jerking motion before turning around. "Sorry, you scared me. I, I, um, I was fishing. It's Eddy. What are you all doing?" He silently reprimanded himself for asking the obvious.

They both recognized him and Mrs. Samples, seemingly satisfied that Eddy was harmless, lay back down.

Shannon remained watching. "Are there like real fish in there?"

"Yeah."

"And, like you catch them?"

"Sometimes."

Her expression was incredulous. "Can I try?"

She descended the ladder like a newborn calf, her legs delicate and wobbly. When she reached the ground, she wiggled her toes into a pair of yellow flip flops. Her skin was the soft pink of rose petals, but in some places, she had started to burn.

His eyes traveled to the thin white lines impossible to ignore, the untanned areas around the strings of her bikini bottom had shifted;

she had not even double-knotted them. Eddy bet she didn't wear shorts under her uniform like all the other girls at school did either.

Mrs. Samples yelled down to him, "Good, take her. She doesn't need to bake anymore," and then spoke to Shannon, "What? You know you're going to freckle."

She walked down a thin rutted path towards the creek, stopped, took off her flip flops, and then pitter-pattered from rock to rock until she finally made it across to him. Another image to take with him like the one from yesterday. Eddy offered his hand. She was slick with sweat and suntan oil.

"Thanks. Sorry."

"It's fine." She smelled like the beach. Lawrenceton felt bigger, bolder as if its tiny sign with a population of sixty-seven suddenly tripled. Yet, he felt awkward in his new town, more awkward than he had ever been in his entire life, and now with her so close to him, he forgot how to cast.

Rather than landing in the deep pool of water before them, his line landed in the broken branches washed behind the creek. He was forced to cut the line and start over. He handed his rod to Shannon in defeat. His bravado vanished. She held it limply, questioning her next move, and then handed it back and said, "It's okay...hey, do you like Billy Idol?"

"Sure."

"What's your favorite song?"

Eddy knew who Billy Idol was, but in this moment, he couldn't think of one song title and blurted out, "This is boring. Let's go swimming."

"Shut up! You have a pool? That's so rad."

"No. I mean here."

"Here?" Shannon didn't exactly sneer, but she eyed the creek suspiciously.

"Yeah, why not?"

"Aren't there snakes?"

"Nah."

Eddy ran across the rocks and jumped into the darkest part of the creek.

"Oh my God. You're crazy," she yelled, but plunged after him, and then screamed as she emerged fom the ice-cold water, "Holy shit! It's freezing."

"Watch your language, girl," Mr. Samples' voice came out of nowhere. Neither of them had noticed him walking from the trailer to the creek. His hair was longer since the last time Eddy had seen him. Shirtless, in cutoff jeans, he canted his right leg to the side while his eyes peered at them in the creek as though he was making some calculation about the scene before him.

Shannon pushed back strands of wet hair from her face. "Why? You say it all the time."

Eddy prayed silently, *don't do it, please don't do it.* He knew she couldn't stop herself, though. He'd seen it firsthand. A family brawl at Fritz's Gas Mart and Eddy and his family had witnessed it. Back then, Shannon was just the girl at the gas station, a stranger screaming into another stranger's face, goading him, "What you gonna do? Hit me? Go ahead. Do it." Now, she was real, and they went to the same school and were even in the same grade together.

"It's different. I'm an *adult.*" Mr. Samples pulled a pack of Marlboro Reds out from his pocket and loosely flipped a cigarette from the pack. "I've earned the right." His eyes bore into Eddy's as he put the cigarette in his mouth. He didn't light it. He stood, examining Eddy as if he were marking him for later. He reached into his other pocket and pulled out a lighter. He mumbled, "I know you, kid?" with his cigarette in between his lips while flicking the metal wheel with his thumb several times but his lighter refused to ignite. He tossed it in the tall grass and fished out another one from the back pocket of his jean shorts.

Say something. Something. But nothing came out. His teeth had started to chatter. "Shannon, I'm freez—"

"Isn't it your naptime?"

Shit. Shit. Eddy backtalked some to his own parents but had never been openly hostile to an adult. He whispered "stop" to her, but she didn't hear it, or chose to ignore him.

Mr. Samples quickly pulled the cigarette from his mouth and directed it at her like he was pointing his finger in warning. "Watch yourself." Then he grinned, a grin without any humor and said, "You like showing off to your boyfriend, girl?"

"Like he's not even my boyfriend. We go to the same school."

"Oh yeah, he ain't?" He nodded at Eddy and winked. "Ask him if he thinks he's your boyfriend." He wore the look of a dad who'd caught his daughter's boyfriend squirming out her bedroom window.

"Uh, no, sir. We're just friends," Eddy said.

"*Sir, sir?* You hear this, Shannon? At least you pick respectful ones. Maybe it'll rub off." He knelt sitting back on his haunches, so they were all eye level now. Eddy stared into the creek water. "I'm heading to work."

"*Work?* Where?" Shannon asked.

"Dirt tracks in Farmington."

Eddy looked back up at Mr. Samples. His cigarette was lit now; he took a long draw. Smoke poured from his nose, and then he held out the pack of cigarettes in Eddy's direction, offering him one.

"Mr. Samples, uh, I'm, um, I'm not old enough."

Dale snorted and said, "That's what I thought." He shifted up, glancing over both their heads into the woods behind the creek silently puffing away and Eddy realized he was waiting for Shannon to ask him about his new job.

"So, what did they hire you for?"

"Flagman."

"Really?" Eddy said. "Cool."

"I think so. Wanna come?"

"Yeah! I'll go." His dad had promised to take him several times, but usually apologized later because he needed to pick up an extra shift at the plant. He imagined sitting next to Shannon in the stands with no one else around and Mr. Samples focused on the tracks. It was perfect and had fallen into his lap — a date where he didn't have the embarrassment of asking her out. There was one time in seventh grade they'd gone roller skating, but she hadn't treated it like anything other than the school kids hanging out. This would be different.

"Not tonight, I gotta fill out paperwork." He studied on his cigarette. "Waivers and shit." He drew another drag, flicked an ash, and continued speaking. "Kind of a sudden thing last weekend. Damn flagman had a heart attack right up there in the stand." Dale clutched the left side of his chest, stuck his tongue out to the side of his mouth, stumbled forward, and then acted as if he were about to fall over. "Sumbitch fell on the track. Almost got run over. Helluva sight. Caused a pile up." He giggled — high-pitched and fiendish and then started coughing on the smoke, but even still, he took another drag. When he finally stopped hacking, he coughed up phlegm, spat, and then tossed his barely smoked cigarette in the creek near Eddy. "Goddamn things are gonna kill me one day." He turned around and walked back up the hill to the trailer.

Shannon rolled her eyes and when he was out of earshot said, "Like let me know when, Dale...God, he's so disgusting. What mom sees in him...and a *flagman*? Is that even a real job?"

"Sure. I mean, um a fun job." Eddy shrugged. "You know what a checkered flag is, right?" He was hoping she'd say "no", so he'd have something to teach her about.

"Yeah, I get it, Eddy. But do you really want to go with him?" she splashed him.

"Hey, stop. That's cold."

"But." Splash. "Don't you think..." splash... "he's a total dickwad?" Splash.

"He was a dick at Fritz's." Eddy splashed her back, but harder than she had him. She was being playful. He had meant to be playful too, but it came out wrong, like when his mom said he got too aggressive with his sisters and reminded him they were girls and didn't like to play rough.

She rubbed water from her eyes. "Shit, Eddy. Who's Fritz?"

"You know? Gas station Fritz?"

Eddy saw the truth wash across her face. It was her mom, Mrs. Samples, who he had seen wildly tossing out suitcases from the back of their Chevy Blazer, telling their new town, "Thanks for the welcome party, but we're not staying!" Shannon's social debut was an ass beating from Dale. The entire town knew. And now he'd stupidly brought it up.

"Okay then," she mumbled.

"Sorry. I thought you knew it was me."

"Uh-nope. Like I wasn't really paying attention."

"I'm sorry...I didn't..." She hadn't recognized him from the gas station two summers ago. All this time, and she didn't know him.

Shannon scanned her backyard, avoiding eye contact. "This water is too freaking cold."

He watched her wade over to the shallow part of the creek. Her strawberry-blonde hair clung in dark red streaks like tentacles down her back. Agreeing to the races was an impulse from a boy, but bringing up Fritz's was even worse.

Not bothering to put on shoes, he gathered his things and marched up the hill through the overgrown grass. Rebel eyed him suspiciously from under the picnic table but didn't budge, too hot for even his wrath. She hadn't said goodbye.

He travelled down Highway Y, and the whole way back home berated himself for being so stupid. The asphalt felt like a griddle on his bare feet, but he didn't even care if he completely seared his skin off. He resented everything about Lawrenceton at this moment. The church, the rectory with the old ladies, the cemetery where his family would all end up, where he would end up. Tomorrow was Sunday and that meant Mass, and him as an altar boy. He was sick of getting up early, sick of ringing the church bell. Everything was always the same.

When he got in, his mom was dicing onions, and he knew immediately what she was making. Meatloaf, peas, and mashed potatoes. She had a two-week menu that never varied. He headed straight to his room.

"You catch anything?"

"No," he hollered behind him already in the living room.

"Hey, get back here."

Eddy groaned but turned around.

"After you clean up, you need to take the trash out, and don't forget Friday you're supposed to cut the grass at the church. Ms. Lena and Ms. Holda said there's shrubs needing attention. Are you listening to me?"

"Yes, I heard you. The grass, I know."

"Then speak up. What's with the attitude?"

"What did I do? I said yes. I know all this already."

"Oh, you know everything now."

"Well, it helps you remind me every day."

In slow motion his mother scraped the onions from her cutting board into a bowl with breadcrumbs and ground beef. She took her time washing her hands, hunting a dishtowel, and then drying her hands, before turning around to face him. "Oh, Eddy. *Look at you.* You're dripping on the floor. You've tracked in mud, and why aren't you wearing shoes. Abby just mopped. Go put those in the garage. *And...,*" she selected an egg from the carton on the counter and cracked it lightly on the side of the bowl, "don't smart me."

"I'm not, but I know all this," he said opening the door leading to garage off the kitchen. A wave of summer heat blasted him. He tossed his grubby shoes in the corner on an old piece of frayed carpeting they kept for this reason. His feet were in worse shape. Black on the bottom, but she somehow hadn't noticed. As soon as he shut the door, she was on him again.

"So, where did you go today?"

"Uh...the creek."

"Yes, but who were you with?"

"What do you mean?"

She squeezed ketchup over the mixture. "Mr. Schmidt said he passed you coming from the Samples and offered you a ride home, but you didn't want it."

"What are you spying on me?"

"No, but I don't want you hanging around that family."

"Uh, well, as she's in my class, rides my bus, goes to the same church I'm not sure how that works."

"You've been smarting me since you got back. I don't want you picking up bad manners." With her hands, she blended the meat with the seasonings. "I hear that man practically lives at the Dew Drop."

"Can I go now?"

"May I? Yes, go ahead."

Before going in his room, he heard her say something about a "shower" and "wet clothes." He slammed his bedroom door.

* * *

The week toiled by with more fighting with his sisters and chores from his mother until it was Friday morning. Eddy opened the garage door and dragged garden tools out. The rest of the summer was going to suck. He'd ruined it with his stupid mouth. He walked the tools down the street and placed various sizes of pruning shears on the bottom church steps. Then, he went back to the garage to retrieve the lawnmower. The drudgery of the task before him made each step back and forth between his dad's garage and the church pound into his head until he had a headache.

Worse yet, he couldn't start the stupid mower. It was only 9:00 and he was already dripping in sweat. Every pull of the crank and sputter of the mower enraged him. He was close to kicking it, when

Ms. Holda screeched behind him, *"Ehdeee, did yooou* check the *gaasss?"*

It was more than he could take, and he snapped, "Yes, *yes!* Ms. Holda. I checked." But then he felt bad because she was old, and her entire life centered around her sister and St. Lawrence Church.

"Oh, okay. I just thought...I," she switched, "I brought some iced tea. It's going to be a scorcher. Make sure and take breaks, son."

Nicer, he said, "Thank you, Ms. Holda. I will. I brought the pruning tools, too."

"Thanks, Eddy. You're a good boy. I tell your mother and father all the time. Well, I won't keep you."

After she was out of sight, he leaned down to unscrew the gas tank cap. Empty, which he knew the second Ms. Holda suggested it.

By noon, he was exhausted but finished. He didn't take breaks, only short stops to gulp down tea with his hand on the dead man cable, wanting to be done as quickly as possible, heatstroke or not. After putting away the garden tools, he went back to get the lawnmower, praying the ladies didn't hear the mower's engine stop and want to chat. He wanted to cool off in the creek. Instead, he washed his face, his burnt shoulders, and his legs spackled with chopped grass and boxwood leaves with the garden hose. It came to him quickly then. Other than where Dale parked and their homemade path from the road to their trailer, the Samples' yard looked like it hadn't been cut since spring. He took several large gulps from the water hose. From where he stood, he could see Ms. Lena waving from her porch. He dropped the hose and raised his empty tea glass, indicating where he'd leave it on the church steps. He should walk it up the hill for them, but spotting the overgrown bushes around their porch, he didn't dare risk it.

He waved back and yelled, "Got to take the mower back."

"Okay, thanks Eddy. Did you want something to eat? We made ham sandwiches."

"Too hot to eat!" His mother would be scandalized by him for having a conversation in which he had to shout. The alternative meant getting trapped at the rectory with the ladies. Once, he was forced to view photo albums of faded ancestors and times long gone for two hours straight.

It took an eternity for her to go back inside, but as soon as she did, he unscrewed the gas cap and filled the tank until the gas overflowed. It was church gas he figured it could go for neighborly charity. Eddy sort of jogged the mower down the length Highway Y towards Shannon's wanting to avoid any townies who'd report on his whereabouts to his mother.

They were just now spreading oil on their long legs and his eyes darted between Shannon and Mrs. Samples, a mature version of Shannon. Her dark amber hair was a little past her shoulders. She was still young, and he thought she must have had Shannon at eighteen or even younger.

"Hey," he called up to the roof. "I thought you might want your grass cut, Mrs. Samples."

It was sweltering. His T-shirt was plastered to his chest. He wished he could have changed. "I was at the church today already, and I noticed the other day it was getting kinda high."

"That's so sweet to offer. Our mower died." Mrs. Samples smiled down at him. "If it's not a lot of trouble. *And* call me Wendy. Dale is just Dale, too. We're neighbors."

"No trouble."

Even though the grass was thick, and the yard was uneven, he felt like he had made an upgrade from the church ladies who kept adding to the list of items he could do for free.

Shannon and Wendy came down from the roof to harvest fragments of lost treasure, some of which the mower found — aluminum cans, a Frisbee, chunks of a wading pool, tennis balls for Rebel, abandoned toys from the previous owner. He went back to the garage to get the weed whacker. If he kept up like this, he'd destroy the blades.

Two hours later, beat, and even more sunburnt, they were finished. Garbage bags waited by the cinder block steps near the front door for Dale to take to the dump.

"That made a big difference," Wendy said. "Thanks, Eddy."

"Yeah, like we can actually walk around without stepping in dog shit," Shannon added.

"You and your potty mouth, Shannon. I hope you don't speak like that at school."

Eddy eyed the stretch of their creek with longing "Think I can jump in?"

They spent the remaining afternoon in and out of the creek (even Wendy, but mostly just to dip her feet) until Dale came out.

He sat on top of the picnic table, smoking, surveying the yard, and said, "You guys sure know how to wake someone up, don't ya? Sounded like a damn circus out here. Rebel barking his ass off. Lucky if I got four hours of sleep." His voice increased in volume as the complaints continued. "Probably fall off my stand and get run over, but the yard *sure* looks pretty." And then he spoke directly to Eddy, "You must think we live like pigs. That why you come over here, clean up my yard?"

"Dale, stop. He was being neighborly, and we do live like pigs. You need to stop throwing your cans everywhere, and when you head in, take those bags to the dump."

"I got work. I ain't got time to play house with you three tonight," Dale spit on the ground.

Eddy's mother and father bickered over silly things, but nothing that made him feel he should leave the room. They were small frictions and like stepping on a cat's tail, quickly over. The tension between Dale, Wendy, Shannon and now himself was palpable.

Eddy heaved a trash bag over his shoulders and started towards Dale's Blazer. Dale came up quick behind him and yanked the bag out of his hand. "I got it. You get on home. We're done here. And here." He shoved five dollars in Eddy's wet shirt pocket. Eddy shook his head no.

"Just take it. You worked your damn ass off."

"I never said I wanted to get paid, *Dale*."

Something registered across Dale's face. "What happened to sir, or Mr. Samples, chief? You were all bunny rabbits and bullshit the other day, and now it's just Dale, huh? Are we on a first-name basis, *son*?"

"I told him to stop with the Mr. and Mrs. stuff, Dale."

"Oh, *you did*. Well, I kinda took to it. Wendy, tell him to take the money."

"Eddy, please take it," Wendy said.

And then Shannon. "Yeah, you should take it."

Dale grinned, "You'd be wise to listen to the ladies, chief." He shoved the five bucks into Eddy's shirt pocket hard. "See, a little pocket money feels good, huh?" And then Dale got close to his ear, so close Eddy could smell stale beer and smoke on his breath and whispered, "If you get the urge to cut my grass again...don't."

* * *

The summer continued, but now its earlier sluggish decline sped up and as each day edged closer to the start of school, Eddy felt more aware of time passing and the need to solidify something with Shannon.

They'd meet at noon and travel down the creek into territories familiar to Eddy — favorite places known only to him, places he named, and pointed out to Shannon.

"These are holy lands," he told her. "See the steps. Don't they look like steps to a pyramid?"

Millions of years of floods had eroded the limestone and the various shades of gray stone gave it the appearance of a staircase or hundreds of tiny steps climbing from the creek bed. Eddy explained how he looked it up in the encyclopedia: a pyramid in Tulum,

Mexico called the Temple of The Descending God where Mayan tradesman came to pray and burn incense before traveling inside the jungle to larger ancient cities.

The further they traveled into the landscape, untouched and verdant, the more comfortable he felt with her, and he revealed things he'd never told anyone.

"I think God is from Missouri," he said.

"What?" She asked, but she wasn't making fun of him. She asked like she just needed proof.

"Where else is it so beautiful? It's like you can smell the colors. Just stop. Close your eyes. Breathe in through your nose."

They both stopped walking, closed their eyes, and inhaled the earthy smells of the forest, a palette of mineral-rich soil and morel mushrooms. A melody of water trickling over moss-covered stones along with a breeze murmuring between tree limbs formed a soft song of it. Drones of insects whirred around their skin, drowning in their sweat. Eddy swatted his neck.

"Let's go," he said.

They came to the widest part of the creek and stood over a plateau. "When it floods you can't cross here, but someone, see, here," Eddy pointed to a cable wrapped around a white oak tree. "Someone strung this cable across the creek."

Shannon tentatively felt the thick rusty cable that had scarred the bark where it had become deeply embedded, tight as a tourniquet, and was now part of the tree.

"Your dad?"

"Nope. I asked. It's been here a long time. There's something I want to show you on the ledge. Do you want to go down, *or* we can climb across?"

The cable stretched across the creek bed a good twenty feet in the air and wrapped around its twin brother, another oak. It wasn't a huge drop, but it would hurt if they fell onto the larger rocks or gravely bed where the creek had dried up in the summer.

"I can do it," she said.

Eddy went first to demonstrate. He reached his hands as far apart as possible to clear more cable and he got across quickly. He was proud of his time; her presence urged him to move fast. When he landed his feet on stable ground, he called for her to come. She easily swung from hand to hand until she was about two feet out and he then reached around her waist and pulled her over the remaining way.

Her back was slick with sweat. He wiped his hands on his T-shirt.

"Sorry," she said.

"It's okay."

From here they climbed up the ridge to another sacred site, what he called "Hollow Tree" for obvious reasons.

Eddy slid his body sideways into the entrance of a large water oak. Lightning had struck it, but it was a stubborn old tree and refused to die; the injured part formed a cavity big enough for Eddy and Shannon to fit into. Eddy pulled Shannon in. Soft wind rustled the canopy above them. The blue sky and sunlight soaked through the leaves spreading a shadow on the dry earth like a great gray lace.

When he came here in the mornings by himself the world was dew-damp, and he would sit inside Hollow Tree digging his fingers into the wet earth. Sometimes, he dug deep enough to find earthworms, but Eddy wasn't like a lot of boys his age who enjoyed torturing insects. On days when plumes of rain pelted Highway Y and then an hour later the sun came out and cooled the asphalt, steam would rise from the hot road, smoke-like, as if there were a thousand tiny volcanoes erupting, and Eddy would collect worms off the road. He carried their shriveled bodies — once plump and purple — to the safety of the grass, hoping he'd saved them.

Sitting inside the protection of the tree, he felt the composition of life and land. Yet Eddy's sense of ownership was bittersweet as though within the rich dark soil grief remained. He'd discovered remnants of those who came first. The land was consecrated by

Chickasaw and Quapaw, who were later forced from it for his ancestors, for himself, he worried. He had a prized collection of arrowheads and a few primitive tools inside his top dresser drawer he wanted to show Shannon. Everything he ever wanted was right here. His Mayan Temple, Hollow Tree, the Fourche a Du Clos Creek. He belonged to them, he hoped, and now Shannon was part of him, too.

They sat with their backs against the trunk, with their arms wrapped around their knees on the warm dirt bed. Dried-up leaves from last year's fall clung to their sweaty legs. Eddy brushed them off her. Shannon found a GI Joe figure Eddy had forgotten there at the beginning of the summer, but now he could not fathom ever wanting to play with it again. He carelessly tossed the figure outside the tree. He untangled a twig from Shannon's hair and brushed off dirt from her forehead before he leaned in and pressed his lips onto hers. He did not know if he should move his lips, but she knew this dance and he followed her lips until she abruptly stopped and crawled out from the tree hollow.

They walked home in silence.

* * *

Two days later, Eddy sat in the back of Dale's Blazer which was much like their yard before they cleaned it up. Empty beer cans and fast-food bags containing half-eaten hamburgers in various stages of decomposition littered the floor. A quarter of the windshield was stuffed with similar items. While driving, Dale shuffled through the mess searching for his chewing tobacco. He'd taken the top off the Blazer, so the back two seats were open to the wind and hamburger wrappers flew up and outward towards Eddy until they hit the open road. Dale yelled for Shannon to pick through her side to find his Red Man. No one bothered with conversation; the wind was too loud, or Dale would turn the radio up a notch when Shannon or Eddy said something to each other. But he didn't mind any of it, because tonight he was going to ask Shannon to be his girlfriend.

Thirty minutes later, Dale pulled onto the dirt road leading to the St. Francis County Raceway — a 3/8-mile, oval dirt track in Farmington. He parked, turned to Eddy, and said, "Listen, I can get one of you in for free, but not both. Policy thing. There's a driver's meeting before the race and all the drivers must be in no later than 6:00, so you should be okay. If some sumbitch gets hisself locked out, they ain't racing tonight. That means there may be some angry drivers hanging out and you don't want them catching you neither."

Eddy didn't know what he should be "okay" about or why he should be worried about angry drivers, but Dale continued, and it became clear.

"See that building there by the stand?" Dale pointed to a building covered in gray aluminum siding. "There's a gate back there, but if it's locked, you're going to need to climb the fence. When you see *that* man." Dale pointed at who Eddy assumed was the owner of the track. The man ran-walked, stopping every ten seconds to give someone instructions. *"Right there,* shut *that door."* He pointed to a door. "You head over to the back." Dale spoke to him like they were planning to rob a bank. "Now, you see that other man — the one in the vest, that's Vance — he's the ticket guy, and listen here, son, don't let him catch you. He'll tear you a new one if he catches you."

Eddy's eyes followed Dale's finger. Vance was a heavyset man. He wore a white tee under a denim vest he'd made from cutting off the sleeves from an old denim jacket. His shoulder and arms hung like he was once the star football player ten years and sixty pounds ago.

Eddy never cheated at anything in his life, so the prospect of sneaking in without paying hadn't occurred to him. He wondered if it was something everyone just did, and suspected Dale jumped many fences. Did people sneak into the movies? He imagined him and Shannon hiding out in the bathrooms, and then watching a second movie for free. Is that who she wanted? If he snuck in now, would it lead to other crimes? He wanted to say he could pay. He had his own money, but Shannon didn't seem to follow the same code and leapt from the Blazer and waited for Dale to come around to take her in. It felt like a test he needed to prove to them he could pass.

"So, hang tight, buddy."

He watched them walk together to the gate. Dale made some introductions to Vance. He could tell Shannon was laughing by the way her back moved even though he couldn't hear her. Something had shifted between Dale and Shannon; it made him uneasy. Dale draped his arm over Shannon's shoulder in a fatherly way and she allowed him to lead her into the building, as if it were "Take you Daughter to Work-Day," and not some redneck dirt track. He imagined Dale saying, "Ain't this sweet? Look at us. My girl follows me everywhere." Eddy preferred it the way it was before with clear lines drawn and enemies known.

From the back seat, he followed the drivers' movements with his eyes. They hung back shaking hands, slapping backs until the last man slipped into the building and Vance shut the door and placed his wooden stool directly in front of it.

The console display read 6:10. Vance wouldn't budge. He remained seated on his stool, spitting in a cup, guarding the gate like some redneck St. Peter. Eddy willed him to move. Nothing. It felt like an hour, but only five minutes had passed, and then Vance finally rose. Eddy felt tension tingle up and down his spine. It was time. He got out, shut the Blazer door lightly, and then sprinted alongside the chain link fence, constantly looking back to see if Vance had gotten sight of him, praying he didn't turn around. Vance ambled towards the concession stand.

This is good. This is good, Eddy thought.

He made it to the gate, but it was locked as Dale suggested it might be. It wasn't a high climb, but now he noticed there was barbed wire wrapped around the top of the fence. Dale hadn't mentioned that. He figured it was on purpose.

"Crap, Crap," he whispered to no one as he stuck the fat toe of his tennis shoe into the chain link fence. He had one leg over the top of the fence and was trying to lift his other leg over without getting his jeans stuck to the barbed wire. It was hard to see with only the distant light from the parking lot. "Shit." His shoelace came undone in his race to the back fence and had gotten caught in the spikes of the barbed wire. It occurred to him that Dale always wore boots — easier to toe into a fence and no strings to catch on anything.

The position was so awkward he decided it would be easier to pull his foot out of his shoe and retrieve it once he made it over. He leapt, faltered in his landing, but didn't fall all the way, stabilized himself with his hands, and then quickly climbed up the fence again, now on the right side, or wrong side depending on opinion, and yanked at his shoe. He was sweating hard, his mouth was acrid, dry, and the fluorescent floodlights waiting to tell on him hummed above. Someone flipped the switch and like an escapee from prison Eddy ducked and covered his head as if his arms could hide him. He surveyed his surroundings. He was safe.

Eddy stood up and walked rapidly in the direction of the stands, his socked foot picking up pebbles and dirt. He saw Dale talking to Vance, and then he saw Dale pointing in his direction, ratting him out. He didn't know if he should run back. Vance would reach him before he could make it back over the fence. He decided to keep walking. It had to be a joke. Dale and Vance approached him.

"You don't like paying, boy?" Vance had the deepest voice he ever heard.

"Um, well. I. No."

"Um, well, I, No," Dale mocked. "Answer the man." Dale wasn't joking.

"I, um, I have money. Do you want it? I know him. *Mr. Samples?* Tell him, *sir?*"

Eddy fumbled in his pocket for the wadded five-dollar bill Dale had given him for cutting the grass.

"Sir, huh?" Dale smirked.

"You know this fool?" Vance asked Dale.

"Now that I think on it, he does look familiar." Dale rubbed his chin. "Yeah, I know 'em. Aren't you one of Shannon's running mates."

"Man, Dale. You say he's her friend? But I hate these sneaky sumbitches who think they can outsmart me."

"Yep," Dale agreed. "Nothing but an ass beating to curb it."

Eddy held out his sweaty crumbled five dollars in the direction of Vance. Vance lurched at him and yelled "boo" in his face. Eddy recoiled and instinctively threw his shoe at Vance, a lame defensive attempt. He was expecting a strike from Vance that didn't come.

It was Dale who went for him from behind and Eddy was unprepared. Dale grabbed him around his neck, shoved his head hard under his arm into a headlock, and rubbed his fists into his hair. It didn't hurt. Dale was laughing hard. Vance too.

"I got you, boy. That was so damn funny." He let him go with a push and he fell on the grass and quickly leapt back up.

"You should've seen your face." Dale snickered, pleased with himself, and then both men doubled over again.

"What the heck, buddy? You threw your dang shoe at me, kid!" Vance picked up Eddy's tennis shoe and handed it to him. "Sorry, kid."

"That was the funniest fucking thing I've seen in forever. Goddamn. I thought you were going to shit yourself. Did ya'?" Dale asked.

Eddy got the joke. He looked past the empty stands that would fill up in the next hour and was relieved to see Shannon wasn't there, and hopefully hadn't witnessed this.

"Let's see those pants, chief. Do a twirl." Dale twirled his own finger.

"Ah, give the kid a break, Dale."

"Shut up," Eddy said. He had enough of Dale and stomped away. Dale hollered some more jabs his way. He'd never met anyone like him before. He was an overgrown boy, a bully. His whole body quivered with anger inside and out. He hated him.

When he didn't find Shannon at the concession stand, he walked back to the stands and climbed to the highest bleacher. She didn't seem to be anywhere, and he wondered if she *had* seen what went down and went back to the Blazer. He hoped she was as disgusted as he was. He scanned the entire track one more time. This time he found her. She was sitting at the bottom of the flagman stand, leaning in, her long legs sweeping back and forth, talking to two race car drivers. He ran towards her and waited behind the two drivers for her to acknowledge him. She waved weakly and kept talking to the drivers. Five whole minutes passed, maybe more, while she flirted and totally ignored him.

His body felt disconnected with the realization she had not been watching for him or waiting for him. She hadn't gone back to the Blazer. And with this knowledge he saw himself as a participant in a game he came too late to play. He turned to walk away and saw three more drivers, all walking in the direction of Shannon. Eddy recognized the same hypnotic pull he felt weeks earlier in the summer, slogging up the Fourche a Du Clos Creek, searching for the source of music; it was what now beckoned these young men.

The race hadn't even started, yet Eddy heard the engines roar, and the grime of dirt was already building up on his face from dirt sprayed off the tracks. He'd have to sit through it while Dale stood above the circus of speeding cars like a proud boy marching into battle with nothing but his flag for a weapon. It had not even begun, yet the winner was chosen—it wasn't Eddy. He felt cheated like when he knew he'd gotten an A on a test, but instead his teacher handed him a paper, with a red-inked "D" in the upper right-hand corner. Cheated, like when the news promised snow. The kids didn't mind carrying extra homework to cover a week of missed school days. Come morning, he enjoyed the sound of his bleating alarm, for once, so assured he was of no school, until his mom called from the hallway to get ready in her smug, satisfied way, and he thumbed his blinds open. He couldn't ignore the dry ground, the iceless branches, and later the screech of the school bus. He felt so utterly cheated.

He put his head between his hands, covering his ears. Why did I change paths that day? He shook his head. Why? Why me? And, for some reason he thought of one those 1960's beach movies he suffered through with his sisters. They were always the same — a girl, a guy, a bad girl, a bad boy — and then in the end, good triumphed over bad. The good guy got together with the good girl, and they both ended the movie singing some ridiculous duet about summer love. This was not the case here. Eddy would have to agonize through the race, the drive back, and Dale would drop him off defeated with a sure-as-shit grin plastered on his face.

St. Damien of Molokai

The Sisters of the Most Precious Blood inhabited a neat little household overlooking St. Agnes School and Cemetery in Bloomsdale. Sister Bienenkönigin reigned as principal over the school, demanding the same level of order she asked of herself, her fellow sisters, the teachers, the students, and one of her few extravagances — her beehives, that were kept behind the nuns' house. The hierarchy at St. Agnes School was like a bee colony, in her opinion, with herself ruling as queen bee. The sisters she lived with, and non-secular teachers were drones and the students, worker bees. Everything usually functioned seamlessly under her direction. That is, unless outside parties were introduced who didn't follow *her* rules.

This is what was happening now at St. Agnes with a particular eighth-grade girl named Shannon Lamb. The girl was an intruder, an interloper, with California ways, who continued to disrupt the natural order of the school with her outlandish behavior. If there were more girls like Shannon Lamb, eventually the order Sister Bienenkönigin instilled at her school would, like a bee colony, simply collapse. Invading hornets were known to wipe out an entire colony. The bees or her students would not just move away to build a new hive, move to a new home or town, but would completely fail, and this is what she feared more than anything else.

Sister Bienenkönigin had read cases of worker bees flying off and not returning to their hive. There was a well-known case of it in the early 1900s on the Isle of Wight that occurred across the ocean and before she was born. There were reports of colony collapse in Louisiana in the mid-1960s. Scientists said it was due to the weather, pesticides, pathogens, and poor nutrition. Whatever the cause, it reversed thousands of years of instinct.

Sister Bienenkönigin decided that on no occasion would this occur on her watch. What would the sisters at the motherhouse in O'Fallon think this Christmas if they didn't receive a jar of her honey? It was her annual tradition, and she was above all things a devotee of ritual, rule, sacrament, and tradition. There were only the old ways. And one event, more than any other event, warranted strict adherence to custom — the sacrament of Confirmation — which Sister Bienenkönigin navigated, or at least *tried* to navigate, with St. Agnes's eighth-grade teacher, Mr. Diener.

* * *

During the months preceding eight graders Confirmation and the arrival of the archbishop from the Archdiocese of St. Louis, the class spent every afternoon in Catechism. They fasted Wednesday through Friday (on plain white rice and water), and on one occasion even made a trip to the motherhouse in O'Fallon. The nuns took Confirmation very seriously, which is not to say that First Confession and Holy Communion were a cake walk, but the girls and boys were going to officially be indoctrinated as adults into the Roman Catholic Church. Another, equally important aspect of Confirmation was the selection of a new name — the name the children would be called in heaven once the archbishop anointed them with holy oil.

"So, listen up. By next Friday, seven days from now, you will have decided upon a name, and you will have completed a *full* two pages about why you chose your saint or martyr whose name you selected. This is serious business. Two *full* pages."

Mr. Diener turned away from the class and picked up a piece of chalk. On the blackboard, he wrote "saint or martyr," underneath that, he wrote "research history on saint or martyr," and under that, "reason for selection."

Earlier in the day he made his annual pilgrimage to the supply room where he kept a box containing a stack of pamphlets provided by the archdiocese. When he was hired as the eighth-grade teacher at St. Agnes, Sister Bienenkönigin told him one of his responsibilities was the selection (or guidance in the selection) of the children's Confirmation name. It was she who suggested he contact the archdiocese. Mr. Diener wrote a letter specifically asking for "guidance on assisting Catholic children on their spiritual quest to select a suitable Confirmation name," and presented the letter to Sister Bienenkönigin, who made a slight change in word choice, and told him to mail it. The archdiocese sent him a box with well over a thousand pamphlets. He only had eighteen kids in his current class and with dwindling numbers every year, Mr. Diener did not want so many pamphlets. The sheer number overwhelmed him so much he wrote the archdiocese a second time and offered to return at least half of the box. He never heard back.

Mr. Diener waived a pamphlet in the air. "We have a limited amount of these, so keep up with yours. This means do not lose your pamphlet."

While Mr. Diener made his speech, he stood before the line of desks holding kids. He methodically counted out five, four, four, five, slowly handing out the pamphlets to the first in line before moving to the next formation of desks.

When all the kids received their pamphlets he said, "Your St. is part of your spiritual journey. He or she will travel with you from the moment of your Confirmation until you enter heaven, *if* you enter heaven, so I stress to you that you do not merely pick the easiest saint or martyr to research, but one who speaks to you."

Most of what Mr. Diener said was found in the pamphlet, but there would be some who would not give the pamphlet a second glance after receiving it. When Mr. Diener was finished passing out the pamphlets, he sat down at his own desk and said, "You may take five minutes to look over what I have just given you but do so in silence."

The girls were the most excited about choosing their new names. They could finally be what their own parents had denied them. The possibilities of three syllable names and French spellings, accent marks, and the letter "q," seemed exotic, something generally not, allowed on the premises of St. Agnes. No less than three girls would bring in papers on Sainte Jacqueline and then argue amongst themselves over who had thought of her first. What was not expected and certainly not common was a girl choosing a male's name and worse yet, the name Damien.

* * *

On the following Friday afternoon while the children were at recess Mr. Diener nonchalantly flipped through the papers. For the past twelve years he'd presented kids with the process of Confirmation names without a hiccup. He eyed the stack of essays and math quizzes that had accumulated in his makeshift desktop organizer and dreamt of a weekend free of grading. On the top of the stack was Shannon Lamb's essay. He skimmed her paper, expecting something odd — the girl had a thing for the macabre and had specifically asked about female martyrs who had been decapitated. He'd suggested Winefride or Susanna. She chose neither. Of course.

Nope, not me. Not my problem, he thought, and put her paper to the side to grade the others.

When the last bell rang, waves of green plaid and white button-up shirts dashed towards the door all at once and Mr. Diener didn't even bother to remind them about forming a line. They knew better and they knew he knew they knew better, but children were Philistines and would sooner their classmates leave bloodied and bruised than allow one to get out the door before them.

When the school was marooned, he rose and strode towards sister Bienenkönigin's office near the back entrance of St. Agnes. Her light was on, her door open.

Dammit.

He slinked into the minty-green tiled bathroom. The boy's bathroom sat to the right of her office. He was used to concealing himself here, often ducking inside if he saw the familiar navy-blue habit crest at the top of the stairs at the entrance across the hall. He hated the simple, black rubber-soled shoes the nuns wore that allowed them to sneak up on him. After four minutes passed, he peaked out the door. Her light was off.

Yes, he should have questioned the girl about her name choice, but instead, Mr. Diener put the paper into a folder with a small note expressing his concern, slotted the folder in her mailbox, and scurried down the hallway to flip off his lights.

* * *

The following Monday, sister Bienenkönigin read Mr. Diener's note and part of Shannon Lamb's essay and put them both back into the envelope where she'd found them.

Shannon Lamb
May 5, 1985
Mr. Diener

Father Damien of Molokai

Father Damien of Molokai was a Belgian Catholic priest who led a mission in Hawaii. On the island, he taught the natives about the faith of the Catholic church. What Father Damien was mostly known for was his commitment for caring for the leper colony quarantined by the government. The government misunderstood leprosy and falsely believed it was very contagious. Father Damien spent the rest of this life until he eventually contracted leprosy, building homes, hospitals, churches, dressing wounds, constructing coffins, digging graves, and sharing the leper's pipes and poi.
I am choosing this individual's name because...

She'd had enough. Damien was not a saint nor a martyr. The girl was odd, made odder by her deliberate attempts to be different. She always did the opposite of what everyone else did. She shaved the side of her head in seventh grade and wore double piercings in only one ear, but this was the final act. She would not embarrass her and the entire community of Bloomsdale in front of the archbishop, and that was that.

She knocked on the eighth-grade door, opened it before Mr. Diener responded, and motioned with her hand for Mr. Diener to come and speak in the hallway.

In a hushed voice Mr. Diener said, "We're taking a test, Sister."

"That's fine, but afterwards please send Ms. Lamb to my office."

His expression went from worried to relieved. He was a decent teacher, but he was not one for confrontation. That girl was clearly running the show.

* * *

"Come in. Sit," she said not looking up from the letter she was writing. The girl sat silently as she ought to. Sister Bienenkönigin waited a full minute before she spoke, hoping the girl would reflect upon why she was now here in her office. When she was finished, she informed the girl she was disappointed. She had not taken the job of picking her name seriously.

"You'll need to write a *new* paper...you've wasted everyone's time..."

When none of her words seemed to make an impact on the girl, she said, "By this Thursday..." Still nothing. "Meaning you need to pick a new name. What was your second choice *from the pamphlet?*"

"I don't have one. I don't under —"

"Think about it today and tell Mr. Diener this afternoon before school is out. There were plenty of names to choose from. All the other girls selected from the pamphlet. Anne, Beatrice, Ruth." The girl literally huffed when she said "Ruth." She told her she may return to class and stop being a fuss to everyone.

When the final bell rang and day was over, the school halls took on that silent quality sister Bienenkönigin so loved and looked forward to each day. She rose from her desk and fluttered down the now dim hallways to Mr. Diener's classroom.

Back in the mid-1970s, enrollment at St. Agnes had peaked at two hundred fifty children. In those days, even when the school was vacant for holidays it seemed to vibrate from prior activity, as if the hum and buzz of a full school threaded like electrical wires inside the walls, the doors, the floors. There was always a door being shut, or the sound of children's shoes tap-dancing down the stairways. The scent of children lingered even during summer break, but the truth was the town of Bloomsdale was dying, and with its depleting population the school suffered. The school, much like a beehive, would slowly but surely experience one less student, one less teacher, until nothing remained but empty buildings — an empty hive.

Sister Bienenkönigin leaned against the doorframe of the eighth-grade classroom with her arms folded across her chest observing Mr. Diener put his papers in his satchel. He hadn't heard her approach. "So, do we have a new name? What's it going to be, Mr. Diener? Not Ruth, I assume." She chuckled.

Mr. Diener seemed startled upon hearing her voice. His expression took on a defeated look as if he hoped to escape the classroom without running into her.

He snapped the buckle of his satchel. "Maybe, she just needs some time to mull it over, sister. Have a good evening."

My goodness, he cannot be trusted to complete the smallest of tasks.

* * *

Sister Bienenkönigin's desire for order subsisted in every facet of her life and even though she had to share living space with the other sisters it was clear who ruled the house. Generally, the nuns got along well, and it was a quiet house. They made up for lost prayers not recited in the day at evening time, usually alone in their prim rooms amongst their essentials — a twin bed, a nightstand with a petite lamp sitting upon it, a kneeler with a crucified Christ, a Virgin Mary, or a saint overseeing their praying. In good times they clicked rosary beads together. In bad times, there were episodes of breadcrumbs and stray cardigans scattered willy-nilly. These were the times that made sister Bienenkönigin cringe as if one of her school children was chewing open-mouthed and smacking into her ear. These indiscretions reminded her of when she once lived on her aunt and uncle's farm in O'Fallon amongst noisy cousins, chickens, and cattle.

Back in 1961, the young Bertilda Bienenkönigin lived in two worlds. There was the dirty farm polluted with the earthy smells of cows and chickens who constantly bleated, clucked, or moaned along with cousins who cried, fought, or wanted to be fed and then there was the quiet and sterile world at the Sisters of the Most Precious Blood Motherhouse. They were a contemplative order, who found harmony and stability in reciting prayers and teaching children they'd never have nor wanted for themselves.

Bertilda was fascinated with their history and listened attentively to the perils the sisters experienced before settling in O'Fallon. After church each Sunday, one or two of the sisters would speak to her about their order. Every Sunday recruiting Bertilda a little more.

"Our order was founded in Switzerland in 1845...but we were *forced* out."

"Forced? But why?"

"Boy you are inquisitive. Is she not the most inquisitive creature, sister Dear?" The nun asked the other nun who nodded her head in agreement. "The Swiss Government banned contemplative orders, so our exiled community moved to France, close to the German border, you see. That is how we ended up in Germany."

Bertilda loved it when the sisters used "we" and "our" in her company, as if she were already a member of their secret society, including her with possessive pronouns.

"But how did *we* survive?" Bertilda asked.

"Making vestments for the priests, as we do here. Some became teachers. But again, there was another small dispute." The nun squished her nose up to emphasize the word small. "Between the Catholic Church and Germany, and again...*expelled.*"

"Cast out. Again! What now?"

"Our order moved to America. To Illinois."

"But then how did you end up here...in Missouri?"

"Some differences of opinion, but here we are now. And Tilda," the sister gripped her hand, "we are incredibly happy here."

Expulsion, castaways, disorder. Bertilda Bienenkönigin was hooked. Was not her own situation one of disorder? Was she not also a castoff in the eyes of her family? Her parents both dead, and she, orphaned?

At nineteen years old, Bertilda had no siblings, no parents, no prospects. Aunt, uncle, cousins, farm—she hated all four. She did not inform her family of her decision to join the order. She simply disappeared. Nor did the family search for her. On the occasion they attended church service they saw her amongst her new sisters and were as pleased with the arrangement as she was.

She was merely the product of being unwanted, another mouth to feed when there was scarcely enough for her four cousins. She never owned a nice thing or a room to herself. She traded in her false freedom for security and structure in the motherhouse. Piety agreed with sister Bienenkönigin. The habit did an exceptional job of covering up more than just hair.

Yet, when she had already made up her mind to join, the sisters suggested she take one more week to reflect. It was during this period of reflection she found a rabbit fur coat. On Saturday afternoons, she was permitted to walk to town. While taking a corner around an apartment building, she witnessed something she had never seen before — an eviction. Dining room chairs, a rug, and small stacks of clothes were on display for everyone to see, and already a crowd was picking through the items.

"What's going on?"

"Didn't pay their rent," a man rummaging through a box answered. "Got kicked out."

"You're allowed to, to, to just take it?"

"Hey, don't judge me. Help yourself or move on."

"Won't they come back?"

"Yep. That's why you got to be quick," the man said and jogged off carrying a bundle of dresses.

Two teenaged boys were lifting a wardrobe when the door flew open and the rabbit coat — what was to become a prized possession — literally fell before sister Bienenkönigin's feet.

"Looks like you got a new coat lady. You want it? If not, my sister will."

Years and years of never having, of wanting, of Christmases smiling at cousins opening shiny packages while she received pieces of fruit or a dowdy dress from a second-hand store, all those feelings of craving, yearning for just something, even something minute, just for herself were stored inside a treasure box buried deep within sister Bienenkönigin's heart. It was an empty vessel, waiting for her to put something inside it; all at once her heart exploded with desire.

"No! It's mine."

She snatched the rabbit coat, clutching it to her breast, but no sooner had she gotten the thing she realized she would not be able to keep it. Was she not to give up all earthly possessions? So soft, sleek, and in her size. Just one thing. Can't I have one thing?

She took it to the motherhouse folded into a quilt. When she was assigned St. Agnes, she hung it in her closet, never once wearing it outside the confines of her room.

In that week of soul-searching, she resolved that she would allow herself one petty luxury: her secret rabbit fur coat. Later, once she joined the order and her years passed from being a young nun to middle-aged, she allowed herself another luxury — sleeping in on Saturday mornings, waiting to hear the front door open and close, and then, and joyfully knowing the sisters had vacated the home.

* * *

Sister Bienenkönigin awoke to the sound of birds chirping and she prayed, thanking the Lord for songbirds and a good night's sleep. No sooner had she finished her prayer, than she began to hear the musings of her house. Anger flared inside her squat efficient body. The faint sounds of the sisters chatting, a giggle, and then a door closing. Finally, she thought. She rose and headed downstairs.

Sister Lapin, who ate toast every morning, was mindful enough to put the toaster back under the sink but had a terrible habit of not cleaning up her breadcrumbs. The kitchen was tight. A half-stove and an icebox dominated most of the galley style room. Sister Bienenkönigin didn't tolerate the clutter of appliances on the counter space. It was her opinion that only a coffee pot should be allowed on the counters and nothing more.

As sister Bienenkönigin took the last step from the stairway to a short hallway that led to their shared kitchen, she imagined Sister Lapin smearing butter onto her toast — not on a plate or even over the sink. Each time the butter knife would touch the crisp bread, crumbs flicked off the toast and gathered on the once pristine countertop where she left them for another to clean up after her. This was the kind of disrespect she silently endured. And sure enough, Sister Lapin failed at this morning chore yet again, as she failed to do most mornings, leaving sister Bienenkönigin to wipe the breadcrumbs off the counter into the sink, rinse the sponge she kept for such occasions, and then scrub the sink clean.

One trivial anger had the potential to blow up until what one was angered about (perhaps not breadcrumbs) reared its toothy mouth and growled. Now, sister Bienenkönigin growled to herself while wiping away the crumbs knowing it wasn't the crumbs that bothered her (well, to some degree it was), but something else. It was...*the name.* Days had gone by with Mr. Diener avoiding her, making it obvious that the situation was still a situation, and that she would have to have some dialogue with the girl's mother.

An infection, if ignored, could lead to illness, disease, even death. If she did not address Sister Lapin's breadcrumbs, or this girl's choice of a name so unfit for heaven, what else would start to crumble and deteriorate? Look at what was happening to colonies of bees. Years of poor nutrition and effects of climate on a species over time can devastate them. Did one bee tell the other of his plans to leave? Did some start to complain about the work, the conditions not being up to standard? He told a friend, who told a friend, and on and on. If there were no bees, would there be no flowers?

Had Sister Bienenkönigin read all of Shannon Lamb's paper, she might have learned that the process of canonization was under way for Father Damien. He had remained with his leper colony until he died. But canonization takes time, and Shannon Lamb and Sister Bienenkönigin's tiff would be long forgotten by the time he was sainted as a martyr for charity, the patron saint of lepers and outcasts. Had she read it, she may have identified with Father Damien and his outcast family.

But she had not.

On the way out the door Sister Bienenkönigin hung Sister Abeille's cardigan on the empty hook where Sister Bienenkönigin had conveniently labelled all their names.

"No matter, we'll throw them willy-nilly wherever we want," she said out loud and then for effect tossed Sister Abeille's cardigan on the floor where it sat like a sin before she plucked it back up and put it where it belonged — on Sister Abeille's hook. For a moment she pressed her index finger into the labelled name. Closing her eyes, she slid her fingers across the raised letters and fantasized she was blind and reading braille. But she wondered if blind people did not have an advantage over life, thwarted from seeing all the ugliness.

Then, she opened the door, marched down the hill from the nun's house, and made her way to the cafeteria where the teachers congregated before the first morning bell. She found Mr. Diener sitting in the cafeteria in his usual spot, drinking black coffee from a Styrofoam cup. He was with the seventh-grade teacher, Mr. Lehrer.

Displeasure briefly registered across their faces upon seeing her in front of them. She pulled a seat out and sat down.

"Good morning, gentleman."

"Yes, good morning, sister," the men said in unison, well-practiced at this routine. "How are you, sister?"

"Fine."

Sister Bienenkönigin sat in the chair opposite Mr. Diener.

Mr. Diener began, "Sister, I want —"

"Mr. Diener, there's a letter on your desk, in that lid you use. Make sure Mrs. Samples gets it please." Sister Bienenkönigin took a cautious sip.

"Oh, yes, yes. A letter for her mom. The name. It's, it's not going to —"

"No. It will not work. And if she isn't going to provide a name, we'll be forced to choose for her. A shame really."

Mr. Diener snickered. "She probably got it from *that movie,* you know?"

"I do not know. What is *that movie*, Mr. Diener?"

"No? Well, you would *not* want to watch it, and I, I, I didn't watch it all the way through, awful really." Mr. Diener finished his coffee and was now tearing Styrofoam pieces off the rim and tossing the pieces into his empty cup.

He explained, "There's a movie...called *The Omen.* A kid in it is named Damien...a horror movie.... Antichrist. You know Damien." When Sister Bienenkönigin didn't respond, "You know? Demon. Damien...Uh, these kids are so influenced, but you, um, you, you wouldn't know it, I'm sure."

The man was too twitchy, she thought. Sister Bienenkönigin rose and smoothed down her navy-blue, polyester skirt. Before walking away, she said, "No, I wouldn't know *anything* about the Antichrist."

When Sister Bienenkönigin climbed the last step and was safely out of earshot, Mr. Lehrer patted Mr. Diener on the back. "Man, did you really go there? The Antichrist? *The Omen*! Hahahaha. Things one doesn't say out loud to Sister Evil. What *was* that?"

"She makes me so nervous. Her eyes. She never blinks. I swear."

Mr. Lehrer narrowed his eyes. He would often act out a rendition of Sister Evil if he found Mr. Diener hiding in the boy's bathroom, or even sometimes in the hallway while she walked in front of them, he'd imitate her waddle. Mr. Diener did not particularly like it when Mr. Lehrer made beady eyes at him, mostly because he feared Sister Bienenkönigin would discover his mockery.

"You gotta explain," Mr. Lehrer said, continuing to chuckle.

"Shh, shh."

"She's gone, man. Spit it out."

"There's a girl who selected Damien her Confirmation name."

"Let me guess. Shannon Lamb?"

"Suppose it wasn't that hard to figure out."

"Well, I had her last year when she shaved the side of her head, but what's the problem?"

Mr. Lehrer was one of those teachers who the kids liked. They laughed at his jokes and would probably remember him as a positive role model when they were adults, looking back on their year with him fondly. Mr. Diener, on the other hand, for all he tried could not make the kids naturally like him. They minded him, because if they acted up, he'd tell Sister Bienenkönigin. But like him? Never.

"It's an attention thing." Mr. Diener collected the pieces of his demolished cup and tossed them in the trash.

Mr. Lehrer shrugged. "Probably, but kids will be kids."

"So, she can't use it," Mr. Diener said a little frustrated. Perhaps he had made more of it than he should have, but the bell rang, and with it the start of the day.

* * *

At the end of the day, Mr. Diener gave a sealed letter with "Mrs. Samples" name written in long, angular, cursive letters on the front of the envelope to Shannon Lamb. And the following morning after Mass, the Pledge of Allegiance and morning prayer, the girl raised her hand.

"Yes, Shannon?"

"I have a letter for Sister Bienenkönigin from my mom. Can I take it?"

"May I take?"

"*Maaay,* I take it?"

"No. Just put it here." Mr. Diener tapped the cardboard box lid on his desk with his ink pen. "I'll make sure she gets it. Do you have something for me?"

"I, uh, the letter. It's about that."

"Oh, I see."

The girl dropped the letter into the box lid with some flair and then walked back to her desk in a manner that reminded Mr. Diener of a feline. This drama was becoming epic. He hated squabbles, especially if it involved him.

Mr. Diener would have liked very much to open the letter. The answer to the girl's missing paper and silence about the name was there, but he let it rest (not so peacefully) for three hours before the lunch bell rang. Every time he turned away from the chalkboard the first thing that caught his eye was the letter. It had taken on a sort of aura. At one point, when the children were taking a quiz, he picked the letter up to inspect its seal. It was glued, and not only that, but there was a piece of tape across the back, securing its contents forever from his eyes. He tossed it lightly back into the box. He looked up at his class and caught the girl staring at him. She gave him a wicked little smile. When the lunch bell finally rang, it frightened Mr. Diener so much he jumped back in his chair and made a tiny "ooh" sound.

"Okay, kids. Line up and head down to the cafeteria. I'll be down in a moment. No talking. You're on your own."

When the last kid sailed out, he shut the door to his classroom and picked up the letter one more time. He held it up in the air near the window. Black-inked cursive. But like ancient languages yet to be decoded, the words were illusive. It was not a long letter judging by the thinness and weight. Only one page he imagined. Mr. Lehrer took lunch in his classroom; Mr. Diener went to him now.

"What letter?" Mr. Lehrer asked. He was spreading peanut butter onto a slice of white bread. He kept a loaf along with peanut butter and homemade preserves in his desk drawer. He lifted the bread in Mr. Diener's direction. "Want one?"

"No, no. Thank you. I can't eat now. The letter from the mother. You know, the name." He whispered, "Remember, Damien."

"The demon child? Yes, what's the story now?"

Mr. Diener filled him in and when he finished Mr. Lehrer said, "Wow. It really is the little things around here that get whipped into a meringue."

"Well, it's not my fault. There were instructions, but that isn't why I'm here. Look. It's taped shut." Mr. Diener handed the letter to Mr. Lehrer who turned it around to observe the tape.

"Yep. No getting into this one unless you want to put it in another envelope and do a slight forgery. Of course, Sister Evil isn't aware her name was written on the envelope. I mean she hasn't seen it yet, so it's entirely possible to get away with it."

"You're not thinking we should open it?"

"*Me?* No, I didn't even know of its existence. I was saying out loud what you're thinking."

"Just forget it. Give it back."

Mr. Lehrer passed the letter in the direction of Mr. Diener's outreached hand, pulled back, and then ripped the side open.

"*What did you do?*" Mr. Diener yelped.

"Eh, live a little."

Dear Principal Bienenkönigin,
I received your letter and find issue that a priest (who is soon to be canonized), who worked with those poor rejected souls when they were shunned by their own family, community, and government, and then died from the same disease, staying with his colony until his death, is somehow deemed not worthy of my child's namesake. That

isn't good enough for you? It is for me. Damien is the name she chose, and Damien is what she will have. Stop picking on her.
Regards,
Mrs. Wendy Samples

"Holy shit, man! That was killer, made my day, maybe my week." Mr. Lehrer folded the letter up. "Thanks for sharing."

"You know I didn't mean for you...oh, just give it back," he said stamping one of his feet in vexation.

Mr. Diener returned to his classroom, more agitated than he was before visiting Mr. Lehrer. His hands shook as he put the letter into a new envelope. He didn't dare forge Mrs. Samples' handwriting, and so left the envelope blank. Yet Somehow, the lack of Sister Bienenkönigin's name on the envelope pointed to his indiscretion, so he added a piece of tape to replicate Mrs. Samples' seal. But all his attempts to return the letter to its earlier state felt futile. The damn letter oozed with suspicion. He wanted it gone from his desk. He didn't even want to touch it or put it in her mailbox, but he did.

* * *

Even though the issue of the name was dropped, it was never resolved in Sister Bienenkönigin's mind. The weeks tick-tocked away until they finally arrived at the day before Confirmation. On that Friday afternoon instead of climbing up bus steps or waiting in the carpool lane, the eighth graders remained seated at their desks hugging backpacks and sleeping bags. They were having a sleep-in in the basement cafeteria. On Sunday, they would be confirmed. Tonight, was a reward for their hard work, to be kids, to let off steam. They played charades, ate pizza, and drank soda. It was not Sister Bienenkönigin's idea. Parents were getting increasingly progressive, but she did establish gender borders and a preset "lights-out" time.

It was true Father Damien of Molokai died of leprosy and remained with his outcast colony. One side effect of leprosy being sensory nerve damage, the inability to register pain. Father Damien made his own diagnosis when he couldn't feel the scorching water of his bath. He felt nothing but the surety of death and the end of a community who needed him more than God, but he never stopped wrapping wounds and burying the dead in his leper colony. He stayed to the very end, perhaps even digging his own grave. Sister Bienenkönigin knew none of this about the man; all she knew was in about a day's time, the girl would take his namesake.

Sister Bienenkönigin retired early that Friday evening. She had read Mrs. Samples' note often during the final weeks before the archbishop would arrive. It had not been lost on her that Mrs. Samples had not addressed her as a sister, but as principal. The letter would become a new secret, like her rabbit coat, she kept guarded in her room. She could recite it from memory, if asked to, but was thankful nobody knew, besides her, Mrs. Samples, and probably the girl. Sister Bienenkönigin wanted nothing more than to sleep after fighting a battle she did not win. When she got home, she drank two spoonsful of cough syrup, removed her rabbit coat from the back of her closet, wrapped herself inside it, and went to bed. She fell asleep petting its soft, downy, fur collar.

* * *

In the school cafeteria, the children played Twister, a game that allowed them to innocently fall atop one another. Thighs brushed against thighs, young legs snaked around arms, with lips and breath dangerously close. Maybe, someone slipped their mother's sleeping pills into the chaperone's coffee. *Maybe.* They played and played, an arm giving out over a red dot, a foot slipping off a yellow circle, deliberating grinding into each other's bodies.

"Who turned the lights off?" A girl whined. There was still one goody goody left, but not for long for. Boys pulled out bottles of wine and passed them around until the children were just a heap on a rainbow of dots, giggling, and, tipsy. Their bodies were young, ripe, and glistened like bright new bicycles or Bing cherries recently washed, waiting in colanders to be dropped into buttery pie crusts.

"Truth or dare!" a boy yelled.

"Truth!" the girls called back.

"Is it true you're possessed by a demon, Shannon. Or is it...Damien?" Hoots and howls followed.

Answer him. Answer him, they cawed like crows. *Reveal your true self!* The secret was out.

Someone turned on a strobe light. The room flashed on and off, on and off, faces black and white, bodies jerking in and out of focus.

"Dare!" a boy yelled.

"I dare the girls to run through the cemetery."

"You run through the cemetery!" the girls yelled back.

It would be a shared dare. The children quieted themselves as they tip-toed up the stairs, crept down the hallway to the exit, and one by one left the school.

* * *

Covered by the darkness of night, Shannon led the children up the hill, past the nuns' house where Sister Bienenkönigin and her sisters slept, and into the cemetery. They traveled trance-like, deep into the graveyard, past the last of any lights, past redemption, and while they journeyed, they drank to witchery. Drunk, they began to chant, "St. Damien of Molokai," then, "Damien, Damien, Damien," until it was no longer Damien they called out to, but *Molokai, Molokai, Molokai, Molokai, Molokai.* And finally, they abandoned the priest of lepers and called on another — a primordial evil. Chanting and in their ecstatic state, the name Molokai changed to: "Loki, Loki, Loki, Loki, Loki, Loki, Loki, Loki, Loki, Loki, Loki, Loki, Loki, Loki, Loki, Loki, Loki, Loki!"

Devised by prayer and sacrament to protect and remain undisturbed above the graves—the hardened dirt began to swirl, forming small waves, then larger, until the tops of the caskets could be seen. With bony hands the dead pushed open their coffins and emerged from their watery burial holes — the cemetery, a sea of death and decay. The children's souls were shipwrecked, wretched. Loki invoked, he circled serpent-like around the boys and girls, stinging them with his venom. There would be no Confirmation, no archbishop.

The children tore at buttons and zippers, clawing off their clothes, forsaken to the night. One girl grabbed a boy and kissed him hard upon his mouth, bruising their lips with rot passion. Loki hissed with delight, slithering between the stones and the now unrestrained bodies of the children and the deceased. There would be no Jacquelines, no Ruths, no Beatrices, but an army of outcasts — lepers, destitute and forgotten by the true God, they fell prostrate in worship to the darker god. Loki shivered with pleasure, but wanted more, more, an orgy of dead and living flesh, a necromancer's ball. The wicked flock now faced each other. Corpses bowed low, reached out their skeletal hands and taking each child as a dance partner they began to waltz. They waltzed upon the desecrated graves. Living flesh met dead flesh, more, more, Loki demanded, hipbone against hipbone, gyrating on top of each, they howled in nocturnal pleasure but when they became one the young flesh began to fester. Boils and sores covered the children, mephitic. But they paid no attention to their oozing secretions. They noticed nothing other than their own fetid desire.

It was so hot, so extremely hot, boiling, burning, blistering hot. Sister Bienenkönigin could take it no more. She screamed, "No!"

The children startled; they had heard the nun bellow from her room. They disengaged from their deathly paramours, now set on her ruin. Hordes of plaguey youth spewed forth and descended upon the nuns' home.

No, no, she screamed. *No.* But this time nothing came out. A "no" that had been forever trapped inside Sister Bienenkönigin, eating at her all this time. She tried to form the word. It was for nothing. Yet, even if her lips weren't darned shut, her tongue nailed down, or her lungs full of cement, even if the children *could* hear her silent screams, they would have ignored her.

They stomped upon her hives as though they were immune to the bees' stings and feasted on her sacred honey consuming her entire life's work in a matter of minutes. How could she just watch while they destroyed her hives, her parish, her order?

For her apathy and penance, they now turned their attention to her. Single file, as she liked it, they stood beneath Sister Bienenkönigin's window and sang, *Non, rein de rein, Non, je ne regerette rein.* From the "Os" of their mouths great swarms of bees poured forth—thump-thump-thump—and dashed against her windowpanes. First a fissure, then a crack, and now in her room.

Her wonderful, perfect bees were infected by pesticides, insecticides, disease! They encircled her in marvelous cloud, stinging, stinging, leaving a thousand barbs embedded in her flesh.

And all at once, the bees dropped dead. Their sting — their final act.

* * *

Sister Bienenkönigin's eyes popped open. She was instantly awake. She stumbled to her window, pushed back the curtain, and peered outside. They were gone. She ran out into the hallway, pounding on the sisters' doors and shouting, "Get out, get out!"

The sisters, forgoing their habits, burst from their rooms, trotted down the stairs, out the front door, and around the corner to where Sister Bienenkönigin stood wagging her finger at her beehives.

"See, what they did! They destroyed my hives!" Thinking they must have returned to the cemetery, she directed them to follow her.

The sisters shook their heads. They did not see a midnight funeral march to the cemetery, nor possessed children summoning Loki. Her hives were in tack.

Sister Bienenkönigin was overheated and soaked in sweat. Feverish even. They directed her back inside.

"Why, I've never seen this before," Sister Abeille cooed. "What a lovely coat, but you're very warm. Here, take it off. You are burning up. Come. Rest now, Sister."

The sisters helped her out of her coat and nightgown and handed her a fresh one. It was just a nightmare. No stingers were found in her flesh.

Only a nightmare. She had fallen asleep in her rabbit fur coat.

From her bed she watched Sister Abeille hang up her fur, and thought, it's about time she hung up something for once. Sister Lapin brought her a glass of water, turned off the light, shut the door, and Sister Bienenkönigin was alone.

And though she knew her sisters were outside her door, the children sleeping in the cafeteria, that the school, the church, the town, the whole parish was outside, she felt empty. Her bedroom, only an empty nest, and she, all alone. And she pondered, did the queen bee wonder where her workers went? Did a few valiantly still buzz around her, to the very end, or was she alone at her death with the husks of her colony lying about her?

The High Priestess

The time I spent at St. Agnes Middle School before we moved away from Lawrenceton for good, I never once invited a single friend over to my house. Never a Friday night sleep-over with my "Best Friend Forever," Becca. No slumber parties. This is not to say *I* didn't go to sleepovers or slumber parties, because I did. Many times. And I could easily describe myself as popular, but that status was due in part to the fact that no one at St. Agnes knew my actual living situation — we didn't ride the same bus. We lived in the boonies off Highway Y in a rusted white trailer with a rusted metal roof, no shrubbery, no sidewalks, no clean pathway to the front door (only a handful of scattered rocks), and no driveway unless you counted the deep ruts left behind by my stepdad, Dale's, Chevy Blazer. Our lawn consisted of overgrown weeds full of dog poop and a well-aged, splintered picnic table our German Shepherd, Rebel, was secured to by a thick chain. Rebel barked at every car that passed by until Dale would pull out his BB gun, and Rebel, who recognized the pumping action sound the gun made, would dart underneath the table. By today's standards, it was animal abuse, but back then that was just how country people dealt with dogs who chased cars.

Not only were we outsiders with our outside ways, but we were white trash in the middle of a town that was settled in 17-something and something. We're talking about deep-deep-deep-rooted traditions. And that made us stand out like a bonfire in Antarctica.

In seventh grade we were assigned a toothpick project to build a model of our home. I built an elaborate, two-story, Spanish mansion that I painted pale pink. For its tiled roof, I crumbled up burnt orange, colored paper and glued those wavy pieces on top. Partly, this *was* true. When we moved here, Dale worked for his cousin who had promised to sell us the plot of land for our imaginary mansion. But as these were dealings with Dale, both the job and the land vanished. I lived in two homes in Missouri, one real and one fantasy.

And I carried this dirty secret with me for two years until my mom convinced me to have an all-girls' party on the last Friday school got out for summer — our last time together as eighth graders before high school began in the fall.

My mom was a spoiled child, growing up on the flawlessly outlined grid off Q Street in Sacramento with her own bathroom in her bedroom. This was the 1950s when kids didn't get en-suite bathrooms. She merely had to wake up, eat what was placed in front of her, and go to school, and because of this, she never took too much to tidiness. The day-to-day was completed to perfection by nana, who was never satisfied with anyone else doing the cooking and cleaning.

As for nana, she was connected to an invisible string that yo-yoed between the kitchen and the rest of her immaculate home. When Dale smoked in nana's formal living room, her eyes would become like those of birds of prey — piercing the dirty ashtray. As soon as Dale stubbed out his cigarette, she'd swoop down and whisk the ashtray away. That invisible string propelled her to the trashcan, to the kitchen sink where she rinsed the ashes out, and then back to the sink to now give it a cleaning, too. Before he lit another cigarette, a clean ashtray would be back in position. Not that Dale ever offered to clean his own ashtray out, but if he had, she wouldn't have been satisfied with the job.

When you grow up never having to clean or pick up after yourself, it doesn't just kick in one day. Living with mom and Dale was like living in a permanent version of *Animal House*; I'd given up on communal housework. So, it wasn't just the outside but also the inside I was worried about. I was doomed.

* * *

"Like don't girls *like* just want to have fun?"

Mom thought she was being cute by Cyndi Laupering me. She also enjoyed Culture Clubbing — *Karma, Karma, Karma, Karma, Karma Chameleoning* — me. She'd adopted the vernacular of a Valley Girl to get me to stop saying "like" before every sentence, and she didn't deserve a response. I stomped down the hallway. She followed, but before I got a chance to slam my door, she put out her hand to stop it.

"Come on. Tell me again the name of that movie you wanted me to rent? The scary slasher one?"

"Gawd, what planet do you live on? Who hasn't heard of *Halloween!*" She's the only parent who wasn't aware of movie ratings, too. "Oh, and get *Halloween II*," I said. Slasher films were the best.

Mom twisted her hair. "Like *for shur.*" And when I tried to shut my door a second time, she pulled her cackling witch voice and said, "But...you girls...are going...to...be...*terrified,*" and ended with a Vincent Price laugh.

"Please, *please* promise me you won't talk like that. I'm so serious, mom. You can't talk like that. I'm being for real."

"I promise." She put both hands in a prayer position. "I won't. We're get junk food and your gory movies, and it'll be so bitch—"

"Like these girls have real homes," I said.

"What's that supposed to mean?"

"You know exactly what it means." I hurt her with that.

"Shannon, you need to take a chill pill...Besides, if they're real friends they shouldn't have a problem with where you live. And you'll meet new friends in high school. They aren't going to be lifelong friends."

"Yes, they are."

Mom shook her head at me and gave me the typical parent expression that said she knew so much more than me since she'd lived longer.

"Will you leave? Please, just leave. You're so embarrassing."

"Shanana, you know this is temporary. It's really none of their business anyway. Where you live, how you live. That's superficial shit." She paused to allow me to take in her wisdom.

I heard it all before. The promises Dale and she made to me when we moved from Los Angeles to the sticks were going to take an extra eternity because Dale couldn't find a job...or should I say, keep a job. I knew the land for the new house would never be bought. The foundation would never be poured; it would remain a toothpick pipe dream like the toothpick mansion I built two years ago. It was just a matter of time before we headed to wherever Dale landed next.

"But... I get it, you're embarrassed. You know? I was once the same age as you."

"You'll never get it."

My idea of a real home meant a single-story brick ranch surrounded with boxwoods, a cemented driveway with a mailbox at the end of it (not a PO box because the mailman/woman won't visit) in a subdivision called Cedar Hills or Goose Creek Landing. Even the loser boy who sat behind me at school who called me "Peter, Peter Pumpkin Eater" every day and asked if I liked to eat peters, even *he* lived in a subdivision.

In my real house there would be real steps leading to a real wooden door, and absolutely no cinder blocks — Dale's solution to everything. No one else in town had dead fathers they never met, stepdads without jobs, *or* stepdads for that matter, and cinder blocks holding up their world.

"Listen, don't be so serious. They're not coming to judge."

"Uh, teenaged girls, not judgmental?" I rolled my eyes. "Are you kidding me, mom?"

She threw up her hands. "One day your eyes are going to get stuck up there in your head, Shannon." She walked away, but as she was heading down the hall, I heard her say, "Like *duhhh*, I know how to be good. *Totallee.*"

So, we scrubbed and polished and the lemon Pledge that cut through our primordial dust almost covered the stench of our cigarette-infused couch cushions. The slumlord finally put down gravel; we had somewhat of a "driveway." I suppose it was as good as it could get on that fatal Friday, but nothing was going to transform our trailer into a house.

I felt equal amounts of excitement and dread when I exited the bus with a posse of girls most of whom shared abbreviated names ending in either "i" or "y," and half of them I didn't even like: April (hate), Lori (April's minion and bestie, dislike due to affiliation), Becca (my best), Cathy with a "C," (sweet), Kathy with a "K" (nerd/suck up to April/Lori combo), Shelli (heard she let a public school boy finger her; undecided, but want to hear the whole story tonight), and Carrie (lice in 5th grade; used to like, but never stand too close to he before I start to itch). At least, I was spared my worst enemy, Anna Schmidt (still hate from the live nativity debacle), who luckily spent every weekend for the past six months in St. Louis with her dying grandmother.

When April asked Lori, "Isn't she supposed to live in a mansion? I've never been in one of these before." I was immediately transported to the third Wednesday of each month. Every girl but me left class at 2:30 for the bathrooms to change from their school uniforms into their Girl Scout uniforms. We couldn't afford the Girl Scouts — their fees, their badges, their pins, their minty green smocks, and blue neckerchiefs, and in the winter, their exotic wool berets. Those minutes right before Sister Evil, our principal, announced over the intercom, "All Girl Scouts may change into your uniforms," vibrated with anticipation. April, who pretended to be the troop leader, led the way to the bathrooms but not before asking, "Why didn't you join the Girl Scouts, Shannon? Oh, that's right. You're in 4-H.... the *hicks* need a club, too."

Rebel didn't give the girls much time to take in the outside, however. He yanked violently on his chain and scared the girls so badly they ran shrieking up the cinder blocks pushing against each other to get inside.

I hadn't noticed how light our metal front door was until Shelli apologized for slamming it. "Oops, your door is like hollow or something." She meant cheap.

I could already imagine what lunch next fall at my high school cafeteria would be like. Everyone would be chanting "Trailer Trash." Something like how Ogre from *The Revenge of the Nerds* sounded. Or maybe it was more subtle. Snide "TT's" as I was at my locker, and when I turned around to face the culprit, everyone looked at me with blameless eyes. Was summer long enough for them to forget?

Our front door led directly into the living room where everything was a shade of pecan. The carpet, the couch, the compressed wood paneling that climbed up our walls like unabsolved sin was all dirty brown. The same fake wooden walls led down the hallway until you opened the bathroom door — a tiny alcove covered in a layer of peeling country-blue wallpaper with dancing, dingy, white geese — mom insisted they were swans — and daisies. The same white, textured, plastic-looking, resin material that was used on the kitchen backsplash, covered the shower walls. We never could get the rings out of the toilet bowl no matter how much we scrubbed. All those blaring realities of cheap fake composite that constructed our lives, every manufactured inch, might as well have been graffitied with two words, "Trailer Trash," on the metal walls outside.

And then there was mom, sitting on a stool at the breakfast bar in a neon yellow, oversized, off-shoulder sweatshirt and *my* new, acid wash, denim mini-skirt with "Sister Christian" blaring on *my* boombox she clearly took form *my* room, oblivious to us all. Her right leg rapidly jumped on the footrest, a bad habit which drove Dale into rages which was easy enough. The only redeeming thought was he was working a job in Kansas and wouldn't be home until Sunday.

I flicked the radio off and wide-eyed her.

Mom looked up from a spread of tarot cards laid out on our chipped laminate countertop. "Oh hey, girls. How was the last day of school?" as if a half-dozen girls graced our trailer every day. As if she didn't hear the squeal of the school bus's brakes, or Rebel's barking, at seven shrieking girls, or the front door slamming.

A choir of "Hi, Mrs. Samples," and, "lames" answered her.

"Sorry for interrupting," Carrie said, her eyes narrowed in on the cards my mom restacked and put away in a cedar wooden box. It could have been worse. We could have walked into her waving stinky smudge sticks. Oh, no. That was earlier. I could smell sage in the air. This was supposed to be my day where she stayed in the back and only came out to make the frozen pizza. *And* I was pissed about my new skirt.

Mom waved her hand loosely in the air and said, "*Asss if.*"

They seemed in awe of her. She was the magical distraction who made them stop judging our home. But I had no place for mom, and I announced we were going to my room, ignoring her offerings of food.

Once we were safely behind my bedroom door, they were taken in by all my posters. That goose, goose, daisy pattern from the bathroom used to cover my walls too until I replaced every square inch with posters of Adam Ant, Billy Idol, Boy George, and Duran Duran. But mostly Duran Duran because I was in love with Simon Le Bon...oh, and sometimes John Taylor.

"Gawd, you're so lucky," Cathy said, "my mom won't let me put even one poster up."

"My parents would never let me watch *Halloween*," Kathy said.

I must admit. My room was cool, and it seemed to make the girls forget where my room was. The shame I felt descending the bus steps that afternoon vanished. We crimped our hair and painted our nails Red Velvet with "Flesh for Fantasy" blasting twenty-one times. We confessed the name of who we wanted to marry, and our backup if our true love died tragically. Then, mom cracked my door, to announce she'd made popcorn. "Come on, the VCR is set up, you're all gorgeous. Michael Meyers is waiting for you."

The girls yelped.

"Mom, go away!"

"All right, I'll be in my room if you need anything. Have at it."

"I need to use the bathroom," Becca said.

April piped up, "I'm going with you."

Because my anxiety had melted away, it didn't occur to me to question why April wanted to go to the bathroom with my best friend. The rest of us headed to the living room.

"Your mom is really pretty. I love her hair," Cathy plopped into Dale's chair.

"Mine wear old people clothes," Shelli added. "It's like so embarrassing."

"Yeah, but she does some weird stuff, too," I said.

"Like what?" Shelli asked.

"Oh, I don't know. Weird, or you would think so anyway. I'm sort of used to her."

The tarot cards were put away but were not forgotten.

"Like read fortunes?" Carrie offered.

Kathy stopped smacking her gum and blurted out, "Oh my God, your mother's a witch. Does she cast spells?"

"Yeah, I mean sometimes." I stopped there. They wouldn't understand gris gris or the dolls carved out of red wax that contained Dale's nail clippings and hair (so gross) meant to bind his eternal love to her, but seemed to make him more and more jealous and paranoid. "She's just weird."

"I want my fortune read," Shelli demanded.

The conversation wasn't going where I wanted it to go. The more I tried to put them off, the more they wanted to know, and I had a sinking feeling about a different conversation taking place in our cruddy bathroom between April and Becca. They'd been in there too long. The space was small. It didn't take that long to pee.

The girls persisted with their inquisition into casting spells and Voodoo dolls until I blurted out, "I'm getting my boombox. Just a sec." The only way to end the conversation was to exit it.

Our bathroom was across from my room and parallel to mom and Dale's room. Mom was standing inside her doorframe. She put a finger to her lips when she saw me approach and motioned with her head to the closed bathroom door.

I heard the familiar click of a cabinet door opening, the careful rummaging of nosey girls inspecting the contents of a stranger's medicine cabinet, but more disturbing was their conversation. The dialogue of hypothetical friends. I could tell my mom was mad. She'd been there longer. We both shared the same intuition that made us come to wait beside a closed door.

"Honest. Tell the truth, Becca. If you had known we'd have to stay overnight in a dump, would you've even come?"

April was a virtuoso at making someone look bad for the benefit of herself. Always the one to sigh or snicker or raise her hand with the correct answer while some poor fool held back tears in front a blackboard full of math that might as well been hieroglyphics. If I had my way, I wouldn't have invited her, but mom told me it wasn't fair to exclude one from the entire girl population. I was nowhere near as surprised by April's opinions as my mom was, but when we heard my best friend, Becca, agree with her, I felt as if I swallowed one of Dale's cinder blocks. My best friend was a traitor!

"All this time she comes to my house and never said a word. *Not one word.* I swear, April. Like, *omigod.* That's why she never asked me here. I kid you not, I feel like so cheap now." Funny, how Becca pretended she grew up in the San Fernando Valley, but not one person from her family had left town for over 100 years. She was always stealing my phrases and acting like she came up with it.

"I don't see how you can be friends with someone like that."

"Right. And now that I think back, Anna Schmidt said something about her living in a mobile home, and her dad, or stepdad, had long hair and is never around or drunk, but Anna is, well...*you know*, Anna."

"I get it."

"Yeah, no one even talks to her, so I was like whatever and —"

"Becca, she lied to you. Your best friend."

"It's like exactly like lying. Should I say something? I feel like so weird." So much for "Best Friend Forever Becca."

"Maybe be the better person and give her this one last night together, but when we're in high school next year, you need to be careful who you associate with. One wrong move in high school and you're finished." I pictured April slicing her neck with an imaginary knife.

For almost thirty seconds they stopped talking. I stood in the unnerving quiet, waiting for another knife to the gut, condemned without a trial. And any second the door could fly open, and they'd catch me spying. I backed into my dark room. Maybe they knew we were eavesdropping. But the feeding frenzy wasn't over.

"*Or* I could call my mom and tell her I'm sick, to pick me up, you know? And then you could go with me, and Lori can come, too. I'll just start feeling better before I get home. My mom won't know. And you and Lori can spend the night over at my place, but the rest of these dweebs...can stay." There was April in front of the medicine cabinet mirror, primping her hair, using my lip gloss saying "dweebs" like she starred in a John Hughes's movie.

"I don't know. Is that like *too* mean?" Becca asked.

Mom had enough; she knocked loudly on the bathroom door. "You girls need anything? Come on. The party's out here."

A yelp came from one of the girls, followed by silence, followed by some muttering, followed by a snotty, "just a second" from April. My high school career was ruined, and I hadn't even stepped into the hallways. There was no way I could go to high school if I couldn't even return to my living room. I needed to move.

When the door finally cracked opened, mom blocked the girl's line of vision to my room, so April and Becca couldn't see inside or see me.

"You girls go on in the living room. I need to talk to Shannon for a second."

As soon as she shut my bedroom door I said, "I told you so. I told you so. *See?* This is so stupid. And now they probably think I was listening in."

"Shh, shh." She quickly opened then shut my door to check for lingering girls, then surprised me with the truth.

"You *were listening* in and why do you care what those scheming little bitches think?" She pulled a strand of hair out of my eye. I pushed her hand away. "I'm sorry. You were right, you were. But I know what to do. Just trust me."

"You were the one who told me to invite them. I *did* trust you."

It scared me that she was no longer sugarcoating it for me. At least, her naïve optimism gave me some hope. I could already envision April pulling Lori aside, telling her about what they concocted in the bathroom.

"What am I going to do now?"

"*You* don't need to do a thing. I'll fix this."

"But they're leaving."

"No, *they're not*, Shannon. Give me ten. Get out there and act like nothing's wrong."

The hallway was too short. My feet didn't want to walk. My body became heavy with dread. Out there was a blackhole of negativity. The brutality of a single teenaged girl could bring down a nation.

"I think the ice-cream upset my stomach," Becca said clutching her side for effect, and watching April to see if she was doing a good acting job. "Maybe I ate too much of it."

The first claw tore into my flesh. I had assumed April would make the war cry. Becca initiating it made it especially hurt.

"Yeah, I keep tasting pepperoni. Like I almost threw up. Sorry, I for being in your bathroom so long, Shannon."

Teeth penetrated my hide.

"Yeah, sorry. She *almost* threw up," Becca said. "Me too."

Then Lori moaned and rubbed her stomach. "I'm not sure I can handle a scary movie. Blood and guts."

The first blood was drawn.

The next in line was Carrie — though I don't know how April got to her in the brief time I was with mom — who started to gag. Ever since the lice episode she'd become desperate to fit in, always taking her cue from the pact. Survival instinct, I guessed. "My stomach is way too weak for horror. I don't even like it."

April's lips formed a small smirk I might have missed if I didn't know why she was so pleased with herself.

I was so done. They were feasting on me. Blood, bone, fangs, talons. The full works. And I was mad, so mad. My mind experienced something comparable to an atomic flash. And I heard a voice, like when an angel appears to give a message: *Dale keeps a loaded shotgun under the couch.*

I saw the inner workings of April's mind before me. She was a virus corrupting a system that was supposed to be built upon friendships, and the infection was spreading. Three toppled by the host in mere minutes. I recalled one day in seventh-grade history class, when April proudly claimed her ancestors settled the town. She stood at the half podium Mr. Lehrer placed on his desk to lecture from and read out loud, "My family arrived with the first wave of French colonialists in 1735. In fact, the Bolduc House, which is now the Bolduc House *Museum*, still stands today. It is the site where my ancestors once lived."

There was no way these girls were going to stay tonight not with me, the gatecrasher, the foreigner, the refugee. No way.

And again, another flash — a flash of realization. As if I were in a movie theatre and stayed past the credits, past the soundtrack, the sound of the reeling film in the projector that always made me think of insect wings. The movie stops. The screen flashes white. Only me and an empty theatre. Because I have no friends. An usher flips on the lights. The theatre brightens. I'm back, but I've changed since the deception started spreading. I'll be the final girl here, I thought. I'm not going down without a fight.

The set of Ginsu knives Dale bought mom for her last birthday pulsated right behind my left elbow. The infomercial ran clearly through my head: Dale in his La-Z-Boy, mom and I spread helter-skelter on the couch, hypnotized by Ginsu-carrying samurais sawing through tin cans, hacking through wood with a single blade that could just as well cut a jugular.

I could Michael-Myers every single one of these deceitful, two-faced, devious, fake bitches, turn our trailer into a slasher movie.

Then mom walked in, and the pressure seethed out as though a whistling tea kettle had just been removed from the burner. My wonderful, underappreciated, super-smart mom stood before us, dressed like a Romani gypsy witch. She wore a long, paisley, wrap dress and a yellow fringed shawl tied loosely around her waist. She'd twisted a red silk scarf around her head. Her wrists tinkled with stacks of bangles. She'd applied thick, black eyeliner on her eyelids and stretched the lines into feline slits. There was even a black mole dotted above her claret-stained lips.

My mom, the high priestess, sucked up the pandemonium and cruelty of sly petty girls. The Queen. One Woman. My mom! The girls loved her almost as much as *I loved* her. She was the cure. Healed by the high priestess. My mom, enchanted them, all without breathing a word, and *I* didn't have to kill anyone, because *she* was in the room, and with her a new hierarchy.

She set her deck of tarot cards on the coffee table and proceeded to light candles, directing eager girls to turn off all the lights. When the stage was set, she sat on the floor in front of the coffee table and said, "Who of you will dare to question the universe? You?" She pointed at Cathy. "Or you?" She pointed at the other Kathy, who yelled, "I do!"

"Who wants to be read by the high priestess?"

They lined up like kindergarteners eager to please, excited to be forming lines because what was at the end promised a secret knowledge of their future. Every "I wanna to know if I'll be famous," or, "Who will I marry?" April would counter with, "But we're sick. She gave us food poisoning."

"Dramatic much, April," mom said. "No one has food poisoning. If you don't feel well, go lay down in Shannon's room."

The room had miraculously recovered, all except April who occasionally made sounds of discontent while "resting" in Dale's La-Z-y Boy.

Mom, obliged to reveal their fates, spread out the cards one, two three, four — past, present, future, and what she called the final outcome. Cathy — a career-driven life. The other Kathy, many, many lovers (we all agreed on that one). Shelli would have a spiritual calling. For Lori, fame. An actress. Broadway. Carrie, a large and happy family with no less than two kids who would become doctors. And for myself, I got all the above. Fame, love, fortune, and wisdom. Providence smiled upon all of us, but two.

Then it was Becca's turn. She looked directly into her eyes, and said, "Struggles, oh yes, I see loads of struggles."

"No way. Everyone else got good fortunes. What kind of struggles?"

"Hold on. I need to concentrate...yes, illness." And then mom revealed very matter of fact, "Becca, you're going to get really sick." This got April's attention who she left Dale's chair to stand behind Becca.

"What? *What do you mean?* Am, am I, I going to die...young?"

Mom sat back, leaning against the couch cushions and sort of huffed in annoyance, as if Becca's questions were silly and she didn't have time for them. "Yes, you are."

Images of a too-young Becca in a hospital bed, wearing a kitschy turban to cover her baldness and uttering her last words appeared in the mind's eye of every girl. What would we say at her funeral? Would she be buried at St. Agnes Cemetery? Was it going to happen soon? It was so easy to foresee it. There we all were, placing lilies on her grave. Shedding a tear for *that girl* who died so young.

Becca's lips began to tremble. Her eyes welled up, and mom maybe feeling she'd gone overboard, said, "But wait." She picked up a card with a prancing jester, the fool, and showed it to Becca. "You can change your fate. If you listen to your inner self instead of others, then, your life will be spared. It's the lying, the deceptions, and negativity that fester and make you ill. This is a warning, Becca...to not be a follower. To live an honest life. A big, *big* warning." Mom glared into Becca's eyes. "Take heed."

Becca studied the fool card. "Do you think I'm a follower?"

"Like duh. Move out of the way." April nudged Becca, taking her place before mom, who shuffled and reshuffled and chuckled at us girls and our riches and fame. Finally, she stopped shuffling the cards, and slammed the deck down so hard in front of April we all jumped back. "Cut the cards."

She spread out April's fortune, occasionally making mmm-hmm sounds and explaining, "All major Arcana cards. Very strong cards." April gloated, so self-assured her future would be better than all of ours.

She took more time with April than the others. Mom picked up each card individually to study its art, to divine its meaning before carefully placing it back in position. Once she was satisfied, she placed her hand over the card and spoke as if the card was shooting the vision directly into her hand, up her wrist, through her arm and neck, and out her lips. She presented the first card to April speaking its name, *"La Luna."*

In unison, the girls repeated "La Luna" as if they were her acolytes.

"*La Luna* indicates that you've been walking in darkness. Things may not seem as they really are. You're looking for your path, for answers. La Luna is attuned with the fertility goddess. Its nature is cyclical, like the menstrual cycle."

"Stop, mom. You're so gross."

"What? It's natural. The moon has cycles. See for yourselves. Tonight's a full moon."

Becca bolted to the front door, joined by Cathy and Kathy. They ripped it open and screamed, "It's true. It's a full moon!" The moon hung as bright as a premonition, and I suddenly believed in mom's magic.

"Come back, girls. You're breaking the circle." She continued, "It's more to do with the mind rather than the body. Do you feel like your imagination is playing tricks on you, maybe?" April, always confident, gave it a cursory thought, and responded by rapidly shaking her head no. Mom shrugged and moved to her present.

"The second card is justice." She presented the card to her newly formed coven. "This card represents the laws of the universe. It pertains to cause and effect. Your actions determine your results. You should take caution about the decisions you make. Use good judgment. A karma card, *for shur.*"

I let her have that "for shur." The girls were so engrossed by my witchy mom none of them noticed she was teasing me, and anyhow, she saved me tonight.

She presented April's next card. "This card is your future. The Sun. The child on the horse is you, and see how the sunflowers are facing the child with the light of the sun illuminating them? The sun always rises. You'll be rewarded, April, with whatever it is you seek." She hesitated, concentrating on the sun card a moment longer. "Absolute power will be yours. If it is darkness you crave, you will have your way. If it is lightness, you can have that, too. Now, this last one is your final outcome card."

"Oh my God, April, what does this one mean? It's bad." Becca snatched up April's last card, glad someone else's fate was worse than hers.

Mom smacked her hand away. "Never touch another's person's cards while a reading is in progress."

"God, Becca, don't you know anything?" Shelli said.

Becca squeaked out an apology.

"How odd, coming after the sun."

Mom held up the devil card for all to see, to take in his red muscular body. He was horned and hoofed and wore an impish grin. A man and woman were chained to his dark throne. His forked tail curled coyly around their naked bodies.

I could tell Lori, who was supposed to be April's best friend, was enjoying seeing April squirm. She lightly tapped the back of April's neck to frighten her. April jolted upright and yelled, "I know that was you, Lori!"

"What? What did I do?"

And I thought, how not that long ago I was watching my own execution, a bystander to my own death by mean girls.

"Did you feel his tail whip you, April?" Carrie snickered and pretended she had an imaginary whip to flog April.

Shelli screamed, "You're marked. Look. She has the devil's mark—"

"Stop it. All of you!" April cried, covering a birthmark on her neck we'd seen a million times but until now hadn't realized it was the mark of the cursed.

Mom waited for the girls to calm down and said, "It implies the direction you choose is corrupt. You allow negative forces to control you. If you let them, they will consume you. Like a disease...but I don't think it's cancer or anything...physically life threatening. I don't think so anyway." Again, she paused, letting April soak in the full effect of the possibility of her life or death. "No, not physical. Whew." She smiled flippantly at April, who sat stiffly glowering at her life in four cards. "What a relief, huh? Yes, it's definitely your spiritual destruction."

The girls stared at the devil card in terror, convinced April's fate was marked by evil. Some of them were already nodding their heads in agreement. Had not all of us felt April's wickedness come their way? Did she not this very night attempt to sabotage me?

My mom, probably sensing April didn't care about her dark path, gave one more prediction. She finally figured out the thing that would get under April's skin. "Other than that, it looks like a perfectly normal, boring, insignificant, and monotonous life."

"Where did you get that from?" April asked in disbelief.

"I think I'd rather be dead," Becca said.

April rolled her eyes. "Whatever. It's not true. None of this is real." She stood up. "I don't want to do this anymore. I'm bored."

Mom tsk-tsked her. "Yep, it's already starting to take effect. Boredom."

"This is so stupid. Come on guys. I want to watch a movie."

No one moved.

April had been demoted.

"We should do a séance next," Shelli said.

"Yes! A séance!" Becca, Carrie, Cathy, Kathy, Lori, and Shellie screamed.

"Come on, guys. It's time to watch *Halloween*, besides séances are stupid," April said. "It's all fake. Like she made that up." She stomped back to Dale's La-Z-Boy, falling into it like a sulking child queen.

"April, come on." Lori pulled at April's arms, but April wouldn't budge from her throne. *"Come on."* She tugged some more. "We're doing a séance."

Mom shrugged. "Why did you have me read your fortune if you already knew it was fake?"

With eyes asking for direction, for guidance, the girls looked at mom, at me, then back to April, and then back to mom and then a bevy of high-pitched teenagers yelled, " *Yeah, April!* "

The former queen had been toppled, uncrowned, dethroned, beheaded.

"I think we have the majority, ladies. Form a circle," the high priestess said. "We're calling up the dead."

The Annual Picnic

On the third Sunday in July, St. Lawrence Church hosted their annual picnic. Picnic proceeds paid for upkeep on the church and tuition for parish kids who either attended the elementary and middle school, St. Agnes in Bloomsdale, or Valle Highschool in Sainte Geneviève. Many of the parishioners were farmers with fixed incomes who were often impacted by the weather or broken machinery. Visitors came from all over the Midwest to stuff themselves on fried chicken, kettle beef, and liver dumplings— the leberknödel recipes all known by heart and prepared by German grandmothers. Mothers sewed quilts, baked pies and cakes, daughters served visitors sweet tea, coffee, and dessert in the church basement, fathers and sons set up and manned the tables, tents, and beer booths while grandfathers congregated in lawn chairs commenting on the success of each year. After the visitors ate, they carried their beer-buzzed bodies up a hill to a covered shelter where they played bingo. At 6:00, the raffle started. Shannon was humming "Pink Houses" — what she heard coming from the live band between the echoes of the bingo caller. It was suffocating in the basement. She craved escape, not just from the picnic, but the whole damn town.

This was not Shannon's first time serving. She got a break her first summer when they moved from Los Angeles to Lawrenceton, two weeks before the picnic, but she has served every summer since. Though a little nervy interacting with strangers at first, she was a good waitress and some of the visitors have started tipping her. It nipped at her conscience because she should probably donate it back to the church, but it was only a dollar here and there, so she decided to keep it.

A young man with a Mohawk, dyed black and loose (not glued and spiky like Shannon like Billy Idol) seated himself at one of her tables. Silver loops dangled from his ears. He was tall, thin, and hot — a dangerous type with a serial killer smile. He didn't belong here, but neither did she.

When she topped off his tea, he slipped a twenty in the pocket of her apron. He didn't touch any skin, yet somehow, she felt heat between his fingers and the material. She should give it back she's in the red with her best friend, Eddy Bauman, and maybe now she could get a new tape by The Cure. So, she ignored it, and how it seemed to sear through the soft, thin material of her over-washed apron the old ladies made from scraps. She returned to her serving station, wishing she'd selected a plainer apron, self-conscious of its childish ruffles.

When she thought it was safe to look in his direction, she used the back of her hand to wipe away sweat from her brow and then covered her eyes as though the fluorescent lights above were hurting them. But it was undeniable; she was searching for him, and it was no good because when she found his eyes, they were staring right at her. He smiled. Not with teeth or from ear to ear, just a simple smile telling her he noticed her. The air between them—connective.

Usually, she was the one who stuck out in Lawrenceton, but today he took her place, and she was granted refugee status. Locals eyed her with pity for having to serve the foreigner.

He motioned for her to come back. She noticed letters tattooed on his fingers and deep down she knew she should turn away, leave, her shift was nearly over, but she walked towards him anyway. The sound of ten buzzing fans hummed in her ears, and the hot air felt as though it was evaporating as she got closer to him. She felt faint. The air circulation was poor.

He asked her when she got off. She asked why. He said, you know why. She said, do I. He said, I like you. I think you might like me. She didn't respond. Someone behind her called out. "Miss,

Miss," and she turned away from his table to pour sweet tea, but she felt his eyes watching her, and she wished she had listened to her mom who had told to "stop wearing those shorts, they're too tight and ride up your butt crack," but Shannon liked the attention she got from men when she wore them.

He lingered past dessert, and then when she was busy wiping down her last table, she noticed he had left. She was disappointed and relieved at the same time. After counting her tips, she discovered she had thirty-two dollars total.

Shannon had promised Eddy, poor Eddy who had a crush on her since she moved to town, that she'd come to his tent. He had made over a dozen birdhouses to sell, and she had helped paint flowers and white fences on a few. A lavender butterfly on one.

His tent was near the parking lot; he was hitting up empty-handed people, "Birdhouses for sale! Handmade birdhouses." But they were way past hearing him and only wanted to get into their cars that had baked in the sun since morning and drive home to Indiana or Illinois, or maybe another distant small town in Missouri.

"Hey, looks like you sold a lot." She was being kind. There were only four empty spaces.

"A few. They keep trying to haggle me."

Shannon huffed. "Don't give in. People are so cheap. At a church picnic, too."

"Right. How was the basement?"

"Freaking hot as hell. I made some tips, though." She patted her apron pocket and then realized she was still wearing it. She pulled out the cash, stuffed it into the back pocket of her shorts, untied the apron, and rolled it up into a ball like dirty underwear she was ashamed of. "Do you mind? I can't go back in the basement."

Eddy tossed the apron on a table with his cash drawer. "Really? That's allowed?"

"Not sure, but I can buy *Disintegration*," she said in a sing-song way. "And here." She handed Eddy ten dollars.

"What's this for?"

"Columbia House. Sorry it took so long." She sort of hoped he wouldn't take it.

"Cool. Don't join that crap again." He put the ten dollars in the cash drawer, and she figured he was donating it because that's how he was. "Just buy it straight out."

"Okay, *dad.* But it's not like I ever have money."

"How much you make?"

"A girl never reveals...okay, twenty." A lie.

"You deserve it for sweating your ass off. I wouldn't tell anyone."

With her thumb and index finger, Shannon zipped her mouth. Eddy kept talking, but his voice had started to fade. He was saying something about judgy people. It was all lost, because there was Mohawk again, leaning against the door of a black Chevelle with a bucket of beer on its hood. She wondered how long he had been standing there watching her talk to Eddy. She fidgeted with a strand of hair. The same primal feeling in the church basement had returned.

"You're not even listening to me. Hey, come back to planet Earth." Eddy snapped his fingers in front of her face.

"What? Huh? I'm like so listening, dude."

"What did I say then?"

"People and tips. Wait, like don't look now, but there's some weird dude in the parking lot next to a black Chevelle." She knew the body style because her stepdad, Dale, poured over Chevys day and night.

Eddy turned his head to see, and she said, "Eddy, what'd I just say? He totally saw you. Oh-my-God, he's walking over."

Mohawk strutted, literally strutted across the gravel, taking his time but on point. She saw all of him now: Doc Marten combat boots she wanted forever for herself, but couldn't afford, another tattoo on his forearm she didn't catch in the church basement. Shannon picked up a birdhouse pretending to be interested, and then he was there, right next to her.

"Yo, sup, man?" He gave Eddy a high five, but Eddy missed his hand the first time, so Mohawk offered another high five.

"Whoa. When did you get here? What'd you do with your hair, man?"

Shannon hated it when Eddy tried to sound cool, but it hit her that somehow Eddy knew Mohawk and now she wanted to know how that was even possible.

Mohawk rubbed the top of his head, laughed, and said, "Last night."

"No one told us."

"Yeah, it was late. Mom didn't know either. Scared the shit out of her when I unlocked the door and walked in."

Shannon didn't know if she should introduce herself, or walk away, but was starting to feel out of place and decided to leave.

To Eddy, "Catch you later, alligator."

Later alligator? Stupid, stupid, stupid.

"Wait, Shannon. Stay. Hey, this is my cousin, Victor. Victor, this is Shannon." Eddy was beaming as if he had introduced her as his new girlfriend.

It didn't fit — them belonging in the same family. Victor held out his hand for Shannon to shake. The formality felt off.

"When you done here, cuz?"

"I guess when I sell everything."

"Shit, that'll take too long. I'll help you out. How much is this one?"

"You don't have to."

"I want to. I'll give it to mom." Victor looked at Shannon and said, "You pick."

For some reason, this decision weighed heavy on her, like a mind game, the kind of game you play with yourself when you have a crush on someone and you tell yourself if you make it back to the TV before the commercial was over your crush will like you, too.

She handed him a little white chapel with a miniature copper bell in the steeple and a yellow bird on the roof that is far too large for it. Eddy started to put it in a bag, but Victor shook his head no. He would walk it over to the car, and then he asked if they wanted to go for a ride, except he was only speaking to Shannon.

"How old are you?" she asked.

"What's that got to do with the price of tea in China, baby girl?"

Shannon couldn't help but smile.

"He's twenty-two." Eddy seemed miffed.

Victor said he needed to get away from all the old people. They would come back for Eddy. Twenty minutes. Tops. He would even wait for Shannon to tell her mom she's going on a drive with Eddy and his cousin.

Shannon decided against telling her mom. They both knew they wouldn't be coming back in twenty minutes.

Victor opened the door for her but before she got in, she peered into his sideview mirror.

"Pretty," he said.

Victor spun his tires, tearing out of the gravel parking lot. A few people noticed, and she thought, let them look. It was late afternoon, the beer was still pouring, and the old-timers and dads had started sipping under the table.

She turned the station to KWIX, all New Wave. He didn't seem to mind, and then because she was bold and his stuff was just as much hers, she opened the glove box and began pulling out its contents.

Black Sabbath cassette. Yeah, she thought, he had that Satan worshipping thing about him. He kept it simple, though. No pentagrams or skull rings, no stacked, black, rubber bracelets she thought ridiculous on a boy. Just a black tee and dark blue Levi's.

Marlboro Reds. She had snuck her stepdad's cigarettes from time to time, but she preferred menthol. She told him this, and he offered to stop at the gas station. He would take care of her now. He'd do anything for her. She belonged to him.

A letter from the Navy. She opened it. Discharged from service. That's where he had been. A pint of Jim Beam.

"I see you carry the essentials."

He laughed. "Yep, you got that right, baby girl."

"Why'd you give me a twenty? It's more than the cost of dinner."

"Needed to get your attention. It worked."

"You kept staring at me? Don't you think that's just a little bit creepy?" She squeezed two fingers together in front of his face to emphasize "little."

"Are we playing now? Is that how you want to go at this?"

"You *were* staring...just saying."

"Just saying," he mocked her.

"Stop."

"*Stop.*"

"I mean it."

He stopped and then asked, "What else should I stare at? You're beautiful. I wasn't sure I was at the right picnic. Where you from, 'cause I know you sure as shit ain't from here."

"LA."

"Yes, *you* are. Did you forget your wings there?"

"That's not going to work on me, you know?"

Shannon took a sip of Jim Beam. Victor took the bottle from her, had a longer draw, and then cradled the bottle between his legs near his crotch.

"Like I could get drunk off one sip...besides, I drink."

"Why? You got sorrows?"

"Whatever. I have a stepdad." An image flashed before Shannon's eyes of her mom's face, bloodied and bruised. Then another image of her stepdad — splayed out on the couch, the national anthem playing, and finally the TV going fuzzy. When Dale was sleeping, his eyelids never fully closed, and they reminded her of crocodile eyes — half open and predatory. "His name is Dale." She reached for the bottle between Victor's legs he allowed her to take it back.

"Is he that bad? I can take him out."

"Oh, right. You're so special forces."

Victor's voice became serious. "What if I was?"

"Were you?"

"Hell no. I hated that gig. Someone always telling you what to do, what to eat, what to wear, when to sleep. I hate people telling me what to do, but I'm all done, and now I'm free." He momentarily took his hands off the steering wheel and flapped them like the wings of a bird. "Where's your real dad?"

"He's dead."

"Oh, I'm sorry. How'd he die?"

"Vietnam."

"Man, the military sucks. What branch? That war was such bullshit."

That was what everyone would say to her when she responded with "Vietnam," and it bothered her because it sounded like they were saying his death was bullshit, but she never knew him to know whether it was bullshit or not. Her mom didn't talk about him. Him, Peter Lamb. He was attractive in the photos, kind eyes, but there were never any pictures of him holding her. He was killed before she was born. All she had from him besides half his DNA was his last name.

"He was in the Army." And then she added, "If the military is such bullshit why'd you join, then?"

She handed him back the bottle, he took a nip, leaned over her, and put the bottle back in the glovebox. Guess I'm done, she thought. The rules between them were getting laid.

"Why else? Get out of here."

"For sure."

"If I stayed here. I'd probably be in prison. You know that idle hands stuff."

"Yep, my stepdad was in the Airforce, but I don't think it did him any good...so, you're bad news? Should I be afraid?"

"Nope, not anymore," and then more intently, "Do I scare you, babe?"

Yes. In a good way. In the way I l to be scared. She shook her head no.

They were a good distance down Highway Y. She wanted him to slow down but wouldn't admit it. They were coming up on the intersection where the school bus made its last stop before dropping her and Eddy off at St. Agnes School.

"Where are we going? I don't want to meet your mom."

"She'd love you, but no, she's at the picnic."

He pulled into the parking lot of the Dew Drop Inn. Dale's hangout.

"We can't go in there."

"Come on. One beer and we'll go back."

"They're not going to serve me."

"What are you sixteen...fifteen?"

"I'll be seventeen next year," she said hoping it made her sound older.

"You're old enough for a kid."

"Shut up." She paused for a beat. "My stepdad hangs out here."

"Is he here now?"

She looked around at the mostly empty parking lot, but she knew his Blazer would not be parked there, because he came by the basement earlier with some skank woman, he said was named Tina who was going to take him to get cigarettes because he couldn't find her mom who had the keys. Blah, blah, lies, lies. Dale never lied in short sentences, but no matter, her mom was the type that thought even the Devil wasn't past redemption.

"*No*, he's at the picnic with your mom and mine, Eddy, and everyone else." Where I should be.

"Well, I think you should be with me and I'm here. Come on. I know these folks. There won't be no problem. Promise."

Victor sidled over to the passenger's door and reached over her body for the door handle. His forearm brushed her thighs, and that same heat that penetrated her apron when he slid the twenty dollars in her pocket, intensified with flesh touching flesh. He came around the car where she had already crawled out. The Chevelle was much lower than Dale's Blazer. Then he draped his arm over her shoulder, cradling her neck in a loose chokehold, and guided her towards the entrance. Possession was powerful and she understood in that moment why her mom liked that feeling from men.

The Dew Drop Inn on Old U.S. 61 was once a mill and later converted into a bar. The wooden siding had multiple layers of white cracked paint. A neon red and white Budweiser sign hung from the second story, near the window where Shannon had seen "For Rent" at one time. In the countryside where people had long driveways and acres and acres of land, it was the last light you would see for twenty miles either way.

Shannon never thought she'd ever set foot in this place. Mostly bikers and semi-trucks stopped in from St. Louis, on their way to Cape Girardeau and beyond.

They walked past a large window air conditioner propped up with two by fours where it whirred nonstop and dripped water onto the gravel.

Inside, it was dark and musty and reeked of old smoke, the kind of place that stayed on your clothes and hair even if you only walked in and walked back out. It was a one-room bar. There were two box fans going at high speed. One was wedged between the sill and an open window; strings of dust blew out but clung to its screen. The other fan sat on the bar top directed on a female bartender who was wiping down liquor bottles with a white rag. She looked familiar to Shannon.

Victor aimed Shannon in the direction of a booth with a window, although the shade was down. Aside from bartender, there was a man sitting at a high top who looked like some ancient bygone wizard of the darker variety. He squinted when the door opened. Light streamed over his weathered forearm that he contemplated briefly and then silently picked up his empty glass and jingled it at the female bartender. Shannon had the feeling people came to hide out here.

The bartender called out to Victor. "Hey there, want a Bud, Vicky?"

"Yeah, make it a bucket, would you Tina?"

Tina, the cigarette woman with Dale. Shit. She did know her.

It didn't take long before Tina set the bucket on the table between them. "You two hungry?"

"I'm not. Been at the picnic but get whatever she wants."

Tina tapped her ink pen on her order pad. "Bet you forgot my liver dumplings you promised me last night?"

"Nah, I didn't forget you, girl."

"They in the car? 'Cause they'll get spoilt in the heat."

"I'm going to get them later. Bring them back, see?"

"Yeah, sure." Tina glanced at Shannon. "I've seen you. Your daddy know you here with him?" She pointed her red pen at Victor.

"*Step.* Did you help Dale get his cigs alright, Tina?"

"What's all this about, ladies. Come on."

Shannon gave Tina a dazzler of a smile. "May I get a basket of fries, ma'am?"

Tina snorted some and said, "Sure, honey." She shook her head, walking away.

"Cheers." Victor tapped his bottle on Shannon's. "So, Shannon. What you are doing here?"

"Someone invited me on a ride."

"You are enjoying it?"

"More or less... *Vicky*."

He beamed at her. His teeth were even and very white.

"A girlfriend?" Shannon nodded her head in the direction of Tina.

Victor leant into the back of the booth, stretched his legs underneath the table, and wrapped them around her ankles. Shannon would have leaned back too, but the vinyl upholstery had been repaired with electrical tape and the sticky side had come lose and something was scratching her shoulder.

"Baby girl, I'm never going to lie to you, and nah, she's not a girlfriend. She may have been friendly, but I swear it was all her. You don't have to worry about anything."

He was profoundly serious, and she wanted to believe him in this moment. But there was a slight inflection between lies and truth Shannon has learned to detect. Subtle. But Shannon knew it. What Victor was saying from behind his teeth, what his full lips were forming, those words made from his tongue could have sounded like the truth. She wanted to believe him, and yet, there was that inflection that warned her not to. She shoved it down.

"I know," she said, but fixed her eyes on the jukebox.

"Good."

He pulled out a cigarette, lit it, handed it to her, and then lit one for himself. He began speaking some more of his truth, romancing each word.

"When I saw you, I thought, well, here we go. This is what everyone talks about. Never felt it, not once. I thought I want to know every bit of this girl. Not just physical. I can see you think it's all I want, but it's not. It's right to be suspicious, though." He stopped talking to take a drag. "You're a good girl. I can tell. Wouldn't want it any other way."

"Don't call me a good girl. I hate that. I mean it."

Shannon's neck started to burn, and she knew red was creeping up her face. Her ears were hot. She knocked away his feet and scooted out of the booth. "Where's the bathroom?" Victor used his cigarette to point to a hallway between the bar and kitchen.

The lady's bathroom was surprisingly clean, probably from never being used, and smelled very strongly of perfume. Shannon tossed the cigarette she hated into the toilet and sat down to pee. There was a curtain around the sink. Underneath — a curling iron, Aqua Fresh, tampons, a makeup bag, baby powder. Tina's bathroom.

She washed her hands, took several paper towels out of the dispenser, wetted them, and wiped down her face, her arms, and her legs. She was sticky with picnic sweat. She lifted her shirt to smell her underarms. Under the sink she found Tina's deodorant and perfume. She looked closely in the mirror at herself.

When she was eight, she once climbed the tallest diving board at the YMCA swimming pool. Her legs just took her up the ladder, but by the time she walked across the gritty board she was trembling and too terrified to climb back down. She would have to jump. Her toes clung to the edge of the board. She couldn't jump. Kids lined up on the ladder on the other end of the diving board. The lifeguard yelled, "One at a time! I told you guys before. One at a time!" The kids behind her shouted for her to jump. A boy walked forward; he was acting like he was going to push her, so she leapt. She remembered nothing of her time in the air, and only recalled breaking the surface of the water, and feeling more alive in that moment than any other moment of her life. She felt the same way now staring into the mirror, except her ponytail made her look too young, and no one was here to push her.

She pulled out the rubber band. With Tina's brush, she brushed out some tangles and then sprayed perfume in her hair. Tina had nice boobs, she thought. Shannon was naturally lean in all departments, but she knew people thought her pretty. She contemplated her large indigo eyes and flawless skin. "But no boobs," she said to the mirror.

She started to open the bathroom door, hesitated, shut the door, and then wetted more paper towels, adding some soap. She pulled her skintight shorts down to wipe between her legs.

"LA Woman" was playing when she came out. Victor was adding more money to the juke box.

"You smell nice," Tina said, tossing her basket of fries on the table in front of her. She didn't leave immediately, as though she was waiting for Shannon to say sorry or something.

Shannon may have felt shame, but for the beer and liquor in her system. She didn't care what Tina thought. So, what if she used her perfume? She wouldn't respond to Tina. She made her face completely blank. No emotion, she thought. Life, or maybe survival, required pretense. All the bad must be tucked away in a secret closet in your head. Fold it, hang it, store it away, deal with it when you run out of space; she was young and had a lot of space left.

She wasn't drunk, but more than tipsy. Victor selected more songs, The Eagles and Neil Young, the stuff her mom and Dale still listened to. Not anything current, but she recognized the songs, and even sang some lyrics.

They talked about nothing and everything as if they hadn't seen each other in years and had so much to catch up on — music, places they'd been, who and what had wronged them, where they were going now, and Eddy. When Eddy came up, they both understood it was time to go. Plus, some hardened picnic goers trailed in, and Shannon was nervous someone would eventually spot her.

Victor led her to his car and put her in the passenger seat. Seconds later, he was in the driver's seat and then grabbing her face with both hands and kissing her. Somehow, he managed to pull her over the console and onto his lap without stopping. They both were breathing hard, and then he was undoing her bra, and it was too much, so she pulled back, and sunk into the passenger's seat.

He started the Chevelle. It was getting dark now. They were heading away from the sunset. About a mile before entering

Lawrenceton, Victor pulled off into a dirt road that at one time went somewhere, but she knew nowhere tonight. He turned the engine off.

He rested his head on the steering wheel. He said he wanted to cry. She agreed. He said he wanted this more than anything; he knew he could convince her to come with him, but he just wanted to do the right thing for her. She kept asking him why, what? Why can't he stay here? He had to keep going down the road, if not tonight then tomorrow, or the next. They belonged together she told him. He yelled at her, to make her stop telling him the truth they both knew, and then he told her to get out.

For a moment, she thought he was leaving her here on this empty road with empty promises, but he came around and forced her back on the hood. He pushed and pulled on everything she had. He had one insignificant breast in his hand and was jabbing his tongue into her mouth. He yanked at her zipper, tugged her shorts down, and pushed his fingers into her. And she was naked like never before. It hurt. Not their agreement, but Shannon stopped asking herself what she was doing. This was it. On the hood of a Chevelle with a stranger. She was a cliché. She was a kid playing with a loaded gun.

But in part, Shannon wanted this more than Victor. It solidified what everyone already suspected of her. She could quit pretend-fighting. He was inside her. The incessant rattle of crickets roared in her ears, then suddenly stopped, as if someone realized they had been on all day and flicked the switch off. She heard cars rushing by, and she imagined they had stopped and lined up with their headlights on bright and were watching Victor pumping himself in her and accusing her of wanting this all along. She wanted to yell out, stop it, stop him, but they refused her any help. She deserved what she got. Hadn't she asked for this? Didn't she willingly get into his car? Why should they intercede here?

Victor was zipping up his pants, asking if she was ready. But only when she heard his voice, had she noticed the weight of him had left her.

She felt Victor's hand on the top of her arm, pulling her toward the passenger door. The crickets began chirping again, reminding Shannon where she was. He opened the door, and he nudged her in. When he turned on the ignition, the lights flashed bright in the interior, and they gazed at each other for a moment. His chin was broken out, and there were purple moons under his eyes. He had the quality of a fugitive.

"Here, you this fell out of your pocket." He handed her a wad of money, her tip money. She stared at it laying in her lap but didn't make a move to collect it. The interior lights faded out. He backed the Chevelle onto Highway Y.

He hit the on button to his stereo. "Pink Houses" was blaring. He didn't turn the station or turn it down, though the song didn't seem like his thing and then she vaguely recalled hearing it earlier today when things were different than they were now. She wanted to turn it off, but resisted because she didn't want to speak, and he might protest.

He parked off the side of the road in front of the church. The picnic was over. People were cleaning up. He leaned over and kissed her one more time, deeper and harder than before, to say he could do that to her. He didn't open the door or reach over her for the door handle. She understood his silence and got out.

In the graveled parking lot of the church, she watched him through the open passenger door while he flipped through stations. "Wait."

She obeyed. But she hated the discord of flipping stations.

He finally gave up the radio and turned it off. Again, he said, "Wait." He started fumbling behind his seat with one hand. She heard the minute tinkling of the church bell. He reached her the birdhouse, and she took it — like the prize from a carnival —from winning at balloon darts or the ring toss—the birdhouse was an oversized teddy bear, cheap and flammable. He said something about getting her number from his cousin. She couldn't' meet his eyes. She looked down and noticed a to-go container with half-eaten liver dumplings on the ground. Ants were already crawling on it.

"Eddy has your phone number, right?"

But she heard something else, a lack of interest in his voice, and she didn't respond, just stood next to the open passenger door holding her consolation prize. She wanted to slam the car door, resisted the urge, and pushed it lightly shut. He drove away.

She thought, bye Vicky. She thought, see you later alligator, and she chucked the birdhouse across the street into a ditch.

Road Trip

Tina was what some might call a home girl. She'd never been outside the state of Missouri — never further than the Lake of the Ozarks when she was young. Goose Creek Lake was around the corner if she wanted a lake. She lived where she worked, in a studio apartment above the Dew Drop Inn off Highway Y and Old U.S. 61. It was the local for most and a stopover for some who were desperate to eat somewhere but who would never return. In the afternoons, Tina walked down the metal stairs from her studio apartment over the bar, and somewhere around 2:30 a.m. she climbed the same set of stairs and got into bed. Sometimes, she brought a man with her upstairs. For the past six months, Dale Samples climbed her stairs.

It wasn't that Tina was fast; The Dew was convenient for meeting men. She didn't see the point in driving to some overpriced bar in St. Geneviève to meet some guy who would inevitably not work out. Her best friend, Lindy, worked with her and even though the men were not the choicest, they were plentiful.

Tina was *just* cute, cute in the eighth-grade kind of way that doesn't translate into adulthood. She wore thick black eyeliner around her blue eyes which she believed highlighted her turquoise blues and at one time may have, but now made her look more road hard. She was petite with some extra around the hips, but all this was forgiven by her darling smile and her baby-girl voice that had the effect of making her sound guileless. It was the type of innocence that appeals to a certain type of man who looked at Tina as someone who needed saving from the rest of the rednecks who hung out at The Dew. So honeyed and sugared a voice if they lasted long enough to be called "boyfriend" they'd told themselves there weren't many before them though she'd seen the better part of thirty-five and the man drinking beer in the barstool next to him knew what her bathroom wallpaper looked like. Many knew the pattern of her wallpaper.

She loved working at The Dew. It felt good being the only decent looking available woman twenty minutes in any direction. Her attitude towards men was much like most men's attitude towards women. Maybe she could stop smoking or drink less. If it weren't for the job and someone always asking her, "Hey doll, take a seat, have a smoke? What you drinkin, darlin?" Maybe if she had to try harder.

Her days and nights passed, and another line crept around her eyes, but mostly Tina marked off time by whether it was cold or hot outside, because she never let the ice completely melt before she started on her tan. She was a regular at Bronze Bunz Tanning Salon in St. Gen. where Dale's stepdaughter, Shannon, worked. Tina liked to tan on Fridays before her shift, so she would have a nice glow for the weekend. Dale wasn't a member. He worked weekends at the liquor store ringing up customers, stocking, and wheeling out kegs for high school boys getting drunk down some dirt road off the Mississippi River, where cops didn't bother to go. He dropped Shannon off before her shift, leaving them an hour to spare before his shift started.

Tina noticed Dale as soon as she exited the glass door. The window to his Blazer was unrolled; he was smoking a cigarette. She walked inches away from his open window, getting a taste for the smoke. It had been three days since she last had a cigarette, and she was jonesing bad. She reached into her purse for her gum.

"Girl, you gettin real dark."

"That's kinda the point."

"Going get cancer cooking your insides."

"Says the man smoking a cigarette."

"Want one?"

It became a thing for them to talk and smoke after she got out of the tanning bed.

Dale was good-looking and a charmer, a dangerous combination. Golden caramel skin. Nordic blue eyes. Thick toffee-colored hair.

The type who got out of trouble with a grin and a wink. Then one night, Dale showed up at The Dew and charmed free drinks and a later blowjob out of her in his Blazer in the parking lot. He didn't really have to push her head in that direction. She was going there one way or another.

The thing about Tina is she had never been in love. There were boyfriends, but nothing like what she had with Dale. Every time he bitched about his wife, Wendy, and his stepdaughter; her heart shriveled up until it became so small it stopped beating altogether. It was like a hardened dried-up buckeye that only filled up when Dale was nearby. When its last wrinkle puffed out, she gasped — an awful choking air which hurt more and more with waiting. Waiting for a sound, a sign, anything that said he loved her like she loved him. If there was a curse, she could have put on him to make him feel the same, she would have chanted it. If there was a prayer, she'd already prayed it. Never being lost in love, and it being forbidden love, she ignored anyone who told her, "This Dale thing is a bad idea." He was going to leave his family. He was coming to her because that was all she had hoped for. That's how hope works.

* * *

On the Saturday after New Year's, the Dew was dead. Tina decided to close early. She counted down her cash drawer while Dale stacked chairs on tables and complained bitterly about Wendy. Every nasty word built a bigger and bigger house for them in Tina's head: a yellow two-story trimmed in red and white with a huge wraparound porch, and a little girl dunking Barbies in an aquamarine, plastic splash pool. She envisioned Dale cutting the grass and Tina resting in a lawn chair, hypnotized by the hum of the mower, soaking up the sun. Then the mower would cut off and Tina would watch Dale drink from the water hose. He'd catch her watching him, Tina, his new wife who had had his *real* daughter. Their eyes would recognize each other. All of what came before would vanish into this new life where the complexities of ungrateful wives and spoiled stepdaughters did not reside. They weren't even neighbors.

Tina blurted out, "Why don't you just leave her? We can be happy. Me and you?" She pointed to the empty air between their bodies and said, "This thing we have going on."

Dale placed the chair he was holding in his hand back down on the floor and straddled it, seemed to contemplate her proposal, and then responded.

"I *am* leaving."

He got a job at Lockheed in Marietta, Georgia and was leaving in two weeks.

"Were you going to tell me, or just one day you're gone? *What?* Should I even notice you're missing?"

"I just told you. Hell, I just found out I got it, so there was nothin to tell."

"I guess that's it then."

She took a stack of bills and threw them in his face. Hard, or as hard as a stack on a slow night could be thrown. They sputtered, weak without volume, and fell nowhere near him. The dramatic effect was lost; the cash lay strewn on the floor three feet away from his boots. A stripper would have ignored it, but Dale did not ignore it. He came up behind her and grabbed both her shoulders and this made Tina feel like he wanted her.

"What the fuck's wrong with you? We'll see each other." He walked her into a corner and wrapped his hands around the back of her neck, possessively. "What? You'll miss me?"

She pushed his chest. "Is Wendy gonna pick me up at the bus stop?"

"That's what this about then? No, honey, she ain't coming." His lips were on her neck now and his hands had moved down. One grabbed at her breast while the other unzipped her jeans.

"I'll send you a Greyhound ticket," he murmured into her ear. "Just lemme get settled."

For those two weeks before Tina left for Georgia, she drank Slim Fast milkshakes for breakfast and lunch and ate a salad for dinner. She lost thirteen pounds. At Bronze Bunz she splurged on Fire-n-Ice tanning accelerator and upped her membership to an unlimited tan package. Lindy bought a hair frosting kit and after work on the night before she left, she highlighted Tina's hair in her apartment. They jabbered away like girls at a slumber party while Lindy yanked thin strands of Tina's hair through pin-needle holes.

"*Ouch. Goddamn it.* You ripping my hair out, girl?"

"I'm not. Stop. *Don't touch.* These holes are invisible. Grant did mine last time, and I thought the same thing, but it's worth it." Lindy faced her, pulled the cap down tighter, and tied the plastic strings around her chin. "Okay, time for bleach."

"I can't believe you let him do your hair."

"Oh, he's good at stuff like that. Besides, it ain't hard, and you'd pay a fortune having it done."

An hour later, Lindy handed Tina a mirror.

"Dang, you're hot. Girl, I'm going to lose my tips with you all tan, skinny, and blonde. He ain't never going let you leave looking like that." Lindy dug in her purse for keys. "I gotta hit it, though, I was supposed to be home two hours ago."

From the top of the stairs, Tina watched Lindy walk to her car. Before she climbed into the driver's seat Lindy waved and said, "You better come back. Don't leave me with all these rednecks working your shifts on top of mine."

"You know I wouldn't do that to you. It's a roundtrip, anyways. Sides, all my stuff is still here."

"Shit, roundtrip don't mean nothing."

Tina shut the front door and paused for a moment giving the word "stuff" some thought. The neon Budweiser sign outside her window flickered and buzzed to life. It was her nightlight against the dark country skies. A snow globe with the St. Louis Arch sat on her windowsill. She dropped it long ago and had chiseled out the fragmented glass around the edges so you could hardly tell. On her nightstand there was a framed picture of her and Lindy at the last Fourth of July Dew-B-Q party. Both pink in the face and acting crazy, as drunk as the rest of the bar. On her two-person kitchen table sat her grandmother's vase with tiny chips missing around the rim. Giant, fake, white hydrangeas with bushy green leaves hid the imperfections.

She would stay if he asked and leave behind her "stuff," and not say goodbye to friends and family. She imagined filling out Christmas cards to Lindy and Grant and signing it: "The Samples."

The Dew's owner had just put new carpet down, though, and let her pick it out. Pinot Noir. There was some permanence in the carpet, but at the time she hadn't known things were heading this way with Dale, and she had to live her life. Everyone else got to have husbands, homes, and families. Her possessions were broken and glued, and even though no one else saw the flaws she knew they were there.

* * *

Though already September, summer would not break, and the hot air felt like God had cranked up the heater and was blasting it on high. At the Greyhound terminal in Cape Girardeau the AC had stopped working. Grant kept shaking his head and saying, "Tina, you need to find a good man," and, "it sure as hell ain't Dale."

The bus had the faint smell of urine she was accustomed to from cleaning the men's bathrooms at The Dew. Thankfully, it was cold. Tina decided it was best to sit near the driver based on old knowledge that if anything bad was going to happen it would be in the back of the bus. There was a mother with a baby, two young men in military uniforms, and an elderly lady who never looked up from whispering into her Bible. A few men in the back of the bus, probably fifteen years younger than they appeared to be, or acted, cat-called Tina but only for a moment. She knew their type. They worked under the sun, dropped in The Dew, woke up, and repeated.

Every night belly-up to the bar until the job ran out, their funds ran dry, or Tina banned them. Some of them she had slept with, but not anymore.

She lost the old lady with her Bible in Sikeston, the mama, and the military boys in Paducah, but the sunburnt workers remained, and the bus picked up more of their kind, and worse, at her transfer in Clarksville. There wasn't a direct route from Cape Girardeau to Marietta. Tina was so happy about going she didn't care at the time when Grant pointed out how long the trip was, all the transfers, the layovers in cities, and "not little towns like you're used to," he had said. She couldn't drive her car. It was good to get to the grocery store and tanning, but she didn't trust it on a long trip.

Before she boarded Bus Forty, it had started to pour and the aisles were slick with muck from work boots. The odor coming off the workman, who came straight from the construction site foregoing showers, was unforgiving. Her jacket was in overhead storage. As soon as she stood up, the cat calls and comments began and didn't relent until the bus pulled into another station and the men became preoccupied with whatever new interest was boarding at the time. Inevitably, it started again: "Dang, girl. You're hot," or, "Want to share my seat?" It was worth getting her jacket. Anything would be better than smelling a festering bus for the next fourteen hours. She covered her nose with her sleeve and breathed through her mouth.

In Jackson, TN, a man boarded who reeked of booze and nearly landed in Tina's lap but managed to fall into the last empty space a few seats behind her. The back people had merged, combining with the middle so that the bus was almost entirely full of rowdies, drunk on MD 2020 they kept low between their seats. It was the only thing the bus driver warned people about. "Don't make me kick you off my bus, 'cause I catch you drinking. You drink before you board my bus. Not on my bus." He was good on his word and kicked the guy who boarded in Jackson off in Nashville, where Tina had a two-hour stop before connecting to another bus that would take her to

142

Chattanooga. He followed her out repeating, "Hey pretty lady, hey pretty lady," like a wearisome parrot and then, "Hey, I'm talking to you," and finally, "bitch, fucking bitch," when she wouldn't pay him no mind.

The Nashville station was packed with all kinds of people coming and going, but Tina couldn't tell if they looked like normal people. She was so far past connecting with folk that for the most part she kept her eyes on the ground. It was just too dangerous to make eye contact. The Nashville station might as well have been another bar off Broadway. She heard about the honky-tonks on Broadway. These people weren't just drunk. They were high. They were low. The walking dead, bus zombies: a man with an IV still attached with tape to his vein and wearing nothing but a hospital gown and slippers; a homeless lady arguing with the coffee machine Tina didn't dare go near; a couple of street musicians with empty guitar cases singing old time country songs — "Jolene" and "Delta Dawn" — Tina normally would have appreciated, but just made her feel sad.

At The Dew there was a regular named Raymond, a Vietnam vet who kept to himself aside the one time when he overdrank and started a fight, a fight he couldn't finish. He gave Tina a creepy feeling, but he tipped all right and usually minded his business. He had *malum in se* tatted on his forearm; the ink was faded, but you could still make out the words. He told her it meant evil itself. He'd gotten it in Nam. This place — the bus station in Nashville — its residents made her think of him and his tattoo now. None of them you'd want to be left alone with.

She was relieved when she heard, "Boarding bus two, thirty-seven to Chattanooga. Boarding bus two, thirty-seven to Chattanooga." She didn't know if Chattanooga was in Tennessee or Georgia, and she didn't care. Every stop was a wasteland for the lost, but it was the last stop before arriving in Marietta where Dale would be waiting. Again, she found a space closest to the bus driver, avoiding the back full of roughnecks. She couldn't remember the last time she rode a bus. In

143

high school probably, but if she made it back to The Dew, if Dale didn't ask her to stay, she promised herself she'd never ride another. She didn't want to think about those "ifs" right now. She was thinking crazy anyway. All her stuff was in her apartment.

When the bus arrived in Chattanooga the driver hollered and then turned and watched as all the lost souls he had gathered, emerged, and descended the stairs like they were walking into hell, but really going to the station to wait, to board another bus, to meet family.

When Tina didn't budge, the driver said, "Hey, darlin, I ain't leaving for here thirty minutes."

"I know. Just don't want to miss it is all."

"Well, the rules are when I leave everyone's got to leave. Go stretch your legs. It'll be another two hours before Marietta."

"Mister, I don't wanna stretch my legs. I just wanna stay here until I hear you say 'Marietta' and then I'm getting off."

The bus driver looked her up and down and asked, "How's the bathrooms back there tonight?"

"I don't know. I was in Nashville for two hours. I went then."

"I won't risk it," he said and then after a bit, after summing Tina up with her little girl voice he decided she was safe. "All right, I'm going to shut the door with you in it. Just stay put."

Tina nodded and fixed her eyes out the window. She knew he was doing her a kindness, but she couldn't even respond.

The sun came up as they were exiting Chattanooga. At least, there was that. Tina watched as unfamiliar towns passed by her through the bus window. One indiscernible rundown town after the other slipped by with no distinguishing landmarks and Tina wondered if they had places like The Dew, or were their townsfolk so foreign, so different than hers.

Tina was dozing when the bus driver announced, "Marietta, next ten minutes, Marietta, ten minutes," but was wide awake when he continued with, "For the rest of you city dwellers, Atlanta, Forsyth Street is leaving in twenty minutes."

She experienced a surge of pleasure not afforded her the last fourteen hours and nineteen minutes. She got up to go to the bathroom. She wanted a shower, to brush her teeth, a bed. It was 11:10 a.m., and she hadn't eaten real food since she left. Someone threw up in the sink. She hovered over the toilet seat and peed on her new Chic jeans. Tina didn't need to look into the piece of metal which served as a mirror to tell she was well-marinated. She started laughing, hysterically laughing. Even when she sat back in her seat she kept laughing, and no one paid her any attention. It's what a road trip on a Greyhound bus ticket does to a person, and only a day ago Tina thought she was holding a lottery ticket.

She stood outside next to the back of the bus where the driver was unloading luggage. She pointed hers out and he handed it over, a borrowed suitcase from Lindy. It didn't seem possible it could be hotter in Georgia than Missouri, but it was. She glanced around the bus in the parking lot. No Dale. He wasn't waiting inside, either.

There was a phone booth near the entrance to the station. Three times and no answer. She could cry, but instead went inside and asked the ticket lady if there were any places to eat close by.

"You mean walking close or driving close?"

"Walking close."

"Huddle House is up the street."

"What's that like?"

"I don't know. It's a Huddle House. You said walking close." The ticket lady's eyes glazed over at the man who just seconds ago got in line behind Tina and asked. "*Sir*, you need a ticket?"

The Huddle House was up a hill overlooking the Greyhound Bus Station. There was a phone by the entrance, but she ignored it and sat down in a booth. It smelled of old grease, but the coffee was good. She ordered a patty melt and hash browns — the first real meal she'd eaten in weeks.

So accustomed to the darkness of The Dew — the only thing the bus had in common with her life- that when she had emerged from the shadows of the bus, the sun hurt her eyes, and now the lights in the Huddle House seemed impossibly bright. And didn't seem like her sitting here. Some other girl was going through the actions of bus rides and no guarantees, not her. Tina could only look down on this girl, covered in artificial light and feel bad for her. It was as if she was a bystander in her own nightmare.

"Can I get you anything else, sweetie?" The waitress looked like her night before wasn't much better.

"Nope. There goes my diet."

"Oh, sweetie. Don't you know it." She waved her hand at her, "You just enjoy it."

Enjoy it. But she did anyway. Afterwards, she went to the bathroom and threw up. She didn't make herself. It just happened.

It was past noon when she picked up the sticky phone receiver to call Dale. On the fourth ring, someone in the parking lot started honking. She slammed the receiver down so hard she had to check and make sure it wasn't broken. Still a dial tone, and in her anger, she ripped one of her Lee Press-On Nails off. She turned around, flipped the driver off, and then recognized Dale's Blazer with Dale inside, grinning.

He stuck his head out the window and said, "Hey baby, why the bird? Come on, get in. That ticket lady said you were here. I'll get your bag."

Just like that, and nothing else mattered.

* * *

The Moonraker Apartments was an adult-only complex that had its heyday in the 1970s when open sex was the norm and AIDS hadn't surfaced yet.

Dale guided her through wooden planked pathways hidden between Hostas, their stems sprouting ivory flowers, light and feathery, like ruffled birds and Bengal Tiger Canna with blooms as bright as goldfish. Occasionally, he pointed out a pool or hot tub buried into the lush landscape, and she'd smile the smile of someone

146

on their first day of vacation. If Tina had looked closer, she might have noticed rotten wood or chipped stucco, but its aged luster was lost on her. Coming from the bus, The Moonraker was more like a rendering — a façade of resort living, a dream she wanted to believe in. Plus, Dale kept turning around and teasing her. "Look Tina, *the plane, the plane*," and, "Welcome to Fantasy Island."

They came into a large opening, what Tina figured was the main pool. She could hear the faint sound of music during the journey, but now they were in the middle of a full-blown party. Some of the women weren't wearing tops with their bikinis. She was so exhausted she didn't ask, pretended she only imagined bare breasts bobbing around just after noon in the middle of nowhere-she-knew Georgia.

Dale directed her to sliding glass doors that opened into his living room. The floors were covered in a thick grungy shag, except for the sunken living room area, which was done in terra cotta tile. Two steps led down to an oversized couch with a glass table in the middle. On the opposite side of the sunken living room was a floor to ceiling rock wall fireplace bordered by long thin windows that let light in but didn't open. Tina was sure there was a bedroom and bathroom beyond the rock wall. She wanted both and nothing more. It was different than any other place she'd ever been to, and it might have been nice if it weren't so filthy.

The glass table was littered with beer cans and newspapers. A large crystal-cut ashtray sat near the edge of the table and was filled to the brim with cigarette butts. It didn't feel right, all those smoked cigarettes and not one of them had passed between her lips. Lipstick marked the filters in colors she never wore; she was strictly a little Vaseline and Frosted Peach, Maybelline 064. And then there were the Virginia Slims, not her brand and what was that slogan? "You've come a long way, baby." She'd come a long way, but not like that. Seeing the mess around her, Tina wondered if she'd gone in reverse, fast.

Dale pushed her in the direction of the kitchen. It was tiny and felt even tinier because the counters were covered in even more beer cans and half-drunk liquor bottles. The trashcan was full and overflowing and there were a couple of cardboard cases of beer being used to throw trash in if they bothered. He was an hour and a half late picking her up, hadn't cleaned for her, and there was a man leaning against his refrigerator smoking a joint.

"Hey, man. Sorry. The manager was giving us shit about smoking at the pool. This your girl? Old Charles...nice to meet you." Old Charles wasn't old, but Tina didn't care about asking. When he put out his hand for Tina to shake, Dale kind of slapped it away and said, "You don't need to know him." It was rude, yet Old Charles took it in stride and winked at her. It made Tina feel a little better. At least, Dale could be jealous. But then she thought if he asked her to stay, (stay, stay) not just for the week, she'd have to clean this mess and it pissed her off because this was supposed to be her vacation and she'd have to spend it making the place livable.

"Okay, okay. You got your lady with you. I get it." Old Charles opened the freezer and pulled out a bottle of Jägermeister. "I'll just be taking this." Before he closed the sliding glass door to leave, he stuck his head back in and said, "See you later tonight." Tina wasn't sure if he was asking a question or making a statement.

"Dale, I need to use the little girl's room." She prayed it wasn't as bad as the rest of his place.

"Listen to this one. The little girl's room. Come here."

Tina obeyed, but only for a moment. "Babe, please. Stop. I feel gross. This place. *God.*"

For the first time since she'd arrived, Dale seemed to understand her situation. "You're right. Those kids are always coming and going and I'm working twelve-hour days." He reached under the kitchen sink, dug out a garbage bag, and started clearing off the counters. "You take a shower while I get this straight." She started to leave, heading towards where she imagined the bathroom would be, but he grabbed her hand and said, "Hey, everything is going to be all right." And she let herself believe it.

"Is there at least a clean towel?"

"Yeah, yeah. In the closet. No one is allowed back there besides me, and you now, baby."

When she got back to The Dew, she made a promise to herself that she'd never call anyone, baby, honey, sweetie, or darlin again. People had been calling her these names all throughout the trip, some sincerely, but now Dale was saying it too and it meant little after how late he was and the state of his apartment. If it was the other way around, she thought.

The bathroom was clean, or man clean. He must have been serious when he said no one else was allowed past the hallway, and that made Tina feel a little better, and he was so foxy she could just about forgive anything.

* * *

After they made love, Tina fell into a deep sleep. When she awoke, she was covered in sweat — exhaustion sweat. Intuitively, she knew Dale wasn't there. She had lived alone long enough to know what it felt like to be in an empty bed.

It was dark. Aluminum foil covered the windows, and she had no idea what time it was, or how long she'd been asleep. She felt for the bedside table, for the lamp, missed the switch flopping around on his stupid, stupid waterbed. She hated it but didn't say anything because, like The Moonraker, he seemed to think it was something special.

When she found the switch and turned the light on, she suddenly realized a party was underway outside the bedroom door. In the darkness, she had not heard it for some reason, but now with the light on it came flooding in.

She had to pee. The bathroom was at the end of the hallway, past a storage closet or laundry room she did not check to know. She cracked open the door. "Don't Ask Me No Questions" was blasting, and a woman was screaming the words to it; she was so obviously wasted. A man kept repeating, "Dude, dude. Just listen to me." These were all too familiar sounds. She shook her head, talking to herself, "What the fuck? I might as well be at work."

She could just leave, get back on the bus. God the bus, that horrible, horrible bus. She hadn't unpacked aside from her toothbrush and new makeup bag she left in the bathroom.

"Goddammit." She struggled up out of the sloshing bed, pulled herself up onto the hard edge, misjudged, and sank in between the frame and the waterbed. Someone was rattling the door handle. Tina felt a rush of panic; she was naked, and God knows who was on the other side of the door. A woman's voice came through the door.

"Dale, you in there? Open up."

So much for not letting anyway past the hallway, but thankfully he locked the door.

And again, she jiggled the door handle. "Hey Dale. Mandy and I are heading to the bathroom."

What the fuck? Why would he care? The bathroom.

Tina shouted, "Dale's not in here!"

The woman didn't immediately respond. "Oh...sorry...Who's this?"

Tina was going to have it out with Dale. This was fucking ridiculous.

The woman waited all of five seconds and rapped her nails against the door and asked if she knew where he was.

"Good question! No. Do you mind?"

The woman said "okay" in a snarky way, but Tina sensed she had moved on.

The motherfucker left her in a house full of strangers, wasted strangers at that, in a filthy fucking house, and that was just the start of the list. Tina thought about the fourteen hours (over fourteen hours) on the bus she'd never get back. She felt vulnerable, no, *cornered*. And she had made it so easy for him. That bus ride opened her eyes. Oh, she had slipped for a second there, acting out a part she thought she could be. The new girlfriend role. But now, hell no, and she wasn't taking no bus back. Dale would have to pay for a plane ticket. Her pussy ain't for free. If she had to use Wendy for leverage, she would.

While she dug in her bag for a bra, underwear, some clean clothes, she kept repeating to herself, "What the fuck, Tina," saying it over and over, and out loud, though quietly like when she'd forgotten her grocery list and was mumbling to herself, trying to remember what she wrote down while walking down the soup aisle.

She would have loved to take another shower, to get *him* off her body, but that wouldn't send the right message, and she wanted out now. She grabbed her junk jewelry off the nightstand and shoved earrings and a necklace into her jean pocket. Although she didn't need further confirmation Dale was a prick, something made her open the drawer. Tossed change rattled, a cycle trader magazine, and underneath the magazine, there was a farmed picture of Wendy sitting at the beach looking as perfect as she was, and Tina knew he'd hidden the photo because she was coming to visit.

Tina started to shake. Now, she wanted more proof. More proof that he wasn't leaving Wendy. She slung open the dresser drawers and searched through his shit. In his closet she yanked every tee-shirt, every button up shirt, and every pair of pants off their hangers, and scattered his clothes across the floor.

And then under the bed, she found it. A shoebox with dirty pictures of Wendy, and then notebooks filled with what appeared to be every word Wendy ever uttered to Dale. She didn't understand why he would record such trivial conversations, but they were dated and some of them only a few days ago. Whatever they were to Dale, they represented obsession, not for her, *not Tina*, but for his wife.

She knew what had to be done now. In the nightstand drawer she'd seen his pocketknife. It wouldn't be immediate. The vinyl was thick and the blade small, but she felt the tip and it was sharp. A puncture here and there. God, she couldn't wait to see his face.

Already, water was leaking onto the sheets. It was the sloppy work of an impassioned homicide, but it felt good to wreck his room. She swung the door open and headed towards the bathroom.

A woman sat straddling the toilet chopping coke on the lid where Tina had left her makeup bag that was no longer there. Another woman was standing behind her, smoking a cigarette, and flicking ashes into the sink.

"Oh, hey girl. Come in." the woman smoking waved her in as if she'd been expecting her.

"What the hell, Mandy?"

"Steph, calm down, little thing. Look, it's Dale's girl, sorry, what's your name? I forgot he told me you were coming to visit. Sorry, about the door."

"Where's my makeup bag? It was sitting right there." She pointed at the coke. She'd only seen it on TV. Sure, they were drinkers at The Dew, but they were still Midwesterners.

The girl called Steph shrugged and they both said they hadn't seen it. "Come on, come in. We're just shooting the shit, girl."

The bathroom was cramped enough for one person, let alone three. Tina hesitated in the doorway, but Steph reached from her position on the toilet for her hand and pulled her in. Mandy kicked the door shut.

"So, tell us. Is he hung or what?"

"So sexy," Steph said.

Both women erupted into laughter. Then Mandy bent over the toilet lid, snorted three consecutive lines, acted like she was going to gag, like she might throw up, wiped her nose, and said, "Oh yeah. That's exactly it," which for some reason was also uproariously funny to them.

They had assembled in such a way that Tina had gotten shoved against the metal towel rack. She tried to peer at the space on the floor between the toilet and the tub in case her bag had fallen there.

She still had to pee. But she wanted out of that bathroom, Dale's apartment, the entire state of fucking Georgia. All she wanted was to be wrapped in her JCPenney's comforter and to see her Budweiser sign outside her window.

Mandy pointed at the lines of coke with the half straw she held in her hand and said, "Girl, get you some" to Tina and then began speaking to Steph as if Tina wasn't in the same bathroom as her. "Shit, I heard he made her ride the bus."

"You're shitting me? Cheap ass." Mandy handed Steph the straw and Steph leaned over the lid and snorted two lines back-to-back.

"Yeah, yep, yep. And, Steph," Mandy spoke extremely fast, hardly finishing one thought before launching into the next. "Hey, you know I rode the bus from Atlanta to Tampa once, well, I tried to. Remember Lane, I told you about? *Lane*, what a fucking name. You know the thing? You know who. Timmy. Dang, that lying f-u-c-k. Let me tell you, no shut-up, *Steph*, shut-up, let tell you."

When Steph tried to speak, Mandy would slap at the air, sometimes at Steph's hand and talk over her. "I caught Timmy with his dick and balls so far down some girl's throat *and* do you know what he did? Denied it? He f-u-c-k-i-n-g denied it, Ste-pha-nie! That's how he was. Listen, listen he could have his whole dick down her throat, I could be standing right next to them, and he'd say, listen to me, he'd say, 'What? What's wrong, Mandy?' with a look on his face like there wasn't no girl there at all. That's how big a liar he was. He practically had his entire hairy-ass body down this chick's throat. He's so nasty. I swear. Anyway, I got as far as Jacksonville, just enough time to figure out Lane ain't so bad compared to the freaks (she screamed freaks for some reason) on the bus. So, he picked me up. Hey, can I bum another cigarette, Steph? He came and rescued me, mmm-hmmm." Mandy flicked the metal wheel of the lighter several times. "Fu-ck me, this lighter is dead. Are there matches in the cabinet? *No way.* No buses for this bitch." With a razor she dragged out a single line and again indicated that Tina should take it.

"Get you some," Steph repeated.

Not another second in this bathroom with these women who wouldn't stop talking and didn't make any sense, these "get you some girls," not a second more, she thought.

Tina pushed Mandy roughly into Steph, ripped the door open, and ran out. She heard the door slam behind her and "bitch," but she was gone, literally running down Dale's hallway, and then nothing but lunging forward into the sunken living room.

Tina had forgotten about Dale's living room. Her feet couldn't find ground and she grabbed at whatever was in the air. It turned out to be Dale who was standing near the edge of the drop.

* * *

She had a concussion from the fall. She didn't remember the ambulance, only waking up at Kennestone Hospital with a nurse asking her what day it was, what year, and so on.

"What happened?"

"You took a tumble from what I understand, but your boyfriend took the brunt of your fall, which was good for you, not so good for him," the nurse told her.

"He's not my boyfriend." Even though that was true, she wanted to know how Dale was, not because she cared, more so because she didn't care. She'd wished he were at least as beat-up as she was.

The glass table opened the back of his head up and they both ended up in the ER. Between the nurse and the police (some women said she pushed Dale), Tina figured Dale had it about as bad as she did. Someone had already picked him up. She shook her head, thinking, the fucker left me. Not that she would leave with him, but he should have offered.

The nurse asked her if there was someone she could call. She called Lindy who said she'd be there just as soon as she could; it would be at least four days before she could leave, though. It meant Tina needed to find a motel, get a cab from the hospital, and somehow pick up her things from Dale's. It also meant she had to call Dale.

The Georgian Oaks Marietta Motor Lodge was close to The Moonraker — she needed something nearby in case Dale played games and didn't answer or refused to bring her stuff, or if she had to pay another cab drive, or hell, walk. She wasn't leaving her new clothes everything vacation-new, Lindy's suitcase, or her fucking makeup. Mandy and Steph were probably digging through her stuff, taking what they wanted, and throwing the rest away. Get you some, girl.

* * *

It wasn't Mandy or Steph, or Dale, but Wendy who answered and she was not unkind, but a little cold. She offered to drive over and bring Tina's makeup bag and Lindy's suitcase. Tina didn't plan what to say to Wendy, because it was over for her and what Dale's wife thought about something so over in Tina's mind didn't matter now, but she wondered if she was going to get chewed out.

Wendy didn't chew Tina out; except she threw her makeup bag at her and slammed the door. Tina had been in and seen worse catfights at The Dew. Worse things had been said to her. Wendy wanted to know how long, how it started, to verify dates and times and things Dale said, and she understood why his wife asked these things. She wanted to file Dale away like Tina had filed him away, but at least Tina wasn't married to him. She could walk away.

At night, she ordered pizza and watched cable. She didn't have cable at home, and she enjoyed the time to herself. The motor lodge had a pool. She couldn't dip her head in the water, but she could tan all day long as she used sunblock over the small stiches on her forehead.

There was a Texaco nearby, and Tina bought a Styrofoam cooler, overpriced wine coolers, a trucker hat that said, "Shit Happens," she planned to give to Lindy, and a trashy romance novel with "Tempest" in the title. After three pages, she used the book to protect her face from the sun. She doubted she'd ever read another stupid romance again. Highway 41 traffic lulled her to sleep.

Tina slept most of the way back home; the concussion made her tired. When she awoke Lindy schooled her on men, "Men come into The Dew and for the most part are just good old boys wanting a cold beer and nothing else, and then there are those who you don't try and make homes with. Those types are only dropping in. They don't care about what happens in between."

She already knew all this or figured it out before she ate the glass coffee table, the crystal ashtray. There were fragments of glass in her forehead; the doctor told her to let them come out naturally, to not pick at it or it would scar. It was going to scar no matter. It all was going to scar, but it would also heal, and aside from her head aching, she was healing, too.

Tina was half-dozing when she felt the familiar gravel groan under the car tires. She lifted her head over the top of the window and gazed out. It was twilight. The Budweiser neon light above her apartment window was on a timer and had just flashed on. The red and blue lights illuminated the window welcoming her home, and she felt the same feeling she got when the tanning bed lights buzzed on and warmed her naked body as good as any sun.

Calendar Days

Nine months, One week, Four days, Six Hours until Graduation

It was a bitterly cold and raining in March when Dale finally left for Georgia. From the side of the road, Wendy waved goodbye—the raindrops on her cheeks were a good disguise for fake tears. She held her breath watching Dale's Blazer disappear down Highway Y. Soon, he'd drive over the Missouri state line to Illinois, then Kentucky, Tennessee, until he arrived in Georgia, for his new job at Lockheed Martin — his skills from his Airforce days as an airplane mechanic were paying off. Three states away to give her some freedom, to get back on track, make everything okay, although it hadn't been okay for years.

Dale's vacation time wouldn't kick in for a year. With her daughter, Shannon, a sophomore, and Wendy's nursing internship at Sainte Geneviève Hospital where Wendy worked nightshift four days per week there'd be little time to visit, if any at all. Time they both needed away from each other to regroup.

When she was sure Dale wasn't turning around — he hadn't forgotten something, or worse yet, decided against leaving — she exhaled and then she and Shannon clasped hands together and jumped up and down like schoolgirls. They danced on the wet road until their clothes were soaked through, their bones hurt; they felt like they'd crack from freezing.

Running back to their trailer, Wendy yelled, "We're free! We're free!" But she knew they weren't free, that this was a temporary freedom with only three states between her and her husband and their small town. In the moment, she felt a heaviness lift from within herself and that would have to be good enough for now.

A few weeks earlier, when Dale heard back from Lockheed, Wendy was afraid to breathe wrong. Breathing wrong was easy around Dale, though. You could breathe wrong, look wrong, not breathe wrong, not look wrong, and it was all wrong depending on Dale's moods. He had told her so with his fists many times. That was in the past. He hadn't laid a hand on her since they moved from California to Missouri four years ago, but he'd threatened to kill them, her and her daughter, if they ever left him and Wendy believed him. Living with Dale was like living on the side of a crumbling mountain. Each day another boulder fell loose, yet the house remained teetering on the precipice.

She started to feel like it was just a matter of time — not *if,* but *when* he would strike again. And yet, for four years he did not strike her, and the waiting, the anticipation was chilling Wendy. A reader of auras, she observed a suppressed rage hovering around Dale's skin. Mostly, his aura glowered a burnt red, but it had become darker with his moods — a murky bloodied hue, copper, then crimson, until his aura took on a mahogany tone. The spells she'd cast for his success, or jobs, or their happiness were blocked by his negativity.

And months passed with them scraping by on his unemployment check and her intern pay, and he remained sunken into his La-Z-Boy like some sentry on his watch, guarding her every move: *Where are you going? School. Who's on the phone? Cindi. Why'd you get in ten minutes late? Grocery store. Where were you? Work.*

She knew he was depressed so she encouraged him. "You should make a schedule, even when you don't have work. It's not healthy, Dale. Just sitting around. It'll make you feel better."

He'd take a sip of coffee glaring over the rim, never agreeing, or disagreeing, silent, set his mug down, and continue in his current state — shirtless and in need of a haircut, shave, and a shower, concealed behind his newspaper, chain-smoking with reruns of *The Rockford Files* and *Barney Miller* on for background — until she shut up.

Wendy would shake her head at this creature who had become the worst version of her husband. His kneecaps stuck out below the classifieds he rarely glanced at. Blue smoke circled up from over the top of the paper as if a slumbering dragon lived there and not a malcontent thirty-six-year-old man who was at one time very employable and attractive (still was) in the rugged way women went for. She had gone for once.

At noon, the video games began, lasting late into the evening. He hollered to Wendy or Shannon in the kitchen, "Pour me a RC while you're in there," because he couldn't leave *Defender*. If he didn't beat his last score or lost, he'd yell, "Mother of shit!" or, "Goddammit to hell!" at the game. Dale was constantly slamming the controller on the coffee table; he'd broken one of the controllers already, so that no one could play against each other now.

And he kept a scorebook, and God forbid you move it from his end table or touch *anything* on his table where he kept all his necessities: an overflowing ashtray, a coffee mug, his precious scorebook, a pair of grooming scissors, and red ballpoint pens wrapped in a rubber band.

After hours of *Defender,* sometimes *Frogger,* he returned to the disheveled newspapers, and used his grooming scissors to clip out amusing articles for Wendy and Shannon. The clippings littered the refrigerator door, stuck behind magnets, until Wendy tossed them after a couple of weeks went by. If he noticed a missing article he'd bark and threaten to throw all their shit away.

Wendy found cups of pee in coffee cups and glasses sitting on the floor near his La-Z-Boy.

A normal person would leave. At her age, a normal person wouldn't have parents who paid her tuition and some extra. Her internship paid for rent and groceries, and no more. Their checking account existed barely above negative. Their credit was shameful; if she had the money, she'd be happy to pay for things on time. And they maxed out the credit card to put Dale up at an extended stay motel in Georgia until he had enough for an apartment. But that meant two rental payments.

Wendy yo-yoed between hoping her marriage was salvageable and concluding it was over. One day she'd convince herself that once Dale got steady work the arguments over money would fade, and he'd get back to acting like a decent human being. Men need work. The next day the nagging part of her said, "Come on, Wendy. Get real." While Dale could get good jobs, he wasn't good at keeping them. He didn't mind living paycheck to paycheck or getting calls from creditors. His solution was: "Just don't answer the phone."

There were a zillion little clocks ticking inside Wendy's head: Dale's departure day, Dale's ninety-day probation period, Shannon's last day of high school, her graduation date from nursing school, the day she and Shannon would pack up and move to Georgia where her family could get a fresh start, the day she'd have her own income and be able to support herself and her daughter, and if needed, the day they'd escape Dale.

Thirty-two wasn't old. She still had her looks. Her auburn hair was one of her best features. High cheekbones. All the right curves. Men flirted and asked if her daughter was her sister. She could meet someone else. Yet, a fantasy man seemed less and less tangible. What did Gloria Steinem say? "Some of us are becoming the men we wanted to marry." Wendy was never a good feminist, though, and doubts flooded her until she'd persuaded herself that in nine months, one week, four days, and six hours Dale would turn it around and she would feel comfortable moving to Georgia. If babies could grow and be born in that timeframe, surely her husband could change.

Last night, the night before Dale left, Wendy handed him a calendar from the local funeral home. The cover featured a black and white photo of a couple standing in a flower garden with an inscription under the photo: *Shafer Funeral Home, established 1898 by Karl and Maria Shafer.* She flipped to the month of April. The photo was taken in a garden. Karl Shafer wore a pin-stripe suit and fedora and faced the camera with his hands clenched at his sides. His wife, Maria Shafer, took on a more natural stance. Although it was black and white, Wendy imagined the blooms behind Maria were those of a yellow forsythia tree and the flowers near her feet, Easter crocus. Maria's faithful terrier pawed at her calves. The photo said, "This is my domain," and she casually attended her garden as though unaware the photo was being taken at all. There was a stack of calendars on the counter at the nursing station. Wendy took home three.

When she gave Shannon her calendar, she sneered and said, "Sort of morbid, mom, but I like it." The summer before high school, Shannon had morphed into a Goth, dying her beautiful strawberry-blonde hair — women would pay good money for — black cherry, and coating her already porcelain skin in bone china foundation. If she wasn't wearing the Valle High School uniform, she dressed in all black now, and refused to shop anywhere but the Goodwill, a blessing for Wendy's budget. Plus, the closest mall was sixty miles away anyway. Shannon came home with two garbage bags of clothes and proudly said, "I got all this shit for forty bucks. Can you believe it? They're giving it away."

Last night, Wendy brushed Shannon's hair out of her eyes and said, "I don't get this black lipstick thing. You're such a pretty girl."

"Don't pretty girl me, mom." Shannon leaned onto the breakfast table, making handiwork out of Shafer's picture.

"Oh my God! Look at what you did to the poor Shafers. I thought these two were so sweet, too. Look Dale." Wendy displayed Shannon's artwork to Dale. The Shafers now had devil horns coming out of the couple's head. The terrier's tail was forked.

"It's an improvement if you ask me."

"Ahh, Dale, not you, too." That evening with a new job and money on the horizon, Shannon and Dale almost acted as though they enjoyed each other's company. Though, Shannon was probably being civil because she was happy Dale was leaving. Occasionally, they had a sort of camaraderie. In those moments, she prayed they'd turned the corner, but one or the other's temper would flare up. She felt defeated by them, always trying to encourage them to do things together. Sometimes, she just wished they would fake it. It was exhausting navigating their relationship.

Wendy studied her calendar. Did the photographer tell Mrs. Shafer to act mesmerized by her flowers, because women were supposedly drawn to romantic ideals at that time? Maria was the frivolous one who tended children, home, and garden, but *Mr. Shafer* must be serious. Death was a somber business, reserved for men who either dealt it out or, like Karl Shafer, dealt with it. Were the flowers Maria's contribution to the business? Wendy imagined Maria carefully selecting white spray roses, larkspur, green gladioli, and button spray chrysanthemum. With practiced hands she effortlessly wove them into arrangements, later draping the flowers respectfully over a casket. What a tidy life the Shafers had carved out for themselves in their town. Everyone knew and respected the Shafers. You had to respect a family who had been burying the townspeople for over one hundred years.

With a push pin, she stuck the Shafer calendar into wood paneling in the kitchen above the breakfast bar. She wondered if she'd ever have a marriage that looked like theirs, and though she didn't expect a family legacy, she also never expected to live in a dingy trailer or need to steal condiments to save a penny.

And now today was irreversibly here and Dale gone. And yes, she was happy.

"I'd be even happier if I could take a hot shower!" she yelled into the closed bathroom door. "Come on, Shannon." She pounded on the door. "I'm freezing to death here." She heard the shower turn off. "And you better have left me some hot water."

"Sorry, mom. It went cold before I even got the conditioner out." Shannon opened the door. She was blotting her hair with a wet wash rag, trying to get the rest of the hair conditioner out without subjecting herself to icy water.

"Again? I told you five minutes tops." She flung her soggy clothes into the hamper and wrapped her wet hair with a towel Shannon handed her. She stood before a space heater, rubbing her hands over her arms and legs. It did little to relieve the cold. They never turned the real heat on. With three space heaters going nonstop during the winter, she was surprised they hadn't burned the trailer down. And what would the town think then?

When she was finally dry, she climbed into sweatpants and a sweatshirt and walked out to Dale's end table, borrowed one of Dale's forbidden, red, ballpoint pens, walked over to the Shafer's calendar, and slashed through today's date, marking an X, as if there were buried treasure there.

Eight months, Ten days until Wendy and Shannon Move

Dale called on Sundays when the rates were cheaper. This time, he called a little earlier than his normal time and Shannon picked up, and for once he was glad to speak to her. Wendy had casually mentioned during their last conversation that Shannon didn't want to come to Georgia, that she wanted to finish out high school there. They were acting fishy again like the last time they tried to leave him in California. It had gotten ugly, he overreacted, but she had provoked him. And from then on, if they had the slightest disagreement, she'd pull out a suitcase and leave it out for a few days as a symbol. Or she'd tear through the house pulling pictures down and boxing them away as though at any moment she'd be gone.

"So, your mom said you wanna finish there? Why the change?" He was seething. Teenaged girls were so cunning. Shannon had dug her claws deep into Wendy.

"I don't know."

I don't know, I don't know. Her answer for everything.

"It's a pretty big deal for not knowing."

"I mean like I have friends here. It's not much longer."

"For you maybe, but for me it's a helluva long time. When did you get friends?" he asked. "You said you hated it there."

"Whatever. I have friends."

"Eddy Bauman? The neighbor kid doesn't count. Who else? Name one."

"...I'm getting mom."

"Yeah, hey, wait, wait. I didn't mean it like that. I'm sure you have tons of friends now. Hey, what time did your mom get in this morning?"

"I don't know."

I don't know. I don't know. She sounded like a Goddamn bird, calling out the same annoying tune. He hated songbirds. In the mornings and hungover, their chirping was like missiles going off in his head.

Shannon huffed into the receiver. "Maybe 11:00."

"*Eleven?* Doesn't she normally get in at 10:00?"

"Yeah, I guess. You know I sleep in on the weekends. Who knows? Who cares?"

"Uh, *I care.* But you said 11:00, right? That's a two-hour difference. Was it 11:00 or later?" Dale rubbed his neck where tension was building.

"It could've been midnight. Like I have no idea, Dale. I was asleep. I don't keep up with her. You want to know, ask her. Mom! *Mom!* Your husband is on the phone and he's asking about when you got in this morning."

"Hey, stop. Don't say any —"

"She's coming."

Dale heard Shannon set the phone down. Selfish little bitch. Here he was sacrificing for them, working out of state to send money while they both finished school, and the little brat couldn't be bothered to answer him. That kid had a smart mouth he smacked a few times with Wendy boo-hooing. His own daddy whipped him with whatever was handy — leather belts, a garden hose, tree branches, shoes. Wendy let Shannon cuss, too.

"What the fuck is taking so loon?" Since he started living on his own, he began talking to himself. Sometimes, just under his breath. Sometimes, full arguments with Wendy about Shannon. "Dale the bad guy, the villain, always the one in the wrong." Wendy loved to push his buttons, begging him to fuck up so she'd have a reason to leave him. It was as if she was dangling a rat over a hungry snake. The snake's tongue senses dinner, coils, ready to strike, but right before it strikes, she lifts her hand, and slams the screened door to the terrarium shut. The snake is addled. The problem was, Dale didn't know if he was the rat or the snake. He sure as shit wasn't the puppeteer.

He heard the padding of Wendy's feet, her breath, her hello. God, he missed her. "Hey, baby girl? What you up to?"

"Reading. What about you?"

"Is that why you didn't answer the phone? Must have been a good part if you couldn't answer. Why'd it take so long to get to the phone?"

"Uh, I don't know. I didn't hear the phone. I was studying."

"You didn't hear the phone? Where were you?"

"In the bedroom. Why?"

"Oh, nothing. Just want to know what you're doing so I can picture you. I miss you. Hey, talk to me."

"Not now. Shannon's watching TV."

"Come on. What're you wearing?"

"Dale, stop."

"Tell her to go to her room."

"She's not three, Dale."

"Goddamn, she's always in the way."

"Screw you."

"Yeah, I wish."

She laughed, a little more playful.

"I love you," he said.

"I love you, too."

Hearing her voice soothed his mood; he decided not to mention the time discrepancy, but he wasn't forgetting it either. Instead, he started calling at random times.

In addition to the Sunday family call, he started calling every morning at 11:00 on the dot, whether Wendy worked a shift or not, and then again at 4:45 when she was supposed to be up getting ready for work.

"What's the rush? It's only been twenty minutes."

"Yeah, Dale, but I need to stop by the store and pick something up first."

"What? What store?"

"Why does it matter? Seriously? I need to get off the phone. This month's bill is going to be a fortune."

"I'm not worth it? You don't want to talk to your husband?"

"I do and I *did* talk to you once today." She sighed. "It's just adding up...did you send the check yet?"

Dale hung up without saying goodbye. He knew the phone bill was high because he fucking paid for it. Paid double for everything. They had two households, but that never stopped Wendy from asking for more money.

* * *

Shannon lay on her bed, her feet splayed against her wall and with her big toe she traced Robert Smith's face. There was something building between Dale and her mom. Paranoia, obsession, jealousy. He's started drinking again in Missouri, but mostly beer-drinking and not Jekyll and Hyde booze drinking. Soon, there'd be accusations if there weren't already. Maybe she's cheating. She could marry a rich doctor.

She rolled off her bed, flipped the tape in her boombox, and turned the volume to the edge of what would piss her mom off. The lyrics to "Heaven Knows I'm Miserable Now" by The Smiths filled her room.

She lifted her mattress, pulled out her journal, and began to write where she had left off.

Dale's acting weirder than usual. Hate him. Mom might be cheating on him. I'll never end up like her. As soon as I graduate, I'm heading to New York. Kids at school suck. Got in trouble for eyeliner the other day. The nuns made me wash it off!!!!!!!!!!!!!! Eddy is still crushing on me. Sometimes, I think I ought to just let him have me, so he'd get over it, but it would be like having sex with my brother. But he's sweet. I don't know what I'd do if I didn't have him. Go insane. Ted Pelletier winked at me. What does that mean? I thought only old guys winked. Anyway, he broke up with April. HAHAHAHAHA! I heard she was devastated. I don't know. He's cute. I'm working on getting my mom to stay here until I finish high school. I don't want to leave in the middle of high school and not know anyone again. I wish she'd just leave Dale. Asshole.

She scribbled flowers and vines around the word "asshole" until she heard her mom yelling for her to turn the music down.

* * *

The only time Wendy had to herself was driving to and from work and she used this time to reflect.

She couldn't control being around doctors, or that they were college-educated and had money. Never mind if the morning report took longer or she made a quick stop for milk. Dale insisted these were excuses, eventually calling them outright lies.

And there was shame. Her parents never approved of Dale, but the shame of a divorce and another failed marriage bothered her...even though she was widowed before, somehow that marriage counted, too. Plus, Wendy hated being alone. She wished she were one of those women who professed independence. What was it teaching Shannon?

They couldn't go to the movies without careful budgeting, and it was always a matinee with Wendy stuffing her purse full of cans of Diet Coke and homemade popcorn beforehand. Shannon never said a word, ignoring the Goobers, the overpriced Milk Duds encased in glass like sacred relics — look, but don't touch.

"Honestly, the gas station has a better selection, and you can get so much more compared to the movies," Shannon said when Wendy pulled over at the local gas station, Fritz's. Still, Shannon only put one Kit Kat on the counter though she saw her hesitating over the TWIZZLERS.

"Shannon, get some more candy."

"Seriously, I'm fine mom. We got all that popcorn, too."

During ten seconds of quiet, between the previews and the main attraction, Shannon opened her can of Diet Coke. The ssss carried over the sounds of people munching on popcorn. There was a girl Wendy recognized from Shannon's eighth-grade sleepover. *Lori something?* The girl didn't turn around, but snickered, and said, "How cheap" for the rest of the theatre to hear.

More than anything she hated the self-prescribed limbo she put herself in. The last time she was alone — when Peter died — she fell apart. She needed to do something, had to do something, that gave her a sense of control.

She pulled off Highway Y onto the gravel dump that served as their driveway. Rebel began to whine. Poor thing. Chained to a picnic table. They lived similar lives. She filled a bucket they used for his water bowl, scratched behind his ears, and then trudged up the cinder blocks steps.

The pity party followed her inside. Her eyes roamed to Dale's chair and end table, almost expecting to see him waiting for her. An idea was forming in her mind.

She plopped in his chair. *His chair.* A regular Archie Bunker here. Why do men get their own chairs? She didn't have her own chair. She picked up his scorebook and flipped through the pages as if the numbers and dates could decipher what her next move should be.

She was pregnant with Shannon when Peter was killed in Vietnam. It became her descent into despair. A concerned friend made her an appointment to see a psychic. It was the early 70s in Southern California, but Wendy was doubtful. Her friend encouraged her, "Wendy, everyone has a healer. I go to two shamans. It's no big deal. She'll get you out of your funk."

The psychic was named Mary. Wendy was anticipating a Madame with an exotic last name, and home that reeked of patchouli. Instead, she found a quaint home near Redondo Beach with a newly mown yard, abundant amounts of Shirley Temple peonies—their sweet and spicy bouquets mixing with the perfume of the Mary's lemon trees.

They sat on the patio, drinking mint tea, acting like old acquaintances, and Mary told her a suicide spirit had attached itself to her. "Your grief is so palpable it has attracted negative energies." She held Wendy's hand while she spoke. She had a warm solid grip as opposed to Wendy's hand that had gone damp and cold with this news.

"Fill the void with your daughter...and your practice."

"Really, a daughter?" She had hoped for a girl.

Wendy left with a black velvet bag full of stones and later discovered a group of men and women who practiced a combination of ancient Pagan traditions blended with New Age spirituality. She felt powerful celebrating moon cycles, studying herbs, learning about astral projection.

Then she met Dale — Dale with the steady job, Dale who acted like her ten-year-old daughter was awesome, Dale who was so attentive and sexy. She thought she'd found her soulmate. But Dale was one person when they got married and an entirely different one after the vows. How many love spells had she cast on him? His version of love was tainted with obsession, violence, and jealousy.

Spells to find employment worked, but she'd never mastered one that kept him working.

To get rid of a lover, freeze him out of your life.

She clambered out of Dale's chair, jogged to the bedroom, and dug through some tees Dale had left behind. With scissors, she cut out a figure from his T-shirt and then sewed various items of Dale's into the doll, to create a poppet. She tore up the pages of his scorebook and stuffed the legs with paper. She would have put his cigarette ashes into the doll, if she hadn't dumped them already, but his handwriting would serve its purpose, or any items close to him. Wendy didn't even have to chant curses into the doll. He'd do all the work himself next time he called. When the poppet was finished, she stuck it in the freezer.

Six Months, Six Days until Wendy and Shannon Move

Dale's fear went far beyond the calls and interrogations. He started keeping a notebook to track Wendy's time. If Wendy drove the speed limit, and she always went over, but if she didn't speed, she should arrive home within fifty to sixty minutes' time give or take bad weather. The math was simple. It didn't lie.

For the most part, the times matched, but there was a clear pattern on Fridays. On four Friday mornings in a row, she was late. He also knew she had left the hospital, because when she didn't pick up at home, he called her work.

"Really, Cindi? Over an hour ago? She didn't say she was going anywhere?" Dale marked the time, 10:38 a.m., in his notebook, noting she'd stayed thirty-eight minutes past her shift.

Cindi took reports from Wendy in the mornings and Wendy often said how much she liked Cindi.

"I bet she stopped at the grocery store. You know, yes, yes. That's right." Cindi spoke as though she was trying to convince herself.

Dale double-checked the Shafer calendar. No doctor appointments. "You don't happen to have the number, do you, for the grocery? I don't have a phonebook and information has gone up."

There was a long pause before Cindi spoke. He pictured her hand covering the mouthpiece, her mouthing his name and rolling her eyes at the other nurses.

"Um, well, let's see. Can you hold a sec, Dale? I gotta grab the phonebook, and I think it's in the supply room."

Dale had driven by Sainte Geneviève Hospital plenty of times. It was a country hospital: no towers, no mazes of floors, no parking garages. All the serious traumas were flown to St. Louis. Sure, there was an ICU, but how bad could it really be? He imagined Cindi stomping around the nurse's station, stomping to the supply room, finding the phonebook, stomping back to the nurse's station, angrily flipping through the pages, rolling her eyes at another nurse, and pointing to the angry, red flashing light on hold that shrieked, "Dale, Dale, Dale." Eventually, she found the number he asked for, but instead of picking of the phone, she sat her wide ass in a swivel chair for two minutes, just spinning around, taking up his time. He was hundreds of miles away with a wife who was carrying on. What did they think about that? Or were they all whoring it up and bragging about it between rounds, sipping coffee while they bitched about their husbands? For five minutes, forty-seven seconds Dale waited listening to brassy jazz. He was sure she did it on purpose.

"Hey, Dale. You still there? Sorry about that," she said in a voice which was anything but sorry. They were all the same. He heard Wendy's last conversation in his head, "Quit bothering the nurses, Dale. We're busy. People are dying." But what she was really saying was this: "You're a paranoid alcoholic and when I'm done with school, I'm getting out of this town and I'm leaving you."

"It's no problem, Cindi, and hey, I'm sorry. You're busy, and I wouldn't ask, but I worry about her and Shannon being alone like that so far out in the country."

"It's fine. I understand, but, Dale, I'm saying this for your own good and for Wendy's sake. You call a *lot,* and we are *busy* with patients. This has got to be the last time unless it's an emergency."

He squeezed his red ballpoint pen until it cracked and red ink spilled over his fisted hand like he'd been in a fight. *Oh, you scolded me, you fucking heifer.* He felt his jaw tighten but he wouldn't apologize again.

"You ready for the number?"

Dale tried the home phone one more time. His next conversation was with an idiot cashier at Rozier's Grocery who kept him on hold for so long he hung up. When he called back, there was a busy signal. He tried the home phone again, but there was still no answer. It was almost noon.

If she gave two shits about him, she'd call him when she got home first thing, but the slutting bitch never called him. He was always the one to call. She said it was because she knew he would call, but just once, just one fucking time, it would be nice if she took the time to call and check on him. He rang Rozier's again.

"I was on hold for three minutes, buddy, waiting on you before I hung up? This is a long-distance call. Are *you* going to pay my bill? Some real customer service you got."

"I'm sorry, sir. When I got to the phone, you had already hung up. Was there something I could help you with, sir?"

"I sure as shit hope so, buddy. I'm looking for my wife, Wendy Samples. Is she there?"

"Wendy Samples? No, no one by that name works here, sir."

"No! I know she doesn't work there." Dale reared his arm up like he was going to punch the wall but resisted. "She shops there. You'd know her. She's 5'4, redhead, pretty."

The manager kept repeating, no, no, no. Rozier's Grocery was the only grocery store in a town of population nothing. Family owned and run probably by one of the original German families who came to Sainte Geneviève after the French sold it off — he was sure of it with that Kraut name — there was no way Dale believed this guy didn't know who he was talking about. He saw the eyes of those church-going men at St. Lawrence memorizing her ass, her boobs. Wendy wasn't a run-of-the-mill type even when he met her in LA where everyone was gorgeous, naturally, or not so naturally, she stood out.

"Come on, man, everyone knows everyone in town, so don't act like you don't know her."

"Sorry, sir. Nope. No redheads today." He paused. "Sir, what's this about?"

Dale slammed the receiver down.

He dialed the home phone again.

"Hey, Dale."

"Where the fuck have you been? I've been calling all morning, and don't give me that shit you had to go to the store, 'cause I already called over there. It's afternoon. You're over two hours late. Cindi said you left like normal, which makes me wonder what the fuck time is normal, Wendy? Who is it? Which doctor? Is it Dr. —"

She was gone. He hit redial. It rang. She picked it up then hung it up. He hit redial again. She picked it up and, again, hung up. He hit redial. She picked it up and hung it up. This was the hangup game she was playing at. He hit redial. A busy tone. Thinking he hit redial too many times and had messed up the line, Dale dialed the number manually. A busy signal.

* * *

Wendy hung up and left the phone off the hook. What were they going to think at the hospital? He was going to get her written up.

The busy signal was alarming after working a late shift. It vibrated in her ears, penetrating her skull, and when she couldn't tolerate it anymore, she unplugged the phone altogether. She sat on the wooden stool in front of the breakfast bar in a daze and then couldn't remember what she was doing before she sat down. She couldn't sleep now, too wired. She flipped through one of Shannon's

Seventeen magazines she had stolen from the hospital lobby to her horoscope from four months ago, and while she read, her tongue searched for the line that used to be on her front tooth.

She finally went to a decent dentist, not quite in St. Louis, but not a country dentist either. She could barely tell where Dale had broken her front tooth off one night in LA before they moved to Missouri. The one and only time she'd call the police on him, and he only spent two days in jail before he was back home making promises to her and Shannon.

Funny how your tongue can detect the slightest change. Eventually, the impulse would subside, and she'd get used to the new cap on her tooth. The new tooth, though minor in the grand scheme was the beginning of things, a new start. But moving to a small town, a do-over, was supposed to be a new start, too.

When Dale reached the point of no return, his irises changed from blue, to gray, to white. The eyes of a man with a very nasty plan. She'd blamed herself partially for that night. She was trying to make him jealous because he'd gotten so drunk and had flirted with several women at a New Year's party a couple of days before. Of course, because he didn't remember, and if he couldn't recall, how could he feel remorse? When the opportunity arrived to give him a taste of his own medicine days later, she rang her friend, and they pretended they were going to meet some guys at a bar — fake guys, fake bar. Dale was listening in on another line — a new habit of his.

Wendy didn't expect the freight train that came tearing down the hallway, ripping through the locked door of their bedroom, and fists and flesh and bone and teeth and blood happening so quickly and all at once she didn't have a moment to be scared or even to realize she was on the other end of his rage, or that it was her flesh, bone, teeth, and blood. And then his apologies and promises and her fear that if she didn't accept his apologies and promises, the man with the nasty plan behind his eyes wasn't going to take "no" for an answer, so she stayed out of fear.

But he also sobered up and became, for a time, the man she had met and later married. Dale went six months sober, kissing ass — even to Shannon — before she agreed to move to Missouri. Then they moved and she was glad because there were so many temptations in Los Angeles. The isolation of the countryside is what they needed so they filled their suitcases with secrets, folded their lies inside dresser drawers, or hung them in closets. Playing pretend house. But only for so long.

Now their dirty laundry had gone too long on the clothesline, through showers, sun, snow, and seasons becoming dirtier and dirtier, worthless, and lonely like some forgotten sock that remained on the line year after year for the whole town to view.

There was no money to get her tooth done right the first time; it was a different color than her real tooth, which had never been this smooth, but now it matched, and as much as she tried to find the line, she couldn't.

She flipped through a different magazine, giving Dale a few more minutes. All the girls were so young with perfect mouths full of white even teeth. She thought she could sleep now so she plugged the phone back in.

She hit the hook a couple of times, dialed Dale's number, covered the earpiece, and spoke. "You don't remember I had a dentist appointment today. To fix my tooth you knocked out. I'm tired. I've been up all night and it's almost noon, so I'm going to bed. You sound drunk, so when you sober up, we can talk." Then she left the phone off the hook, walked down the hall, and fell into bed with the operator saying, "If you would like to make a call..." She didn't have the energy to go back to unplug the phone and eventually the voice stopped.

* * *

He had not forgotten about the dentist's appointment. It was written in red ink in his notebook under the yellow highlighted column for appointments, but he'd put it down for the following Monday. He scanned the other columns, comparing the times. Blue for work. Purple for sleep and getting ready for work. Yellow for confirmed appointments or disputes he resolved. It was the orange column that disturbed him — the empty areas which caused so much internal conflict — those were when the inconsistencies and variations he couldn't account for Wendy's whereabouts were. He now marked off her dentist's appointment, but not before calling the dentist's office, and checking with the front desk.

"Mr. Samples, Mrs. Samples left over an hour ago."

"Thanks, I was just worried," he lied into the phone. "With this downpour and the roads being so slick, well you know. I was concerned."

"It's raining?"

It was raining in Georgia, but Dale's mind was halfway in Georgia and halfway in Missouri. "Oh wait, I hear her now. She just pulled up. Thanks."

It was confirmed, but she may have told him the wrong date to confuse him. He was damn good at keeping up with her. He reviewed his notebook again, flipping through the pages, studying his inscriptions with the intensity of a scholar. *Nothing.* Nothing about a schedule change. Unless, he thought, and this was possible, she'd deliberately told him the wrong day, just to fuck with him. Some sumbitch up there was turning his wife inside out and he was gonna find out who.

That Cindi bitch never said anything about a dentist appointment. Grocery store, my ass. Women tell other women every single detail of their lives. Wendy would've told Cindi and the rest of the women on the floor about her appointment. He was positive the entire hospital, including the patients, would know about Wendy's dentist appointment.

She was out whoring with some doctor, and her little bitchy friends were all covering up for her.

176

After mixing up the dentist appointment, Dale wasn't taking any more chances. He bought a hand-held tape recorder, along with a microphone to capture his questions and her answers through the phone receiver. He recorded all their phone conversations now. When Wendy said "goodbye," he listened, rewound, wrote, listened, rewound, wrote — transcribing her load of fiction. There was a name. Dr. Brouchard.

Five months, Three weeks, Five days, and Six hours until Escape

Wendy felt Dale's eyes whitening through the phone lines four states away, through miles and miles of wire. She twisted the phone cord around her forearm, tight like a tourniquet and let go of the cord. It untwisted itself, leaving red curls on her skin. She repeated the procedure. With her ear pressed to the receiver, and "this fucking cord," she cursed under her breathe, that only went at most three feet, she thought about Rebel chained to the picnic table.

Dale had narrowed in on Dr. Brouchard, the night director, who at one time was the resident town doctor for two counties over until his wife died. Mrs. Brouchard was an integral part of his practice. The doctor decided to close shop and work in the hospital environment, but he was a mild-mannered man and eventually retired from doctoring for administration because he simply "couldn't keep up with the young ones." If she were going to cheat, it wouldn't be with Dr. Brouchard.

Dr. Brouchard was the same height, if not shorter, than Wendy, pudgy, with stained teeth from pipe-tobacco, and a halo-like bald patch on the top of his head. He did flirt with the nurses on occasion, even Wendy, but the flirtations were those of a sweet elderly gentleman who enjoyed a marginal amount of female attention and never lecherous.

177

Every call, every day the same until it became so ridiculous, she started laughing, imagining the things he accused her of doing with poor Dr. Brouchard.

"Oh yeah, Dale. It was so good. I'm getting hot thinking about it." Her voice became raspier, *"Ohhh, yessss.* His *big* doctor cock...so much bigger than yours...and he threw all this money, *ohhh,* all over the bed and not like dollar bills, I mean twenties, and I rolled in it. That's right. In fact, we're planning on meeting again, and again, and again. I can't wait. I'm so wet." She held her hand over the phone. If only she could say this. She desperately wanted to say it. Just once she wished she could poison his ears like he poisoned hers. And then a giggle escaped her.

"What's so fuckin funny? You think this is funny, Wendy?"

"Something on the TV."

"You're not even listening to me?"

Nope.

She set the phone down on the breakfast bar, opened the freezer, pulled out Dale's poppet and set it next to the phone. Let it take all the abuse, she thought.

She walked over to the Shafer's calendar covered in red "X's." Five months, three weeks, and five days — this endless countdown before what, where, how, with what money?

This month was another black and white photo of the Shafer home without the Shafers. It was a stately brick. The Shafers had done well for themselves and had added a parlor in the 1930s. Wendy wouldn't have wanted funerals inside her home all that time. Yet, there was stability in death. No turning back. Maybe Peter was better off.

"You there, Wendy? *Wendy!* Are you listening to me?"

She plucked up the phone. "What do you think, Dale? Really? You really think I have time to cheat between school, work, Shannon, and being up on my feet all night, exhausted, and then listening to you when I should be *sleeping?* At the end of my night

I'm covered in poop, blood, barf. You think that makes me irresistible?"

"You're going to make me quit my job, the best job I've —"

"That's righteous of you, Dale," she spat into the phone. "Find a reason to quit. Make it about me, but if you quit, or you lose your job, just know it's about you and nothing I did." Rage, this was rage. "And…It seems to me the only type of people who constantly accuse others of cheating are the *actual cheaters*. You've cheated before."

"Those were different times. Flirting ain't cheat —"

She hung up.

Three Months, Two Weeks, Three Hours until Wendy and Shannon Move

Dale popped two Percocet with a swig of Old Granddad and cleared his throat. He picked up the phone, then set it back down. He was about to lie his ass off and his story needed to be straight.

"Don't freak out, Wendy, but I just got out of the hospital." She would ask what happened. "I don't remember shit. A hydraulic failure. I was knocked out cold by airplane door. nipped my head, they said." Here, Wendy should say, "Oh my God," or, "You're lucky to be alive." He'd agree. "I know. Foreman said I was lucky, too." She'd ask how he got home, about meds. "My neighbor picked me up, you heard me mention Old Charles." She would want to know more about the injuries, his care, long term issues. "I'm concussed. I got two black eyes and a dent in my head. The doctor doesn't want me to be alone. He said someone needs to be with me. Just a few days for observation. I need you, Wendy."

It was early Monday morning when he got back to The Moonraker — Dale had upgraded from extended stay to an apartment complex. Head injury, Kennestone Hospital, Old Charles. All true, except the accident didn't happen at work; it happened at a party in his apartment. When he had his story straight, he dialed Wendy.

His head was killing him. The Percocet hadn't kicked in yet, the ringing gunned down his head.

Wendy didn't answer at 10:00, at 10:10, at 10:15, or 10:45. She didn't answer until 11:20.

"Where the fuck were you? I've been calling all Goddamn morning."

She was breathing hard into the phone. "Good morning to you too, sweetheart. At work. Where else would I be?"

"In a Goddamn ditch, dead, fuck, I don't know. You're supposed to be home by 10:00."

"What's wrong? You're slurring...again."

"I'm hurt, Wendy. You're *panting*," he said.

"I was outside bringing in groceries...I was running to the phone. What happened?"

"Just got out of the hospital. The hydraulics went out on an airplane door, nicked me in the head. Lucky to be Goddamn alive. I need you to drive down...for a few days...someone is supposed to observe me. Just come down."

Three Months, Two Weeks, One Hour until Escape

Wendy went and she saw the signs of Dale's new life — one big party. He'd managed to find some drinking buddies to ease his loneliness. Yet seeing his swollen and bruised face, the forty-two stiches in the back of his head, she felt bad for him. Not bad enough to remain married, though. If that took a few days in Georgia watching him sleep, keeping him unaware of her plans, it was worth it.

The whole airplane door accident wasn't adding up. That would have killed him. Maybe a fight. She'd hate to see the other man.

180

She mulled over his two black eyes and his broken nose as she wiped spilt beer and ashes off the kitchen countertops. There were so many ashes she wondered what small house had burned down. So many shoeprints on the tile. She felt like she was cleaning up a crime scene but believed the criminal was Dale. Under his couch she found large shards of glass, and she asked him, "Don't you have a coffee table?"

"It was a piece of shit. It broke. Sorry, thought I'd gotten all the glass. Maybe you can hunt me up a new one for me. Wood this time. There's a Goodwill on Highway 41."

Next, she hit the bathroom. She looked under the sink to replace the toilet roll and there it was. The evidence was pushed to the back of the cabinet. A pink, polka-dot, makeup bag. Not hers. She dug through the contents—Maybelline, Avon, and Charlie Blue for Women which she sprayed into the air. So, that's what deception smells like.

Dale was snoring lightly in the bedroom. She sat on the edge of the waterbed so as not to sink in and nudged him awake. His eyes flickered open.

As if ringing a bell in front of his face, she swung the pink, polka-dot, makeup bag. "Who does this belong to?"

"I don't know. Isn't it yours? Fuck, you woke me up for that?" He reached behind his shoulders, patting the shelves in the headboard, feeling for the remote, found it, and turned the TV on.

"Dale, why would I ask if it was mine?"

"Where did you find it?"

"In the cabinet under the bathroom sink."

"Hell, Wendy. Probably left over from the last tenant. They didn't do the best job cleaning out as you can see. Just toss it if you don't want any of it." He turned up the volume.

She didn't toss it. Instead, she studied the contents: a plum blush and a frosted cerulean blue and pink-ice combo eyeshadow. Her mind created the palette, and then, as if she were describing a stalker to a police sketch artist, she formed the face of the woman who would wear those colors.

* * *

The next day while Dale was sleeping — fortunately, the concussion and pain meds kept him horizontal — Wendy made coffee, settled herself into a clean living-room, and turned on *As the World Turns*. The opening music had changed. It had been too long since she could just sit and watch TV. The show brought back memories of her mother.

Her parents had a traditional marriage: father provides, mother keeps home. And boy, her mother didn't miss a beat. She was as immaculate as the home she kept. She scrubbed, mopped, polished all morning. By the time her father got home, her mother appeared completely relaxed in a monochromatic pantsuit and a Tom Collins and the aroma of carrots, parsnips, and roast wafting in the air. It was like her mom lived in a *Donna Reed Show*. Not once did the façade crumple. The Sexual Revolution passed over her parents' home as if her mother had painted lamb's blood on the front door.

Marriage was Wendy's out. Peter Lamb was a good husband, and would have been a good father, but he never got the chance.

Dale's phone started ringing endlessly. She willed it to stop. Soap operas, other than her own, were a luxury she wasn't allowed. After the eighth ring, she trudged towards the phone. Even here, plagued by the damn phone.

"Is Dale there?" a woman with a thick country accent she recognized as local, or Missouri local asked.

"He's asleep. May I ask who's calling?" She knew. *Charlie Blue bitch!* There was a long silence on the phone. "Hello?"

"I'm still here...listen, is this Wendy?"

"Yes. Who's calling?"

Another long pause. The woman breathed into phone.

"Wendy, I'm gonna tell you straight. My name is Tina Kruger and I know Dale from The Dew where I work. We've been seeing each other for over a year. I came down a couple of days ago to Georgia to visit and...it got ugly. It wasn't what I expected. Hard partying," and then more defensively as though she were tattling on a sibling who did something way worse than her, she added, "there were other too."

Tina. Her stupid name was Tina. Every redneck Hoosier woman in the Midwest was named Tina.

"Look, I'm staying at Georgian Oaks Motor Lodge in Marietta until tomorrow. I can get a cab and meet Dale outside the office. Not even involve you. Just tell me when. I ain't looking for a scene. I just want my stuff."

Son-on-of-a-bitch. Son-of-a-bitch, son-of-a-bitch, son-of-a-bitch.

"Not involve me. It's too late for that, Tina. You know when you sleep with someone's husband, you automatically involve the wife." The audacity of this woman floored her, but Wendy didn't want a scene either and judging by Tina's boldness, the woman would have no qualms about showing up. "What happened, Tina? He told me the hydraulics went out on a lift and an airplane door grazed his head."

"He's a damn liar. When I woke up there was a big-ass party going down. I knew he'd lied to me then. Like an idiot I ran down the hall and totally forgot about the living room being sunken and ran right into him, and from what the nurses told me secondhand, he fell face forward into that glass coffee table."

"Hey, honey," Dale called from the bedroom, "Who you talking to?"

Your girlfriend! "No one," she yelled. "It's just the TV. I'll turn it down." Luckily, Dale had a cordless phone. Wendy turned the TV down, opened the sliding glass door, and walked outside on his patio. "I'm coming over. Give me the address."

If she could walk out now, she would have. A few more checks from Dale would increase her secret bank account and then graduation and her life would stop being a ticking timebomb. This

Tina felt like a sick fascination to her; she wanted to know all the sordid details.

Wendy stood over Dale and thought, lying motherfucker. She prodded him awake.

"What the fuck, Wen? The doctor said I needed to rest up."

"I'm going to get groceries."

"Well, couldn't you have left a note?"

"You always want to know where I am, what I'm doing, so that's what."

"Did you wake me to start a damn fight?"

"Yes! Bye!" She slammed the bedroom door, the front door, and finally her car door. She found0 Tina's suitcase in the back of the Blazer, under a Mexican blanket.

* * *

The Motor Lodge was a plantation-themed hotel off Highway 41 that was probably a hot ticket in the 1960s but looked like it was far past restoration. She drove up a hill covered in tall, thin, pine trees. There was a restaurant there called The Plantation. The once-white columns were peeling and gray. Trash littered the cracked sidewalks leading to room eleven, but its decaying state fit Wendy's mood, and if Tina were staying somewhere nice, she would have been even more pissed, if possible.

When she knocked on Tina's door a shirtless man in cutoff jean shorts opened the adjacent door, gave Wendy a once over, and said, "Hey. You Tina's friend?"

"Not at all."

"Well, friendly enough if you're coming to see her."

"It's none of your business."

"All right, cool down, thunder. Tell her I'm heading to the Texaco for cigarettes, and I'll meet her at the pool." The man walked behind her jingling his keys. She's quick, she thought. Dale's been replaced. She knocked again. This time she heard, "Just a second!"

Tina opened the door wearing an oversized T-shirt with damp triangles outlined on her chest from her wet bikini underneath her tee. Her hair was heavily frosted. She was tan, so tan the flesh under her neck looked like a potato that had been put in the microwave too long. Tina was small in frame, had a decent body, but her face was worn beyond her years and was decorated with raw red scrapes and two black eyes, one worse than the other, but they were already fading to a jaundice color and weren't nearly as bad as Dale's. She was once cute, but that day had expired.

Tina picked up her suitcase, set it on the bed, unzipped it, and began sifting through its items as though she were taking inventory. It was all so absurd being inside this woman's room. The AC fan blew musty air and everything, including Tina, smelled like stale smoke.

"Well, guess those other girls didn't steal my stuff," she said, satisfied.

Tina came to have fun. It didn't work out as planned, but she'd picked up where she left off and was back on her little vacation. Angry wife, jacked-up face be damned.

"Tell me about the other women," Wendy said, standing in front of the bed, her purse across one of her shoulders and nails stabbing into the faux leather while her other hand pinched the inner flesh of her bicep.

The carpeting was a deep ruby color with dark patches and might have covered a murder scene. The coverlet and headboard were the same color as the carpeting and the furniture — French Provincial. It was gaudy and gouged and a lot like Tina and Dale's faces.

Tina sighed after Wendy said, "other women," as if she had to tell a good friend something that would hurt her. She pulled the last Salem out of a pack, crumbled the pack, and tossed it on the nightstand. She rose, opened the mini-fridge, and got a Bartles & Jaymes Pina Colada wine cooler out and asked, "You want one? Sorry, I'm out of cigarettes or I'd offer you one."

"I don't smoke."

"I stopped, but with this situation," she waved her unlit cigarette in the air, capturing her present circumstances. "Well, I'll quit later." She plopped on the bed, as casual as can be.

"Tina, I don't care if you smoke five packs a day. I brought you what you wanted, now tell me what I came for." She just wanted the truth as ugly as she knew it would be. She wanted to be angry. She didn't want it sugar-coated.

The truth was worse than grass-stained hems on Easter dresses, or graffiti on the White House, and yet, she didn't really need to drive to a rundown motel to hear it from this whore's mouth. Not only was he screwing around on her while she went to school and worked, but he had the nerve to bring Tina down to Georgia to visit him while he accused *her* of cheating.

"I drink, sure I party, but no hard stuff," Tina justified through a mouth etched with such deep lines, she didn't need to explain her ways to Wendy.

The affair had been going on for over a year. First meeting up outside Shannon's work. It progressed visiting at the Dew Drop Inn where Tina waited tables, then to Tina's apartment above the bar, and now Dale's apartment in Georgia.

"According to the nurse, we hit the glass table together. He broke my fall," she said proudly, nodding, tapping cigarette ash into an ashtray she held in her hand.

Wendy had almost fallen the first night on her way to the kitchen to get a glass of water. The missing coffee table mystery and Dale's injuries were now solved.

"All I know is I was trying to get out." Tina took a long drag, exhaled. "I ran, and I guess I forgot, well, I know I forgot." She pointed to her damaged face. "But I remember there were two women in the bathroom doing drugs. I drink. The other stuff ain't my scene...Look, I wasn't tryin to break up your marriage. He said y'all weren't working out, but hell, you can have him." Tina stubbed her cigarette into a glass ashtray and then said in a conspiratorial way,

"Those women I mentioned...they seemed to know Dale pretty well, if you get my meaning." Her voice didn't match her face. It should have been a husky smoker's voice, not so childlike. She could see Dale liking it, though, or other men.

"You could give two fucks about my marriage when you started screwing my husband, so don't act like you care now. It doesn't matter. Just do one thing for me. Don't tell him I know about you two. I need, I really, really need him to keep his job while I finish school. Can you do that?"

Tina eyed her with disbelief. "If you want, but if it was me, I'd kick him to the —"

"Do you have kids, Tina?"

"No."

"Then stop looking at me like that."

Wendy dug in her purse for Tina's pink, polka-dot makeup bag and threw it in the corner near the bed, walked out, and slammed Tina's door — yet another door — though she suspected there would be a lot of slamming doors in her future.

She almost walked straight into the rube from earlier who had apparently tired of waiting on Tina and was heading towards her room with a paper sack.

He said, "Hey, girl. I thought you were coming to the pool."

She turned around and walked backwards for eight seconds, giving him the finger the whole time.

* * *

Her hands shook while she tossed cereal, milk, butter into her grocery cart, but by the time she returned to Dale's apartment, put everything in the fridge, and slammed the fridge door, she was calm.

She contemplated Dale's calendar. Several magnets kept the Shafer's calendar attached to his fridge. He knew her schedule better than she did. Some dates were circled in purple marker, some in red, yellow check marks for other days. Strange hieroglyphics. She flipped to her graduation date and wished she had never written it down. She wanted to mark it out, but instead she threw the calendar in the trash, and walked the trash to the dumpster.

She let him sleep as long as he wanted, trying to avoid him. When he woke up, he stumbled out to the living room, dropped down next to her on the couch, and put his hand on her thigh. She scooted away.

"I'm leaving in the morning."

"What?"

"Quit whining. You're fine by yourself and I can't lose my internship."

"I thought it was already cleared with them, Wendy. When did you have that *conversation*?" He said "conversation" savagely like she had been told to stop having them and now she'd been found out.

"While you were sleeping. Besides, it's one just day difference. And I wrote a check just so you know. It's in the register." If the numbers were correct, Dale had been holding back from her.

"I just sent you one."

"Yeah, and this trip took most of it and your groceries." A stream of curse words sat on her lips like a canker sore. Instead, she thought *three months, three months, three months.*

* * *

Shannon's journal got an earful today.

Okay, so I stayed at Kathy's. Mom went down to Georgia. Oh, and she's not cheating, but Dale was. I knew I wasn't losing my mind. At first, I didn't really notice. Like it was just a freak thing that Tina Kruger drove up the same time Dale dropped me off at work. I remember thinking she had the same schedule as me somehow, except she was tanning, and I was working. Like duh! Anyway, that creep was meeting her at my work!!! Gross. That's when it started. Mom actually met up and talked to Tina while she was in Georgia. Dale got her down there to take care of him because he had some accident at work, but it was all a lie. Not the accident, there was one, but it didn't happen at work. He is such a liar!!!!! I don't see how she

188

can stay even another day with him after that, but she's got some secret fund to escape. Please, please. Don't let her change her mind. I gave her half of my paycheck last week. Eddy is taking me to work now. And he just hangs out at the salon until I get off, or if the owner comes in, and he leaves and gets me McDonald's fries and a milkshake. I'm going to miss him. If we fucking leave!!!!

And I found some voodoo, hoodoo, whatever Dale doll in our fridge. Oh my God!! I'm going to freak out if I don't get out of here. This is how mom solves problems???? Through witchcraft!!!! A doll. Am I the only sane one here? I almost didn't see it. She buried it behind some frozen peas.

She chucked her journal under her bed as if it were its fault her mom see-sawed from day to day. She hadn't been keeping up with the Shafers, so with a red marker she slashed through the two weeks total and then drew blood dripping around the days. Somehow, it made her feel better.

One Month, Four Days until Escape

By the end of October, Wendy couldn't hold back. No woman in the history of female angst could do what she did. She screamed into her new cordless phone. "Don't you have a new girlfriend, *Dale*? How about that Tina skank from The Dew? You know the one with the pink, polka-dot makeup bag you lied about. She's perfect for you. Call her. I just can't."

"..."

"Oh, what? You didn't think I knew about her? *The makeup bag...her clothes...*in the back of your Blazer."

"..."

"Nothing to say? You always have so much to say, Dale."

"Tina is psycho, Wendy. Don't talk to her. She just showed up on my doorstep and then I couldn't get rid of her. You've been talking to a certified nutjob? *She lies.* Wendy, I swear. It's all her."

"That's not what she said when I brought her stuff and how the hell does she know where you live anyway?"

"What? You saw her? What'd that bitch say? That we're together? I'm telling you. She's crazy. Don't talk to her, Wendy. She a Goddamn bunny boiler, you hear? Talking to her just encourages it. She has got some, some *Fatal Attraction* thing for me."

"You didn't answer me. How did she have your address?"

"How do any psychos know the address of who they stalk? They find a way."

"So, your head injury? An *airplane door*?" She couldn't stop herself. "Tina told me it was your coffee table. You lied about that, you lied about her. You bought her a Greyhound ticket, when we, us, your family, needs the money."

"I can't do this right now. I got to head into work."

"You can't do this right now. Suddenly, when you're caught in a lie, you have to go to work. How rich, Dale."

"She's lying to you. That chick is obsessed with me. Like I said, she just turned up. I didn't buy her a ticket. Check the bills. You see anything for Greyhound?"

"Easily paid for with cash."

"When I get off work, we can talk, and I'll explain what happened. It's not like she said or what it looks like. Yes, I lied about the coffee table, but what was I supposed to do? How could I explain the dingbat's showing up at my apartment? She attacked me, Wendy. Stay away from her. We'll talk later."

After she hung up, she opened the kitchen sink cabinet and pulled out an extra-large garbage bag. She was ready to purge. Escape had grown a body and a head. She would no longer be a bystander, sitting back and watching what other people did to her.

She hadn't slept since the day before and though she was exhausted she couldn't stop. She stuffed garbage bags full of clothes she had kept for sentimental reasons, knickknacks, pillows, old blankets, and sheets. They didn't bring much four years ago, but they hadn't gotten rid of anything either.

She heard the school bus and Rebel barking. After a moment, Shannon walked in.

"What's all this?" Shannon swept her hand out as if she were a gameshow girl presenting prizes. "Are we moving to Georgia, *Wendy*?" Her voice was thick with sarcasm. "Did you sleep? You look rough, mom."

Wendy wanted to explain to her daughter about her day. She wanted to say, I finally confronted him. If only she could talk to someone, another woman, someone. "Don't Wendy me, Shannon."

"What the fuck is going on? I swear, I'm not moving to Georgia. You can, I'm not."

"Don't curse...Shannon. And...don't answer the phone anymore, either."

"*What?*" Shannon threw her bookbag onto the carpet. "It's so unfair. I can't use the phone 'cause your husband is insane?"

"No, I don't want to pull you into this. I'm trying to protect you."

"Really? You're worried about protecting me *now*? Since when? He's been a shit to me from day one, but you, *Mrs. Samples*, are too scared to be by yourself." Shannon ripped open the freezer and pulled out the poppet of Dale. "Is this your solution for us?"

"Don't make fun. You know I believe in that stuff."

"Yeah, I know, but does Dale believe? Because someone needs to tell him you froze him out and he can leave us alone now." Shannon shook the doll in Wendy's face.

Wendy smacked it away and said, "Not today. Not from you, too." There was hatred on Shannon's face, and it wasn't the first time she'd seen it.

"You can make all the dolls you want mom, but here's a thought, when you graduate, you can support yourself. You don't need him!" Shannon hurled the frozen doll into the kitchen sink and stormed off. Wendy heard her bedroom door slam shut.

She picked up the doll and put it back in the freezer. Whether it worked or not, it gave her a sense of control.

Moments later Shannon returned. "Listen mom, if we're leaving him, then we got to do it right." She pointed her finger at her like she had already screwed up. "Whatever you do, just keep it together and be ready to vanish when he finds out. And," Shannon eyes narrowed, the blue irises like crushed sapphires, becoming darker and more serious, "if you're planning on replacing him —"

"I'm not cheating." Wendy aggressively worked her hands through her long hair, trying to capture the strands into a ponytail.

"I didn't think so, but you're weak with men, mom. You can't be alone even if the man you're with treats you like crap, treats me like crap, you'd rather be with him than alone." And then in an almost inaudible voice, she asked, "Is it because of my dad? Is that why you do this to yourself?"

"I'm not going there with you."

"That's right. You never do. I literally know nothing about the person I share half my DNA with. One day you're going to tell me…everything." She moved towards Wendy and hugged her tightly, whispering over her shoulder, "It must be for real. I love you, but *Christ*, it must be for real." She pulled away, looking for dissent in Wendy's face. "And there's no way Dale won't know something's up if I suddenly stop talking to him. We need to act normal."

Shannon was right. She never left a man without a replacement, even if he was a filler; she always had one in waiting. She was so lonely when Peter died. A new baby — a baby he never even got to see or hold. She at once replaced him with the next man who showed interest in her, and then another, and another, as if she were reading a series by an author who couldn't write about anything but bad romances.

Shannon broke her trance, shaking her lightly. "Mom? Mom, you in there? You need to get some sleep. Take a hot bath, relax. If Dale calls, I'll tell him you're sick or something."

Wendy reached for Shannon, and they hugged a second time for as long as her teenaged girl would allow.

Shannon said into her ear, "I hope he felt that when I threw him in the sink." They both laughed. "Now go." Shannon let go of her and pushed her in the direction of the bathroom.

It was nice to have someone who wanted to care for her, even though it was her daughter, and it made her feel guilty.

Wendy turned the hot water knob on the bathtub and watched the water stream out. The corner part of the wallpaper, a mixture of daisies and swans against a country blue background she assumed was a lake had come loose and hung a quarter of the way from the ceiling where water from the shower faucet continuously sprayed it. She tugged the paper off the wall. Beneath it, the wall was water-stained with patches of glue, but it looked better than the hideous wallpaper. The landlord would probably take it out of her deposit if he gave any of it back. Everyone wanted a piece.

She hoped listening to the water would numb her, but her mind continued to race. Panic coursed through her body, running in waves, up and down her spine; her stomach roiled. She had a bitter taste in her mouth. She needed someone to talk to so badly; it might as well be herself.

Wendy stood in front of the mirror while the tub filled up, wiping the steam off the glass. "I'm done with your tricks, lies, and abuse, Dale. I just needed you to pay off the credit cards and save enough to leave your pathetic ass. We're done. You'll never get someone as good as me." It'd be a little over a month before she could deliver her speech, or maybe she'd call from a payphone and say this when they were safely away. Probably never, though.

She began to scrutinize the lines around her eyes, the teeny indentations starting to form around her mouth, and she felt for sure she'd be alone for the rest of her life. "It's not about beauty, you idiot. It's respect, support, communication, and whatever," she pointed at herself in the mirror, *"you don't have."* She put both hands around the frame of the mirror and leaned in, pressing her forehead against the glass. She stayed in this position for minutes, looking at herself as close as possible.

"It's okay, Wendy. You're going to be okay. Shannon's going to be okay. We're going to be okay." That afternoon she repeated these words over and over, "It's going to be okay." Then daily she said these words, and as the weeks passed, she visited her reflection and planted her mantra inside herself.

And then, out of the blue, one of Wendy's girlfriends from Los Angeles called to tell Wendy she'd finally left her asshole husband.

"*Ha*, Katie, there must be something in the air, because I'm leaving my asshole husband, too." Wendy groaned. "Except, it's not easy leaving Dale. We're going to have to disappear."

"I remember. After that one time, I didn't think you'd go back."

"I thought he'd changed. He stopped drinking for a little while. It was supposed to be a new beginning, but he got laid off and there's no work around here. I'm not making excuses. He has always been Dale, but this is his worst version so far."

"They never change. If they get away with it once, they always do it again. You two can stay with me until you get a job, but it won't take long. They need nurses out here like bad. You can get lost in LA. Or go up north, unless that's too close to your parents or you think he'll track you two down, but I'd love for you two to stay with me." And before Katie hung up, she said, "Wendy, it's going to be okay," and Wendy felt as if the universe had spoken to her.

* * *

The weeks before the final escape, Wendy and Shannon went from room to room, packing what they planned to bring until they were down to living with the basics — two cups, two plates, some silverware, a frying pan, a pot, and the coffee maker. Eddy hauled their bagged-up trash in his dad's truck to the county dump. They could have packed and cleaned the last week, but the task made Wendy feel lighter. As though it was already over, and she and Shannon were far, far away from Dale.

The filth and disorder were part of her depression. With each load Eddy took away, another layer of desperation and depression vanished. For years, she felt as if she had been buried alive. And now, there was someone shoveling away the ground above, lifting her casket from her grave, and that someone was her.

She hired an attorney. She was positive Dale would not sign the divorce papers, but the attorney figured for that event as well, and since Dale had a record of violence, Wendy didn't have to be present for the hearing. Her secret bank account increased to five hundred dollars, but that, and more, went to her attorney. With the money Dale sent, she managed to pay her credit cards down and she closed the joint ones. She planned to close her bank account down last. The local bank would be glad to be rid of her pleas to reverse fees on bounced checks. If all they had was enough money for gas to get to California, an hour after graduation they would be on the road. She would make sure of it.

Wendy's commencement ceremony was the morning of December 2nd. She told Dale it was the seventh. He'd planned to come up for the day and then call in sick to have an extra day to travel. She had applied for a temporary license and was approved so she could work some shifts until she could take her boards in California.

God, she wished she could see Dale's face when he pulled up to the empty trailer. He would terrorize the neighbors trying to discover their whereabouts. It wasn't like the town ever really accepted them anyway, but she liked some of the folks at St. Lawrence Church, her friends at the hospital, and Eddy was a good soul. They prepared him for the worst.

"I'll miss you guys." Eddy's brown eyes didn't look at Wendy, but at Shannon. Wendy wondered if they ever had a thing and hoped

195

Shannon hadn't broken his heart. At least Shannon had someone in town and at school. She felt like such a shitty mom.

Wendy hugged Eddy and tried to give him some money for his work, but he refused so she hugged him again and said, "We'll miss you, too, Eddy, but just say you had no idea we'd moved. Maybe, even act a little shocked. Do your parents know you've been going to the dump?"

"I don't know. I didn't say nothing — can I write you?"

Shannon glanced at Wendy.

"We don't have a place yet, Eddy," Shannon lied; she knew where they were staying. "But I'll write you."

Wendy wondered if Shannon would write him, or if she wanted to put away the past as much as she wanted to, and then she felt even shittier because her daughter lied to protect them.

One week, One day until Shannon and Wendy Move

Dale called Mineral Area College three times in a row and the same chirpy lady gave him the same answer all three times.

"Nope, sir. I'm positive, sir. Graduation is December 2nd. My son is graduating, too, so I wouldn't get it wrong. I have a personal stake if you know what I mean."

"I believe you. It's just this is a surprise. My wife didn't think I'd make it and I was sure she said the seventh. If I say too much, I'll give it away." According to Wendy, her commencement ceremony had been moved up.

"Oh, what program is she in? I wonder if she knows my Timothy. What's her name? I'll have to tell him." The woman babbled on like she'd recently been released from isolation and finally had an audience. "Nope, nope, sir, I have it right here. I'm looking at the date and it most certainly is December 2nd."

Wendy could throw all his calendars away, lie about the date, and it wouldn't matter, because her graduation date was branded on his skin, burnished inside his brain. He had her. She wasn't getting away. Finally, he'd found her out and now he was in his truck on the road he traveled almost a year earlier when he had a family and wife who he had a future with, but he had none of that today.

Dale had been on the road since he was a teenager. He left Indiana at fifteen after the last ass-beating by his dad, hitchhiked to Panama City where he easily found construction jobs building hotels, and then sleeping in the same rooms where he had hung drywall that very day. He earned respect the hardscrabble way, through work, boozing, and fighting, and left Florida for California three years later as a man. His last job was picking lettuce in northern California alongside migrant Mexicans before got his GED and joined the Air Force. He hated the military, though it gave him a trade, and he knew where he was sleeping every night unless he didn't make it back to base and then he knew the MPs and the cell well enough, too.

He'd met a lot of women, but none like Wendy. He wasn't willing to lose her to a doctor type. He deserved something good, someone to love him in this whole Goddamn world. He'd fight himself dead for that. To lie belly up like a dog was not in him.

December 1st, Morning, Sainte Geneviève, Missouri

Dale bought a gram of coke from Old Charles, stopped in a liquor store in Kentucky to pick up a bottle of Dickel, and made Missouri in eight hours. By the time he parked in the hospital parking lot, he was shaking hard from the drugs, but it was more than that. He was excited. Adrenaline-fueled rage pumped through his veins. He was finally going to catch her.

At 9:00 a.m., people started to trail out of the employee entrance. He recognized one or two from the church picnic and the infrequent times he attended Mass. He only knew Dr. Brouchard from Wendy's descriptions. Balding and short, but that could be a lie.

He sank down low, his eyes focused on the space between the steering wheel and dashboard. His nose was running, his eyes burned. The weatherman informed him over an hour ago, "We didn't get a fall this year in Missouri. It went straight from summer to winter with no in between." He didn't need no weatherman to tell him this. He'd hit an ice storm in Cape Girardeau. "You got that right, Mr. Weatherman...fucking Missouri," he mumbled to himself.

He watched a troop of men and women in green and blue scrubs half-slide, half-march across the frosty parking lot to their cars. Not one of them was Wendy, and then there she was talking to a woman and a man. He knew neither of them. She waved them off. They both drove away, and Wendy went to her car.

December 1st, Morning, One Day before Escape

When Wendy started her car, a blast of arctic air blew in her face before she adjusted the knob to defrost. She always forgot to move the knob to low heat before she turned off the car. The wipers wouldn't budge; her windshield was covered in a layer of ice. She opened her glovebox. No ice-scraper. She checked under her seat, the passenger's seat, the backseat. One thing she would never need again once she and Shannon were in Southern California.

She got out of the car and opened the trunk. There were a pair of muddy running shoes of Shannon's now dried up and frozen, jumper cables, an extra pint of oil, beach towels, and a couple of cardboard boxes, but no ice-scraper. It was probably on the ground somewhere at the house. She tore the lid off a cardboard box and folded it into a triangle, trying to create some sharpness at the edge to scrape the ice off. She pushed the cardboard across her frozen windshield, managing to create a few lines, but there was no way she could navigate home.

"Need some help?" It was Dr. Brouchard who made a habit of staying later than his shift, usually to talk to a patient's spouse, parent, sibling, or child.

"Oh, I know. I look crazy. I can't find my scraper, and this is the best I can do." She showed him the limp cardboard. He looked amused, but also seemed pleased to help.

"Hold on. You just get back in your car, Ms. Wendy, and stay warm. I have one."

Dr. Brouchard walked to his own car, waved an ice scraper in the air for her to see, carefully crossed the icy parking lot back to her, and began scraping Wendy's frosty windshield. She felt sad for Dr. Brouchard, watching him take care of her as he surely did for his late wife. She bet it was the small moments he missed the most — not the birthdays or anniversaries, but the little things like scraping ice off her windshield, the rituals of a good marriage. He hummed as he scraped.

When she was able to turn the wipers on to clear enough of the frost off so the roads would be visible, he handed the ice scraper through her open window and said, "Hey, I have so many of these. You can keep —"

Very suddenly, Dr. Brouchard's kind face contorted into an expression of revulsion, and for a moment she thought he was upset with her, but then she quickly realized the sound expelled from his doughy cheeks was him absorbing a hard hit from behind. His head struck the inside ledge by her driver's side window. She could feel the cold air breeze coming in where his body had just been blocking the temperature along with the warm blast from the car heater on her cheeks. The ice scraper Dr. Brouchard donated only seconds before sat in her lap.

She peered over her open window at Dr. Brouchard's body slumped onto the ice. His glasses were knocked off and lay a couple of feet from him. Her gaze moved like someone assessing a painting; she surveyed the entire image—loafers, khaki pants, coat—before fixating on the focal point which was no longer Dr. Brouchard, but Dale. This was his artistry. He was screaming at Dr. Brouchard, who wasn't responding; he was knocked out from the first hit.

"You like kissing my wife. *Do yah?*"

Instinctively, she wanted to press the gas pedal, to leave. She saw Dale's leg swing back, heard the thud of his boot as it battered the doctor's fleshy abdomen. Just a nice man who innocently offered to scrape her windshield. To get help meant getting past Dale, and he was terrified. In her head, she screamed, please, someone come out!

Dale smacked Dr. Brouchard's plump cheeks. "Wakey, wakey." Dr. Brouchard came to, his eyes bugged out, totally confused as to why this man was sitting on top of him, spitting angry word in his face. "I'll whup you, you sumbitch.

. You hear? I'll whup you like no one whupped yah before. You hear me?" Dale straddled the doctor's shoulders and began to cram his fist into the doctor's mouth like he meant to stick his full fist in. The doctor protested and moaned, fiercely shaking his head, either to deny Dale's fist or deny what was happening to him.

"Oh, you like it. You like it. That's good. Take it all up now." He leaned in, eye-dueling the doctor. "Suck it, motherfucker." He angled his fist this way, then that, pushing his fist into the doctor's mouth whose lips were stretched wide like a clown's who had outlined his red lips further than his lip line. All the while Dale handed out more false indictments about "his wife." It all seemed so ridiculous. These words. Accusations made at an old man who was past his prime over fifteen years ago.

Dr. Brouchard bit him and Dale leapt back — rattlesnake quick. "Goddamn! You fucking bit me!" He sucked on his bloody knuckle for a moment, then fell back on the doctor. He punched him, winced, eyeballed the bloodied flesh hanging from his knuckle and reverted to backhanding him with his left hand — one, two, three, four times, until Dr. Brouchard stopped fighting back, and even then, Dale wouldn't stop wailing on the man.

"I can't, I can't, I can't." She couldn't listen or watch. With trembling hands, Wendy rolled up her window. She felt like one of those girls in the slasher movies Shannon made her watch: The killer approaches in slow motion, relishing the chase. A girl, with hands shaking, tries to fit her keys into the ignition, drops them. The killer stands calmly, arrogantly outside her window because he knows how it's going to end. Let the girl think she has a chance. Part of the fun. And as soon as her window is up, he smashes through it, drags her body through the jagged glass of the window, and slits her throat.

Still, she couldn't press the gas pedal even with Dale shouting vile things into the doctor's deaf ears. She turned the radio volume all the way up. She laid on the horn and didn't let up. She screamed, but it seemed like someone else was screaming. Maybe there were others screaming and her voice was adding to the sheer noise of it all. It wasn't working. Dale wouldn't stop, and it wasn't enough to just scream anymore.

If she remained in her car, would she be an innocent bystander or a victim? Or would everyone at the hospital, or the entire town say she brought this on herself? The town's murmurings flooded the interior of her car. She didn't even try to help the poor man and she knew what an animal her husband was. Judgements that were louder than the radio, her screams, Dale, or the horn. The verdict was in. Sentenced for being afraid, for being a bystander.

Dale, tired of pummeling the doctor, stood up, stumbled back, and lifted his jean leg over the top of his boot where Wendy knew he kept his knife in his boot. He bent over the lower part of the doctor, unbuckled him, unbuttoned, unzipped, and yanked his khaki pants down to midthigh. "I'm gonna wipe you out, son, you hear me, son?" He tapped the blade against Dr. Brouchard's cheeks. Wendy turned away. He was going to castrate him. This grandfather--he intended on castrating.

Wendy climbed over the emergency brake, over the passenger seat, clambered out, slipped backwards on the ice, regained her balance, and half-running, half-falling, came around the back and tackled Dale. The knife slid across the ice. He hadn't seen or heard her coming, and now they both lay partially on top of the doctor, battling for control.

She seized a chunk of Dale's hair and yanked him upwards, and they slid off the doctor onto the ice and tumbled on the frozen parking lot. She rose, on her knees now, almost to her feet, but Dale elbowed her from behind in the chest. She lost hold of his hair. He had knocked the air out of her. He turned around and tackled her, grabbing hold of her waist. They wrestled on the ice, grabbing at or snatching whatever each other's hands found on the other. She pinched and twisted his skin, dug her nails into his neck. She wasn't going to have to worry about him finding her and Shannon or killing them because they ran away. She was going to free herself or die trying, but he was ultimately stronger, and the element of surprise was over. He pinned her down on the iced asphalt next to Dr. Brouchard, his knees pressing into her shoulders. Wendy closed her eyes and thought, this is what the coroner will see. Dale's hands circled her neck. She tried to pull his hands away and couldn't. An image of the doctor handing Shannon to her when she was born flashed in her mind.

All at once, the pressure of Dale's fingers and hands were torn from around her neck, the stabbing pain of his knees digging into her shoulders was lifted, and the weight of Dale's body was totally gone. She sprung forward like a Jack in the Box and opened her eyes. The air was distorted as though vacuumed away. The previous vision of Dale above her was suddenly replaced with Dale's body being yanked backwards. She inhaled hard sub-zero air, filling her lungs and then started coughing.

The empty space where Dale once dominated her was replaced by a large black man. Time skipped a beat, slowing to twenty beats per minute. The man spoke in slow motion, "Lady   I   are   you okay?" The tempo increased to forty beats. "I've   never   seen anything like this." Then fifty beats, and finally time caught up with her thinking and was no longer delayed. "Are you okay?"

The adrenaline left her body, and she slumped over and sank onto the frozen asphalt and started to cry. Had the layer of ice, then the blacktop fractured open like a thin sheet of ice over a pond where she was ice-skating, if she were drawn downward into freezing water, she would not have resisted. Her pants were soaked through, she was shivering uncontrollably, and her cheekbones felt as if they might split open from raw cold. She inhaled wet, frigid air in her throat and nostrils. It hurt but she was back.

The man who had yanked Dale off her told her she was safe now.

He knelt to examine her with coffee-colored eyes, "You in there, ma'am? Can you get up?"

She nodded and he pulled her up from the icy pavement.

"Steady your breath. The police are on their way. If you need to, count in your head. It helps. My name is Carter. What's yours, ma'am?"

He inspected her neck. His hands were so delicate. Long piano-playing fingers. She'd never seen him before. This stranger who was caring for her. And there was a witness, this kind Carter who would testify she didn't sit idly by while Dale beat the living hell out of Dr. Brouchard — and the other thing he was about to do. She forced herself to look at Dr. Brouchard. His pants were still down. He wore plaid boxer shorts.

Carter said, "Look at me. Not over there."

More people arrived, one of them carrying a stretcher, another a blanket. They lifted the unconscious Dr. Brouchard onto the stretcher, and another gently wrapped her in a blanket.

ER people wheeled him over the ice, back in the hospital she had left only moments ago. Two younger men, the hospital security, had detained Dale, who kept yelling for her.

Carter said, "The officers are going to want to talk to you, ma'am, but let's get you inside, get you checked out." Carter guided her away.

"Wendy!" Dale wailed. He was kicking. He tried to bite one of the men before they forced his head down to the blacktop. Two more men arrived who looked like visitors to help. It took four men.

Dale's cries, her radio still blaring, murmurs from the crowd of onlookers, and now sirens from approaching police cars sounded like some terrible, terrible cacophony of nightmarish sounds. It was awful. But then all the noise stopped abruptly, and she thought, even the devil had had enough.

One of the officers turned off her engine. They ordered the crowd to disburse until it dwindled to her, two officers, and Dale who was inside the back of one of the Sainte Geneviève city police cars, craning his neck to stare at her from the rear windshield like he was a lost little boy the officers just discovered wandering around an amusement park in search of his mother.

Some morning staff, who she'd only seen in passing and didn't know, checked her over, but surprisingly Dale hadn't done her much damage. Bruises and scrapes. Her throat hurt but would heal. She was discharged quickly. One of the officers, an older man, was waiting for her in the ER. He led her out.

"I'm sorry," she said, "but I can't remember your name." She walked beside him to the exit with heads turning left and right to catch a glimpse.

"Officer Hardt."

To her relief, the younger officer and Dale were missing from the parking lot. Officer Hardt caught her expression. "He's being processed."

He offered to drive her to the station, but she insisted on driving herself.

"You're not under arrest, ma'am. You can sit up in front with me. We'll have someone drive your car."

"I know, but no." Part of her wanted to make a run for it. Get Shannon and run.

* * *

The Sainte Geneviève Police Department was a red brick building not far from Valle High School and Wendy wondered if gossip had traveled the couple blocks and Shannon was hearing it from some teenager instead of her. She parked. Officer Hardt was already walking towards her car.

"Come on in and get warm. You drink coffee?"

She nodded yes.

The officer led her to a beige cement block room with beige tiled floors, where a younger officer, who was introduced by Officer Hardt as Officer Lamaire, opened the metal door that had a small square window cut in it, and then pulled a metal folding chair out for her. He sat opposite her at a small table. Officer Hardt walked in moments later with a Styrofoam cup of coffee, three sugars, and two creamers and then asked her to relate the events of the morning.

About twenty minutes later someone knocked on the door. A woman's voice said, "Chevy Blazer," and, "You should look at this." Officer Hardt told Officer Lamaire to come with him. He excused himself and said, "I'll get you a topper, ma'am."

She said, "Sure." He was being kind, but she was exhausted. She just wanted to collect Shannon and leave. "I really need to get my daughter from Valle."

"Is the daughter his, ma'am?" Officer Lamaire asked.

"No, thank God."

Officer Lamaire smirked. Officer Hardt touched Officer Lamaire's sleeve and pressed his fingers into his arm. They both got up and both left.

Thirty minutes later, Wendy glanced at her wristwatch for the sixth time. The door finally opened, and Officer Hardt carried in a banking box marked evidence, with today's date, and "Samples" written in black marker. Wendy tasted bile. Officer Lamaire handed her a cup of black coffee, foregoing the sugar and cream his counterpart had thought to bring her last time.

Officer Lamaire opened the box and pulled out three notebooks, one with a red ballpoint pen stuck inside the metal wire binder, stretching the wire.

"Did you know about these, ma'am?" Officer Hardt pushed an orange-colored Mead notebook towards her. She flipped through it, scanning Dale's data. She did the same with another but

didn't bother with the last one.

"I suspected, but I hadn't realized to what extent." She took a sip of coffee. It wasn't even warm.

"How about this?" Officer Hardt nodded at Officer Lamaire, and he pressed play on a tape recorder. "There were twenty-two tapes in all."

Wendy lifted slightly from her chair into the boxes to confirm the number of tapes were in the box. They were all marked with dates from this year and her name and Shannon's name.

They listened to one of the tapes, their banal conversations, and then Dale's interrogations and accusations over the course of the past year, what Dale claimed was evidence, and apparently, he was correct in his thinking because his evidence had officially become police evidence. She heard her denials. Officer Lamaire was about to turn the tape over, but Officer Hardt shook his head. What was the point of making her listen to all this bullshit?

"We knew he was taping us." She explained how he would tell her to hold on, she'd hear a click like the sound of a tape recorder's off/on button, and then how in the background she heard voices that were her, Shannon, and Dale talking — the previously recorded tape — and then the shuffling sound of Dale going through papers.

"Why was he recording you, ma'am?" Office Hardt asked.

"It's like I told you earlier. He's paranoid. He thought I was cheating on him with every single doctor in town. For some reason, he decided poor Dr. Brouchard was my lover."

Officer Lamaire eyed her suspiciously like she created this mess for them. But of course, he'd heard Dale's version of events when he processed him and now the notebooks and tapes were giving Dale credibility. Even though they proved nothing, the sheer effort Dale took to document her "affair" made the officers suspect.

"You mentioned that your daughter wasn't Mr. Samples' daughter. Is her father in the picture? She may need to stay with him for a while," Officer Lamaire said.

"My husband...died...Peter Lamb. Shannon's father. In Vietnam." She'd lost the ability to speak in full sentences. "You going to write that down?" she asked Officer Lamaire. Why she had to explain herself to this twenty-year-old kid was beyond her. His expression said he had summed her up already. This was a county, a town, an entire population of cousins. Everyone was related one way or another. No one divorced. All the kids had their original set of parents.

Officer Hardt grimaced. "I'm sorry to hear that. I spent some time over there." He took a sip of coffee Wendy knew was as cold as hers. "I got to ask. Was there something going on with Dr. Brouchard? Mr. Samples is convinced and then all this." He patted a notebook with the palm of his hand.

"No, no, no, no. Nothing ever. Christ, never. Dale was cheating on me!" Her voice rose an octave.

"Okay, calm down. Mrs. Samples," Officer Hardt said. "Did he threaten you during this time? Did he ever threaten Dr. Brouchard?"

"Well, sure, but I, I, uh, he probably made threats on the tapes, erm, unless he recorded over it, I, uh—"

"Why didn't you come to us earlier, ma'am? We might have deescalated this situation," Officer Lamaire gave her the same look as before, the one that said, "It's your fault."

"You don't call the police on Dale."

"This wasn't the first time, ma'am?" Officer Hardt asked.

Wendy confessed her whole sordid life with Dale from how he was so attentive at first, wooing her, how depressed she was raising a child on her own, to their whirlwind romance, the drinking, the abuse, their move, their do-over in the country, his cheating with Tina Kruger, which raised the eyebrows of both officers, and now the beatdown of the good town doctor.

"Is this your handwriting, because it doesn't look like Mr. Samples' writing?" Officer Hardt removed the Shafer Funeral Home calendar from the box, put it on the table, stained and sticky from being in the garbage. Dale had dug it out of the dumpster. He knew this whole time she was lying about her graduation date.

"I have the same one in my kitchen." The younger officer snickered.

Her stomach flipped inside out. She asked to use the bathroom.

The lady's room was as beige and as bland as the interrogation room. She splashed cold water on her face. She took in her reflection in the mirror, not a true mirror, more like a piece of reflective metal that projected a hazy image of herself, but it was fitting because that's what she'd become being with Dale.

She returned to the room and asked for an update on Dr. Brouchard. Officer Hardt said, "He's awake. When he's up to it, we'll question him." It was the best news she'd had all day.

Wendy didn't leave the police department until around 1:00 p.m. She told them about the divorce, the move, that she needed for Dale to *not know* her whereabouts. She gave them her attorney's number. They weren't sure about court, or what would be expected of her, but she could leave for now anyway, and if she needed to come back to Missouri she'd have to, or possibly a witness statement could be done on video. They couldn't say, but they had what they needed. Some of this depended on the charges. She gave them her friend's number and address in California.

"You okay to drive home, Mrs. Samples?" Officer Hardt had real concern in his eyes.

"Yes. The coffee's crap, but it's strong."

As Officer Hardt walked her down the dull tiled floors, back to her car, she overheard scraps of conversations between other officers at the station: "The guy was clearly obsessed," and, "Cheating on him," and, "He certainly thought so. I hate domestics."

Officer Hardt ignored the banter, thanked her, gave her his card and said, "He's not getting out any time soon, ma'am. Not after what he did, but when he does, I hope you aren't anywhere near town. Those types never change."

* * *

From the station she drove to Valle High School, where she had a good cry while waiting for Shannon to appear. Shannon's expression was grim. This part of the county already knew. The news would continue to spread like a virus, travel down Highway Y, float down the Fourche a Du Clos Creek, enter their hometown of Lawrenceton, and seep into the walls of the homes.

Shannon inspected her mother's neck bruises with trembling hands and said, "I hate that fucker. He would have killed you if it weren't public."

"It didn't matter whether we were in public or not."

What the fuck happened today? In less than twenty-four hours? Husband, job, school, home. All gone. Though it was her plan to leave all of it behind, it wasn't supposed to happen like this.

When they got back to the trailer, Wendy called her advisor and instructors and explained she wouldn't be walking at her commencement. She made what arrangements were needed while Shannon crammed their possessions into the car. God, she was tired. So tired. She called her supervisor, Judy, next. Dr. Brouchard was going to be okay. He was banged up. Concussion, stiches, cracked rib, bruising, but okay otherwise.

She rubbed her hands over her tired, burning eyes, down her cheeks. "I just need sleep."

"I'll drive. You can take a nap."

"You just got your license and no, I need to do this. We'll stop when we get out of this *fucking* state."

She needed sleep, but she needed even more to put some miles between her and Dale and the town.

"Okay then." Shannon pulled the push pen out of the wood paneling. "You still want your calendar?"

Wendy glanced at the December photo of the latest Shafer couple, no longer in black and white, but in color now. Since she started marking off the dates on the Shafer Funeral Home calendar, three generations of Shafers had gone by with a photographer documenting them all. This time, the husband sat, and the wife stood behind him with both hands firmly planted on his shoulders. Wendy pictured Mrs. Shafer scheduling the photographer, picking out her husband's tie, maybe even instructing the photographer on how they would face the camera.

"Nah, toss it."

"What about our friend Dale in the freezer?"

For a second, Wendy was at a loss. "Oh my God. The poppet...he can stay, too."

"You sure?" Shannon danced the figure in front of her face. "Whatever will our lovely slumlord think?"

"Let him think the worst. Everyone else does."

Wendy contemplated the power of Dale's poppet and wondered if the freezer, the ice storm, and what happened in the parking lot this morning was due to his poppet.

They locked the trailer door and put the key under the mat for the landlord while Shannon freed Rebel who jumped in the back seat.

* * *

When the "NOW LEAVING LAWRENCETON" sign showed on her right. She sped up and said, "Close your eyes and make a wish."

"Mom, you're the most superstitious person I know."

Wendy closed hers. When she opened them, Shannon's eyes were still open, and she was waving.

"Are you saying goodbye to Lawrenceton, or is there actually someone there?"

"No, there was someone. Eddy. He's crying." Shannon wiped her cheeks with the back of her hand.

"But California and the beach. Put some music on. It'll make us feel better."

"Nah, I can't listen to anything right now...it was still our town for four years. Even if no one liked us...and they'll be glad to forget us."

"Some people liked us. Open the glovebox. There's napkins."

Along with the extra napkins, creamers, and ketchup sat Dr. Brouchard's ice scraper. The officers must have searched her car and put it there. It was a nasty memento she didn't want to be reminded of.

"Don't touch it." Wendy reached over Shannon, grabbed the ice-scraper with the tips of her fingers, rolled down the window, ran off the road some, straightened up, and then tossed the ice-scraper out the window.

"That was his ice-scraper, huh?"

"Poor man." Wendy placed her hand on Shannon's knee and squeezed it reassuringly. "They won't forget us." They both started laughing. It was all just too absurd and laughable.

"Yep, there's no one quite like the Samples for making an entrance and an exit," Shannon said. What else could they do, but laugh about it? Shannon pretended she had a microphone and spoke in a news anchor voice, "It's just another day in the life of our favorite white trash townies."

Sainte Geneviève Herald would feature a piece on the incident, Wendy was sure. Lawrenceton was too small for its own paper. Instead, the locals would chat about it after Sunday Mass and even months later the topic would resume at the annual St. Lawrence picnic, accompanied by shaking heads. Only Eddy and the officers knew the real story.

Before turning onto Interstate 55, both Wendy and Shannon craned their heads to look one last time upon the steeple of St. Agnes Church and School, where Shannon attended middle school.

"There's your old school."

If they continued down the highway, they'd run almost smack into the Dew Drop Inn. Wendy imagined Tina bussing tables, an image she enjoyed. The sign for Fritz's Gas Mart came up on the right, the last remnant of town life, and Wendy said, "We'll get gas somewhere else."

"Uh, yeah. Good idea."

She could and couldn't believe they were really leaving. Would there be a mark left on Lawrenceton? Did towns scar? Would she and Shannon store the little town of Lawrenceton away like an old love letter, remembered, but never visited?

"Hey, look at me."

"What?" Shannon said, sounding annoyed. She was back to acting like a teenager.

"We have a lot of time between here and California...You want to hear about your dad?"

"Really?"

"Really." Wendy paused, thinking about where to begin. Instead, she said, "It's going to be okay, Shannon. You know that, right? Here. Hold my hand. Come on. Just for a second. It won't kill you."

Shannon relented and held Wendy's hand. "Keep telling yourself that. You know I heard you in the bathroom... talking to yourself."

"Look at me."

"Mom, don't. Just watch the road."

"No, listen. Don't let go of my hand. Listen to me. It *is* going to be okay...*now.*"

And finally, after so many years, Wendy believed it.

Acknowledgments

I want to thank my husband, Nick Cook, for being supportive on every level, from me quitting my corporate job to pursue my MFA, to dealing with his wife becoming a whacky writer type. I also want to thank my other Cook boy, my son from another mother, but still my son, Harry Cook, for your encouragement and interest.

I want to thank my mother, Suzanne Major, and my father, Ronald Major for making the exodus from California to Missouri because if they had not, I would never have had the inspiration to write *The Bystanders*.

I want to thank my sisters, Aleea Major and Julia Major, who were there during the seven years my parents decided to toss us into something we equated at the time to living like the Ingalls from *Little House on the Prairie*. I want to thank my nephew, Everett Johnson, another creative soul, for listening to me babble about writing and for his encouragement.

Thank you to all small towns, but especially Lawrenceton, Bloomsdale, Sainte Geneviuve, and French Village; these towns gave me the inspiration to write *The Bystanders*.

Thanks to Raymond Adkins and Dr. John Williams, my MFA mentors. Thanks to my MFA workshop folks--Justin Jones, Jennie Mayes, Alyssa Hamilton. Thanks to my AWC workshop ladies: Cynthia Tolbert, Dawn Abeita, Katherine Caldwell, and Nicole Horn-Foerschler.

Thank you, Mandy Haynes at Three Dogs Write Press, for the awesome cover design and support. The universe was at work with us!

Thanks to Michael White for the writerly encouragement and edits. Thank you, Lamont Ingalls and Susan McDonald, for reading and editing. Thanks to Moonshine Cove Publishing for making a dream come true by publishing my first book.

Author's Note: Suggested Music Playlist:

The Bystanders: "California Dreaming" by the Mamas & the Papas

Nativity: "Relax" by Frankie Goes to Hollywood; "Silent Night" by Bing Crosby; "Jingle Bells" by Frank Sinatra; "Like a Virgin" by Madonna; and "Away in the Manager" by Nat King Cole

Summer Love: "Lucky Star" by Madonna; "Girls on Film" by Duran Duran; "Wipe Out" by the Safaris

Saint Damien of Molokai: "Non, rein de rein" by Edith Piaf

The High Priestess: "Girls Just Want to Have Fun" by Cyndi Lauper; "Karma Chameleon" by Culture Club; and "Sister Christian" by Night Ranger; and "Flesh for Fantasy" by Billy Idol

The Annual Picnic: "Little Pink Houses" by John Cougar Mellencamp; "Disintegration" by The Cure; "Jukebox Hero" by Foreigner; "LA Women" by The Doors; "Old Man" by Neil Young; "Hotel California" by The Eagles

Road Trip: "Jolene" by Dolly Parton; "Delta Dawn" by Tonya Tucker; and "Don't Ask Me No Questions" by Lynyrd Skynyrd

Calendar Days: "Charlotte Sometimes" by The Cure; "Heaven Knows I'm Miserable Now" by The Smiths

CPSIA information can be obtained
at www.ICGtesting.com
Printed in the USA
JSHW080020220323
39270JS00003B/26

9 781952 439537